PENGUIN BOOKS

MY TURN TO MAKE THE TEA

Monica Dickens, great-granddaughter of Charles Dickens, has written over thirty novels, autobiographical books and children's books, and her works are beginning to be adapted for television and film. Her first book, *One Pair of Hands*, which arose out of her experiences as a cook-general – the only work for which her upper-class education had fitted her – made her a best-seller at twenty-two, and is still in great demand.

Although her books arise out of the varied experiences of her life, she has not taken jobs in order to write about them: working in an aircraft factory and a hospital was her war work, not research. When she joined the Samaritans, it was the work of befriending distressed fellow human beings which she found compelling, although her novel *The Listeners* came from that experience.

She set up the first American branch of the Samaritans in Boston, Massachusetts, and lives nearby on Cape Cod with her husband Commander Roy Stratton, who has retired from the U.S. Navy, and her horses, cats and dogs. She has two daughters.

In 1978 she published her autobiography, *An Open Book* (to be published in Penguins).

MY TURN
TO MAKE THE TEA

Monica Dickens

PENGUIN BOOKS
IN ASSOCIATION WITH
MICHAEL JOSEPH

Penguin Books Ltd, Harmondsworth, Middlesex, England
Penguin Books, 625 Madison Avenue, New York, New York 10022, U.S.A.
Penguin Books Australia Ltd, Ringwood, Victoria, Australia
Penguin Books Canada Ltd, 2801 John Street, Markham, Ontario, Canada L3R 1B4
Penguin Books (N.Z.) Ltd, 182–190 Wairau Road, Auckland 10, New Zealand

—

First published by Michael Joseph 1951
Published in Penguin Books 1962
Reprinted 1963, 1965, 1966, 1969, 1972, 1977, 1978, 1979

—

—

Made and printed in Great Britain
by Hazell Watson & Viney Ltd,
Aylesbury, Bucks
Set in Linotype Juliana

To
MARY

Chapter One

THE telephone rang. I picked it up, glad of something to do, for there was not much stirring in our office that afternoon, except the spoon in Joe's teacup.

'*Downingham Post,*' I said crisply. 'Reporters' room.'

'There's a lady down here wants to see one of the reporters,' said Doris, who worked our little switchboard in an untaught, haphazard way.

'Oh good,' I said. Perhaps she had brought us some hot news.

'She wants to see whoever it was wrote that piece about the cold potatoes.'

Oh bad. I had written it. I was afraid at the time that I might not have all the facts right, because I had been dozing at the Petty Sessions, but the editor had wanted the story in a hurry and there was no time to check up.

I had hoped to get away with it. Ninety-nine times out of a hundred one did, but this was the hundredth. The lady was in the downstairs office, pacing the linoleum in a threatening hat. She was not the plaintiff in the case I had reported, who had been suing a truant husband for what the police called maintainance. That one had been quite a sympathetic blonde character, and I had been on her side, but this one was swart, with a trembling shadow of moustache.

I kept the counter between us. Doris and Mrs Banks, who handled the advertisements, were on my side of it doing their accounts, and I hoped they might give me support, but they only stared, and Mrs Banks shook out her sleeve in a fastidious way and drew a lace-edged handkerchief from the end of it. I rested my hands on the counter like an obliging shop assistant and prepared to sell the lady whatever she wanted.

'Are you the one who writes the court reports?' she asked, jittering her chin at me. She had some kind of affliction of the mouth, which made her look as though she were chewing all the time on seeds left over from raspberry jam.

'Yes,' I said, although the maintenance case was the first court story I had been allowed to do by myself, and that was only because Joe had wanted a drink before the magistrates did, and had gone away and left me on my own for half an hour before the lunch interval.

'You've made a libel of me,' said the lady. 'Look here.' She put a copy of our last week's paper on the counter, jabbing her glove at my story, which I could not read upside down.

' "Plaintiff, Mrs Jessie Parkins," ' she read, ' "alleged that during a quarrel, her husband emptied a bowl of cold potatoes over her head." '

'Didn't he?' I asked. From what I had seen of the husband, he looked capable of it.

'He may have, or he may not,' she said. 'That is neither here nor there. What is here is that I am Mrs Jessie Parkins. The woman in this unpleasant case' – she rapped the paper again – 'dreadful creature. We know all about *her* – is Mrs Nessie Parkin*son*. So you see what you've done with your vulgar publicity. You've made a libel of me and Mr Parkins, and it's set him right back, just when his legs were getting right. Thirty years we've been married and never a sharp word. Our name will be a laughing-stock when people read this. I've already had the milkman looking at me sideways.'

My heart sank. 'I'm terribly sorry,' I began humbly.

'Sorry isn't enough,' she said, chewing more rapidly on the raspberry pips. 'They oughtn't to let people like you have such licence. What are you going to do about it?'

What indeed? I could feel Doris and Mrs Banks concentrating on me from behind. I was getting nervous. The editor was always lecturing me about libel. I had made many mistakes since I had been on the paper, but none as ominous as this. I apologized to her. I told her that I had meant no harm, that it was a printer's error, a proof-reader's error, a fault in the machines, an Act of God. . . .

'I could sue, you know,' she said with relish, and I thought of dashing upstairs for my coat and leaving the office for ever, although tomorrow was pay day.

'Unless you print an apology. Big enough for everyone to see, though I doubt whether even that will get Mr Parkins over the shock. Thirty years we've been married and never –'

'Yes, yes, we could do that. How would it go? "We regret to announce that in the report of a case in the Magistrates' Court last week, the plaintiff was erroneously stated to be Mrs Jessie Parkins, instead of Mrs Nessie Parkinson. We offer our apologies to Mrs Parkins for any distress or embarrassment caused her." ' I had seen it done in the daily papers. They seemed to get away with it all right.

'Distress, yes.' She nodded the hat. 'And Mr Parkins. His name too. And the address. I'd like his activities for the British Legion to go in as well.' It was going to be quite a saga.

'It will have to go in for two weeks,' said Mrs Parkins. 'Two weeks, or I take action.'

'All right.'

'Very well.' She picked up the paper and her jaw slowed down and was still. The tension in the office broke. Doris giggled and Mrs Banks let out her breath with a little hiss like a tin of coffee being opened. I got away quickly, vowing to take Benzedrine to the Petty Sessions next time.

Upstairs, Joe and Victor wanted to know what it was all about. Someone had drunk my tea, and the office cat had got my biscuit on the floor.

'Apology?' said Vic. 'You're for it. The old man hates putting them in. Says it's the hallmark of second-rate journalism.' He imitated Mr Pellet's crusted accents to the life.

'Well, but surely, if it saves a libel action –'

'I said, he hates putting in apologies,' repeated Vic, who could be annoying when he liked.

'Perhaps I might get it in without him seeing.'

They laughed scornfully. The editor saw every word of copy that was written.

'I could take it in to Harold and get him to set it and fit it in somewhere after Pelly had passed the page.'

'What a hope. Don't you know this paper is the old man's Bible? He lives with it all week and then takes it home Wednesday evening and sits up all night reading it. Cover to cover. All the ads, too.'

'Oh well, I suppose I ought to go and tell him now.'

'Yes, I suppose you did.' Vic picked up a pencil, sucked it, flexed his wrist, made a few passes over a sheet of paper, and started on a headline for the Bowls Club Dinner. Joe sighed and went back to the morning paper.

'Ought to what?' asked Murray, who had just kicked in through the swing door and was hanging up his coat and scarf.

'Go and ask Pelly for a raise,' said Vic, underlining his heading with artistry.

'Useless. I asked him myself last week.' Murray lifted the lid of the teapot. 'You horrible people,' he said. 'You might have waited for me.'

'You can make some more,' Joe said.

'You know the tea doesn't last out if you keep making fresh brews.' Murray had a domestic mind, and worried a lot about whether the tea and sugar would last the week, and whether the milk would go sour if we lit a fire, and whether we could get any more coal.

'I'll make you some more when I come back,' I said. I was sorry for Murray, who never felt well, and who had the sort of wife one would not wish on any man.

'It doesn't matter. I'll go without.' Murray would rather be offended now than have a cup of tea.

I went out of the long, chaotic room where we five reporters wrote and argued and laughed at rotten jokes, and bickered and made our private telephone calls and boasted about what we were going to say to the editor when we asked for a rise. I went along the dark little corridor, which was so narrow that two people could not pass, so that you had to back out if you met anyone, and up the twisting stair, which was also narrow, like belfry steps. You did not have to back down these, because you could always hear if anyone was coming. They made such a noise on the hollow wood.

Mr Pellet made more noise than anyone. He was a short and heavy man, with no waist, no neck, and no spring in his ankles. I was a little afraid of him. No one else was, because they knew that they knew their work and he needed them. I did not know my work and he did not need me, but when he was feeling cosy, he would tell me that in about ten years' time, if I did what I was told, I might make him a useful reporter. The thought that in ten years' time I might still be in Downingham writing notices of Women's Institute concerts and school bazaars was not exhilarating.

The editor was sitting at his desk by the window subbing some copy. It looked like Vic's handwriting – what you could see of it after the mutilations of Mr Pellet's soft black pencil. Although it was a raw March afternoon, with a hint of fog coming in with the dusk, he had the window wide open. Mr Pellet never felt the cold. It was said downstairs that he had a steaming blood pressure, but he was never ill, and had no understanding for anyone who was. It was enough to make you ill if you had to spend too long in his office. Even in summer it got no sun, and in winter your hands turned blue and your face stiffened as soon as you opened the door.

It was a little odd-shaped room stuck in a top corner of the ramshackle old *Post* building. There was only just room in it for a claw-foot coat-stand with one foot missing, a kitchen chair for visitors, the editor's swivel chair that swivelled on a slant, and his scarred old roll-top desk, whose bursting drawers would no longer shut, and whose leather writing surface was chewed into a relief map where he had worried it over the years with his paper-knife. The electric light, with a shade like a dirty white china plate, hung in the wrong place and was hoisted to shine over the desk by a piece of string tied round the curtain rail.

The peeling walls were lined nearly all the way up with reference books, unreadable sagas on Downingham's history, and old, old ledgers and files. Nothing much newer than the turn of the century, for since the paper started in 1890, nothing had ever been moved or thrown away. The shelves and cupboards had long ago reached saturation point, so that all the up-to-date stuff had to be kept inconveniently in the basement. Our reporters' room was half silted up with rolls of old galley proofs which had been collecting dust there since the Relief of Mafeking. No one had yet discovered that I was systematically using them to light the fire, but I would have to do it for all of those ten years Mr Pellet said it would take to make me a reporter, before I made any impression on them.

I was surprised when I first came to this room for an interview. I had expected the editorial office, even of a provincial weekly, to be more impressive. I had expected Mr Pellet to look like an editor, not like a man who prods pigs with a stick on market day. With his large head, broad and curly at the poll like a Hereford bull, his thick clumsy fingers, seasoned by years of cigarettes, like old oak in a smoky cottage kitchen, and his healthy bright blue eyes, he was the most unliterary-looking person I had ever seen. Journalism is not literature, he was always telling me. I thought it ought to be, although the others downstairs told me that when I had been there as long as they had, I wouldn't waste my time thinking up original adjectives which the old man always replaced with some of the tried favourites from stock.

When I told the old man about Mrs Jessie Parkins and the

cold potatoes and the apology, he put down his pen, sunk his neck deeper into his shoulders, looked at me like a bull, and then roared at me like a bull. Victor and young Mike, who were always being roared at, told me that this meant nothing, but it unnerved me. I stood my ground, wondering whether it was the cold or Mr Pellet that made my legs feel weak. I was afraid that he would sack me. I had been thrown out of nearly every job I had ever had in my life, and wanted to hold on to this one a bit longer. I thought he was being unnecessarily righteous about Mrs Parkins, but suddenly he stopped in the middle of a sentence, leaving a vacuum in the air where his voice had been, gave me the sucked-in smile that made him look as if he had not got his teeth in, and muttered, 'Silly bitch.'

'Me?'

He wheezed, which was all he could do about laughing. 'No, her.'

As I stepped back over the icy linoleum to the door, he said, 'Had your tea yet?'

'I was just going to make some more. Would you like a cup?' It seemed wrong that no one took him tea every day, but if ever I took it up unasked, he would wave it away and say that he was too busy to drink tea, even if some people were not.

'Aye,' he said. 'Bring us a mug, there's a love,' and I knew I was forgiven. It was always a good sign with him when he tried to talk North Country.

Chapter Two

ALTHOUGH many people graduate from local papers to Fleet Street with some success, between working on a provincial weekly and working on a big London daily there is a gulf as vast as the Grand Canyon. On a London paper, you are either a reporter, or a sub-editor, or a proof-reader, or a sports writer, or a political commentator, or a woman's angle expert, or any one of the hundreds of specialists who go to make up the staff. That is your job, and that is all you do. You only see your own particular bit of the paper. You don't know and usually don't care what everyone else is doing, and if you were to get a bright idea about someone else's department probably no one would listen to you, so you don't bother to get bright ideas. You are not interested in the paper as a whole. It comes out, you suppose, since you see it being sold next day – although you usually read another one – but of all the infinite details and technicalities that bring it out you are happy to remain ignorant.

You hardly ever see the editor, and almost never see the proprietor, except at the Christmas party, and the annual pep talk, although you feel his presence, because you have to angle your writing his way, and sometimes you have to walk upstairs when the lift doors are chained back after his Lordship's butler has rung through to say that his Lordship's car is on its way to the office.

On a paper like the *Downingham Post*, things are very different. You don't have only one job, you have dozens. You probably have a try at almost every job in the office before you are done, because when Joe is on holiday, someone must do Kiddies' Korner, and when Murray is off sick, you might have to do the leader (non-political), and when Vic is away at Worcester with the town's football team, and Mike covering another match, someone must go and view Plastic Novelties 1st XI v Bingley Engineering Reserves.

Apart from that, in the natural course of events, you do a thousand and one things besides your official job of reporter. You think up headlines for other people's stories, you read proofs, and recorrect corrected proofs, you reword ill-written advertisements and Birth, Death, and Marriage notices (only In Memoriams are inviolate and have to be printed just as they are sent in), and worst of all, you have to rewrite some sense into the rambling reports on darts matches and whist drives sent in by local correspondents from the villages. You also have to take your turn at filling inkwells, fetching copy paper, washing-up yesterday's cups in cold water, and making tea. If you are the only girl, it is nearly always your turn. The only thing you don't have to do is dust, because, although there is an old man who sweeps the floor once a month and disappears no one knows where for the other twenty-seven days, nobody ever dusts a reporters' room. Nobody ever has, and nobody ever shall.

Although you do more work for less pay than on a London paper, you get more fun, because you are concerned with the paper as a whole, and are more directly involved with the adventure of its appearance every week on half the doormats in the county. In Fleet Street, you don't know one-tenth of the people who work with you. In the provinces, you not only know everybody, but you know all their life histories, their moods, their maladies, and can give advice at the drop of a hat on anyone's love problem, having listened to all the telephone conversations and read most of the correspondence relating to the affair.

You see the editor all the time – too much, if he is one of the clubbable sort, who gets bored cooped up alone in his office and comes to lean on your mantelpiece and gossip when you are trying to get some work done. We did not have this trouble with Mr Pellet, but we did suffer sometimes from the proprietor who, far from being a Lord who had to have lifts waiting for him, was an old lady in top-heavy hats and fur round the hem of her coats, who would come tottering through the office whenever she had nothing else to do at home, and tell us tales of her bygone family, who had been known as the Madcap Murchisons.

Then, too, in the provinces, you are not really a newspaper in the strict sense of the word. You are more like a parish magazine. You do not give your readers the news, but only the news that affects them locally. Tremendous events may be afoot in the great world outside, but you are only interested in what happens within your fifteen-mile radius. World-shaking speeches may be made in Parliament, but you are only concerned with what your local M.P. said to the Mothers' Union about the cost of living.

Even when something important enough to be featured in the London papers happened in our district, it was no good to us, because although we tried to persuade Mr Pellet to let us make a big splash with it, he would always say that by the time we went to press, people would have read all about it in their morning papers. He was probably right, but it did seem a waste that time when we had a runaway Duchess, and when a real sex murderer came up at our Assizes. We reported the case, of course, but with scarcely more *éclat* than any other. The sensational stuff had all been done by the London papers, and our lead story that week, which might have been 'RED-HAIRED KILLER SLAYS WIFE, MISTRESS IN SAME BED,' was 'COUNCIL VETOES NEW SEWAGE PLAN FOR BUNGALOWS.'

Poor Mike, who was keen, had gone to visit the red-haired murderer's Mum, and had written an impassioned Human Interest story, but Mr Pellet would have none of it. In any case, he said, Mum lived two miles outside our boundary. She belonged to the *Moreton Advertiser*, which supplied news

16

for the other half of the county. This boundary was rigid, and what happened even just beyond it was considered to be of no interest to our readers. If they thought it was, then let them buy the *Moreton Advertiser*.

One Sunday, when I was bicycling back to Downingham from a visit to some friends, I came upon an accident at a crossroads some way outside the town. One car was on the grass verge with its back wheels in the ditch, and the other was buckled all down one side like tinfoil. There was a body in the road – not a badly hurt one; it was sitting up quite animatedly rubbing its leg and cursing – but still a body. There was the usual miraculous collection of gapers from nowhere, a road scout, a lorry driver, two flushed and vociferous women who had been in one of the cars, and me, fishing my notebook out of my handbag. I had been told to take it everywhere with me, because you never knew. This just showed. You never did know when you might not stumble on a red-hot bit of news.

I had not been on the paper long, and was dead keen. It was just after the *faux pas* of the cold potatoes, and I thought that coming in on Monday morning with a sizzling eye-witness story like this would be just the thing to blot out that memory from behind Mr Pellet's deceptively ingenuous eyes. Licking my pencil, I edged my way among the little crowd. I was not sure how a reporter was supposed to behave on occasions like this; whether to be diffident, or brash, with hat on back of head, as in American films. The road scout, who was trying to pull the wing of the smashed car away from its wheel, looked kind.

'Excuse me,' I said, 'I'm from the *Downingham Post*. Could you tell me how the accident occurred?'

'Press, eh?' said the scout, lifting a face scarlet from tugging. 'You're quick on the job.'

'Just a part of our news service,' I said modestly. 'Could you tell me –?'

'I'll tell you,' said the body sitting on the kerb. 'By God, I'll tell you. Here am I, driving quietly along this main road, which any idiot within miles knows is a main road, even if it wasn't marked Major Road Ahead on all the side roads – and just as I get to this crossing, out comes this lunatic woman, full bat – crash, bang! and I just had time to think: "a woman driver, *of* course," and then here I am with a leg like a bolster and getting bigger every minute. Look!' He pulled up his trousers to show me a white and waxy leg with a bruise coming up below the knee and a broken sock suspender. I tutted at it.

'Might have killed me,' he went on. 'There am I, driving quietly along this main road –' I scribbled away in my home-made code substitute for shorthand, which sometimes made sense to me when I came to transcribe it and sometimes did not.

'Oh, look here,' said one of the flushed women, coming across, 'this isn't good enough. You know quite well the accident was all your fault. If you hadn't been going so fast, I'd have had plenty of time to get across. Don't print what he told you,' she implored me. 'It isn't true. It was all his fault. You say that. It was all his fault. It isn't fair!' She seemed about to cry, and the other woman came and put her arms around her. 'Leave her alone,' she told me accusingly. 'She's had a shock.'

'Had a shock!' exploded the man in the gutter. 'What do you think I've had? Here am I, driving quietly along this main road, which any idiot within miles –'

'Now, now,' said the road scout soothingly, 'don't you go making wild statements, neither of you. Save all that for the police court. And you be careful what you write, Miss,' he told me, 'else you'll be in trouble, too.'

'But I can say what I've seen, can't I?' I forgot that I was pretending to be a seasoned reporter, who would know such things.

'Oh yes, you can say what you seen, but you can't say how it come about, since we don't know till His Worship the Magistrate tells us.'

That seemed a pity, since having seen the woman, I could imagine how it came about, and would have liked to say so. However, I could do a descriptive story, teeming with human interest and emotional conflict. I bicycled home as fast as I could, locked myself in my room and spent two hours writing four hundred words. I headed it 'CALAMITY AT THE CROSS-ROADS'. Joe had told me: 'When in doubt for a head, use an alliteration. Sure fire.'

I had written the story ten times, polished it, sweated over it, decorated it with telling phrases and colourful adjectives, until it seemed to me to be just the sort of thing I should like to read in my local paper on a Thursday morning. I thought it was pretty good – better than any of the others could have done, anyway. Murray, for instance, would have started it: 'At half-past five last Sunday evening –' as he started all his stories.

When I got into the office on Monday morning, Mike was there, sharpening pencils with his overcoat on, for our room was always like the morgue after the week-end. 'Hear about the accident on the Downingham–Glenfield road?' I asked him.

He shook his head.

'Did you?' I asked Victor, who had just come in.

'Do what?'

'Hear about the accident at the Insham crossroads yesterday. Terrific smash. One car in the ditch –'

'The ditch is where I nearly was last night. Near as a toucher,' he said. 'Gosh – coming out of the White Lion – bloody great long-distance coach – missed me by inches.' He was not interested in my accident.

Some reporters, I thought. Never know what's going on right under their noses. But I did. I had been on the job, and I had got a story that would make them jealous.

As soon as I heard Mr Pellet's feet clattering up his little staircase, I took it in to him. Although the room was like an ice-chamber, he was flinging open the window and grumbling about fug.

'Some copy for you, sir.' I laid my effort carefully on his desk, and put his dictionary on it, so that it should not blow away.

He grunted. 'All right,' he said, as I lingered. 'What's the matter? You put any libel in it? You've got to be careful with those darned Guild concerts. The women are after me like hens after a rooster if we don't get in the name of every last one who helped to pull a curtain or shout: "Ho to France!" in the big historical scene.'

'It isn't the concert,' I said, 'it's a news story. Something I saw myself.'

'Good girl,' he said. 'Always keep your eyes open.'

I expanded to his praise. 'It was so lucky,' I burbled. 'I was bicycling along, you see, and there was this smash, so of course I got off, and I had my notebook, and –'

'Where was it?' He leaned forward to read my writing. 'Insham crossroads. Sorry, that's a mile outside our area.' He handed the papers back to me. I could have crumpled them up and thrown them at him, only they would not have hurt.

'What's the matter with *you*?' asked Mike when I went downstairs. I told him.

'Insham? Of course it's outside. That's the *Moreton Ad.*, not us. I could have told you that.'

'Why didn't you?'

'You didn't ask me.'

'I *told* you about it.' We always squabbled first thing on a Monday morning. It was quite stimulating to have something concrete to squabble about.

I remembered that I had to go and cover a cookery demonstration. 'Where are you off to?' asked Joe, as I kicked open the swing door, which had no paint on it for two feet above the ground, and nearly laid him out as he was coming in.

'I'm going to sell a story to the *Moreton Advertiser*,' I said.

'Not worth it. They wouldn't pay you enough to cover the bus fare.'

It would not have mattered if I had sold the story to the other paper. There was no rivalry between us, but a cooperation that I had not expected to find in local journalism. We sold, or even gave each other stories and bits of news quite cheerfully. There was not even much rivalry between us and the *Downingham Messenger*, a smaller paper, which functioned in the same town. We both had our static circulation. Some families took the *Post*, some took the *Messenger*, some took both, had done for years, and always would. The few new people who came to the town were not worth competing for.

We were friendly with the three *Messenger* reporters – a disillusioned man, who had been twice round the world and ended up in Downingham, a callow youth, and a girl with orange lipstick. Although we naturally thought our paper was better, and told them what we thought of their stories, the only serious rivalry between us was in darts matches at the White Lion. Their editor was a middle-aged lady with loops of hair, who had once trained as a lawyer, so we sought her advice on court matters, and she came round to Mr Pellet with furrows in her brow whenever she got in a muddle with her local politics.

The *Messenger* came out two days before us, which was useful, because we could copy some of their stories. Not word for word, of course, but paraphrasing. On a Tuesday morning, we would all read the *Messenger*, scoffing gently at some of their items, but Mike secretly admired the Letters to the Editor, which were much snappier than ours, because their staff were allowed to write some of them, and I secretly admired their Woman's column, which told of such things as new knitting leaflets and spring modes at Harrisons the drapers.

Mr Pellet, who had been disappointed in love long ago and was a misogynist, was sternly against anything like this in the *Post*. I was biding my time. When I had been there a bit longer, I was going to start persuading him to let me have a little bit of space for women. Joe had a Korner for his Kiddies. Why should I not be allowed a niche for house-wives? The time was not ripe yet. I was still an encum-brance, but when I should be more firmly established, I was full of plans for revolutionizing this diehard old periodical. The others had all thought like this once, but had long ago given it up, except at wild moments when their broken spirits showed a rare flash of revolt.

I, who was new, and Mike, who was very young, were always planning how we would run the paper when every-body else was dead or in prison. Between us, we would turn it into the brightest thing in print, which would sweep the country. After all, the *Manchester Guardian* had started as a local paper, hadn't it? We would turn the *Post* into a tabloid if necessary, but not with Mr Pellet about. He was the rock against which all waves of enthusiasm broke and fell back with a frustrated sigh.

On Tuesday morning he came down to us with his copy of the *Messenger*, and marked the paragraphs he wanted to filch. I had always thought an editor was God Almighty, and when I first joined the paper, I used to get up when Mr Pellet spoke to me, and call him Sir. But no one else did, and it seemed to embarrass him, so I remained sitting with the others at the great dishevelled yellow table which was a desk for all of us, and was the wrong height for the chairs, so that everyone except Victor had to sit on telephone books or volumes of the out-of-date encyclopedia.

'Schoolmaster died,' said Mr Pellet, tapping the *Messenger*'s rather blurred print. 'Used to be a great football player. We use some of this. Not all this crap, of course. I sometimes suspect dear old Ruby doesn't know what's news and what isn't. And that Methodist centenary. Have you got anything on that yet from the minister?'

'I thought someone might go round and see him this morning,' Joe said lazily, looking at me, and I made a face at him. I did not like visiting ministers of the Church. Their studies were always cold.

'Don't bother,' said Mr Pellet. 'All the facts are here, and you can get the orphans' party from this too, and Mrs Milliter's funeral. Someone can do those this morning.'

'Poppy,' said Victor, when he had gone. 'Nice little job for you.'

After the first few days in the office when everyone was still being reasonably polite to me, I had been called Poppy, for no better reason than that a Sunday paper was running a crude cartoon about a blonde called Poppy Pink. Humour was as elementary as that on the *Downingham Post*.

Rewriting was supposed to be easy. That was why I was given it. I found it more difficult than writing something from scratch. When I was first given the job, I asked how to do it.

'Change the headline and the first sentence,' Victor said. 'Then you can copy as much of the rest as you want.'

'Oh, no,' said Murray. 'That's plagiarism.'

Vic made a rude noise. He did not like long words.

'You know a lot of our readers take the *Messenger* too. You must make the story different.'

'But how can I when the facts are the same and I don't know any more about it?' I asked.

'Guess, girl, guess,' sighed Vic.

'You use the same facts, of course,' said Murray craftily, 'but you put them in a different order, d'you see? That way, you get an original story.'

'It did not sound like it to me, but I got a pile of clean copy

paper, reached for one of Mike's toffees, and prepared to cere-
brate. After ten minutes, I still had not got the headline. The
one that the *Messenger* had chosen appeared to me to be the
only possible one in the whole of the English language. If I had
not seen it, I could have thought of a dozen headings, but to
see something in print and have to avoid it is to stultify the
brain. 'DEATH OF GRAND OLD MAN OF DOWNINGHAM'
seemed to be the perfect title for the passing of a ninety-year-
old councillor. I tried a lot of other things, but they did not
look like anything you might read in a newspaper. Joe finally
got tired of my sighing and fidgeting and throwing balls of
paper at the litter round the wastepaper basket, which had
been overflowing for days.

He looked up from his melancholy reading of the entries in
his children's Funny Stories competition. 'Want any help?'

'Oh yes,' I said. 'I can't think of what to call it.' The morning was passing and I had done no work at all.

'Let's see.' He glanced at the front page of the *Messenger*.
'"DEATH OF GRAND OLD MAN OF DOWNINGHAM."
Easy. You just put: "GRAND OLD MAN OF DOWNING-
HAM DIES."'

It was as simple as that. It looked well, too. I spent the rest
of the morning juggling with the details of the grand old
man's career, and there again it seemed to me that the
Messenger had put them in the only order possible. Life was
very difficult, and there was more in journalism than met the
eye. At a quarter to one, Vic came back from the magistrates'
court and asked who was coming for a drink. Joe had already
gone, and Mike was putting on his scarf and bicycle clips.
He rode home half an hour to lunch every day, because his
mother said he must have a good hot meal.

'I can't come out yet,' I said. 'I haven't finished these re-
writes.'

'You're mad,' Vic said. 'Finish 'em this afternoon. What
d'you think this is – a stop press edition?'

'But there'll be lots more to do this afternoon. Proofs to read, and Births and Deaths and –'

'Relax,' he said. 'When you have been here as long as I have –'

This was a favourite remark with all of them. It was never completed, but it always meant more or less the same thing. In this case: when you feel like a drink, go and have one.

We went and had a drink.

Chapter Three

ONE week passed very much like another on the *Downing-ham Post*. Since we went to press on a Wednesday, Thursday was the beginning of our new week. We all came in late that morning – later than usual, that is – and whiled away the time grumbling about Mr Pellet, choking up the fire with rubbish from the week before, and filing cuttings in the obituary morgue about people not yet dead.

Joe always filed his nails on a Thursday. He was particular about his hands, although the rest of himself was going to seed along with the brain that had once been going to write novels. He had a trustful, lopsided face, usually badly shaved, with a ridge of sandy whiskers in the groove of his chin. Streaks of damp pinkish hair were spread over the top of his freckled head, and his eyes were a slightly different size, and faded. They became more watery in inverse ratio to the strength of his drinks. Joe was lazy and selfish and a terrible old soak, but everybody liked him. He was so deplorable that you felt that underneath it all he must have a heart of gold, like the prostitute of popular tradition.

Mike always wrote to his girl Sylvia on a Thursday morning – at least, she was supposed to be his girl. They had been going out together for a long time, but when he tried to take things a stage further, Sylvia shied away and left him clutching air.

Mike would not believe the rumour that she was seen out with airmen. 'She's no good for you,' we told him.

'No, no,' he said. 'She's pure. That's why she sometimes won't let me kiss her good night.'

'Ought to be no let about it,' grumbled Vic. 'If you want to kiss a girl, you don't ask her. You just mucking well do it.'

'It's all very well for you,' Mike said, looking very young and despondent. 'You don't wear glasses. If I make a dive at Sylvia, my glasses go for six, but if I take them off first, she knows what I'm up to and gets the garden gate between us. How'll I start the letter this week? Last time I met her, she wasn't going much on me, so do you think she'd take it funny if I put "Darling Syl", as per usual?'

We all gave him a lot of advice, and wrote most of his love letters for him. He rang Sylvia up at her work two or three times a week. She liked that, and would converse quite seductively for the sake of the other girls in her office, and Mike would sit with a silly moony smile on his face, instead of saying the things we told him to. Once, when he was out, Victor had rung up Sylvia and said: 'Hullo, sweetness, don't you remember me? You weren't so stand-off when we met the other night. Gee, we had fun, didn't we?'

Sylvia gasped and said: 'Barry! I thought you'd gone to the Isle of Man.'

'Just leaving, sweetness,' Vic said, and hung up thoughtfully. We did not tell Mike about this. There was no point, for he was besotted with Sylvia's purity, but it confirmed our ideas about her.

Victor did not write to his girl friends on Thursday or any other day. He had several of them – or talked as if he had –

but he would never risk anything on paper, except over-developed sketches which he pinned round the office walls, and Murray hung galley proofs over them. On Thursday mornings, Victor made up his expense accounts, pondering long over how much he could get away with, and rang up one of the fire brigade, who was assistant to the local book-maker.

Murray pottered about on his narrow feet, filing things that no one would ever want to look at again, checking the tea and sugar tins, emptying the wastepaper basket and tidy-ing up his bit of the table, which was fruitless, for no one else ever tidied theirs, and as soon as he had made a clear space, their litter would overflow on to it. Murray was the chief reporter, because he had been there longest, and on Thursday mornings he would spend some time with Mr Pellet in con-ference about next week's paper, and come down looking smug. His spare and secret face drawn down to pursed lips could easily look like that.

I always read the *Downingham Post* on Thursday morn-ings. This seemed to the others the height of folly, but although I had lived with the thing all week and read and reread proofs until I knew most of it by heart, I never could resist seeing my own efforts in print, although they were sometimes scarcely recognizable after the mutilations of Mr Pellet's dusky pencil. I tried to read them with a stranger's eye, and wondered whether they looked amateurish, or whether readers might detect the stuff of genius in the report of Miss Alice Tufton's wedding, over which I had tried so hard, but which had come out exactly like all the other wed-ding reports that ever had been and ever would be in the *Downingham Post*. It was a curious process, like a sausage machine, that made our individual efforts, the product of a variety of brains, go in at one end and come out in print at the other as if they had all been written by the same person.

At half past twelve on a Thursday, Mr Pellet, crowned by

the black Homburg that was too small for him and rocked a little on his curls, would look round the door, wish us Good day and go off to his Fellowship lunch. We would all go round to the White Lion for our weekly darts match against the *Messenger*.

On Thursday afternoons we were free, unless there were any outside reporting jobs. I always had my hair washed. This may not seem very thrilling news to you, but it was to me, after a week in that dusty office, where the desperation of our labours made one frequently rake the hair with fingers that were covered with printer's ink from handling wet proofs.

On Friday morning we prepared to face the fact that we were bringing out another paper in five days' time, and things began to hum a little. That is to say, Joe rolled a fresh batch of cigarettes on his little machine that turned them out like frayed rope, got out his collection of fading notebooks and tried to think of an idea for a children's competition. He had been doing Kiddies' Korner for ten years and had long ago run out of new ideas, but as a fresh lot of Kiddies was always coming along, he could use the old ones over again in due season.

Somebody rang up the ministers of all the various churches and asked them the leading question : 'Post here. Got anything for us next week?' If they could not be reached by telephone, somebody, and it was usually me, had to go and visit the cold homes of the holy, but if you went at the right time, you sometimes got a cup of tea.

It was also somebody's grim task to ring round the hospitals and find out who had died. If there was anyone worth writing about, and we had nothing about them in the morgue, we would ring up the *Messenger*, and if their morgue yielded nothing either, somebody, and it was usually me, had to go and visit the homes of the bereaved. I jibbed at this at first and said I would not go, but Murray said who did I think I was, so I went and, curiously enough, most of the bereaved did not mind. Many of them actually liked it, and here too there was a good chance of a cup of tea. There is always tea brewing when someone has died.

Saturday was one of the busiest days of our week, because there were always a lot of goings on that had to be told in print. Sport, plays, concerts, weddings, meetings, dinners, dances, political speeches – you sometimes had five or six things to go to during the afternoon and evening, and then had to spend most of Sunday writing them up at home.

On Monday, there were all the weddings and funerals and christenings to write up, week-end notices from correspondents at the outposts of the *Downingham Post* empire to be turned into readable prose, and the beginning of the interminable proof-reading, which went on relentlessly whenever you had a spare moment from now until Wednesday evening. It was like the broomstick of the sorcerer's apprentice. Just when you had laboured through a batch, Harold, the foreman, would come in from the comp room next door with a fresh roll of galleys, smiling amiably as if sure of the welcome he never got.

On Tuesday the pace increased and the lino men who made the type on their improbable jittering machines, became a little rattled. Not so much Ernie, who had been doing it for twenty years and could skim over the keys in his sleep, but Ricky, who had only been on the job two years and was neurotic at the best of times. He made mistakes when he was hurried, and this made reading the proofs even more toilsome. They had to be corrected again and again, because Ricky did not always get our corrections right, and when Joe and Vic cursed him, he cursed back and said it was our lousy handwriting. Once he walked out of the building and was seen no more for three days, and Mr Pellet, who had been everything in his journalistic career, took off his coat and put on one of the black ink-saturated overalls and rattled away at the machine until the sweat stood like seed pearls on his brow. We had some rum type that week, because we could not correct all his mistakes. There was not time, and there just wasn't room on the proofs, and there is a Mrs Cody at Insham, who will never forget that she was once called: 'Our Hot. Treasurer, Mrs Cosy.'

So the week went round, with press day, Wednesday, coming round all too soon and catching you napping because you always thought you had plenty of time to write things up.

Much of our time, of course, was spent not in the office writing the news, but out and about collecting it. Apart from Assizes, Sessions (petty and quarter) and Council meetings (urban, rural, and arts and crafts) there was always something doing in Downingham. Not, perhaps, things that you would have attended from choice, but other people did, and so you had to be there to chronicle them.

We shared out these jobs between us. A huge diary was kept in the office and was filled in every week with what was going on, with our initials pencilled against what we were to report. Only Mr Pellet was supposed to fill in the initials, because he liked to be sure where everybody was, but you could suggest yourself lightly in pencil if there was anything which you particularly wanted to attend, which did not often happen. What did often happen was that someone would quickly pencil your initials against something they did not fancy, before Mr Pellet could put them down for it.

Even when he had put them down, they were quite capable of changing the initials when no one was about. I would look through the diary at the beginning of each week, see what I was down for and make a note of it in case I forgot, like that time I forgot to go to Lady Nethersole opening a bazaar, and she was insulted. One Friday afternoon, I saw that I had nothing, so, knowing that Mr Pellet was going away for a long week-end, I arranged to do the same myself. On Friday morning, he came down to us with a green ticket.

'Who is going to the Girl Guides Tableaux this afternoon?' He looked at the diary. 'Oh, you are.' He gave me the ticket. 'Only about four inches, and for God's sake, don't forget the accompanist.'

I looked at the ticket in my hand, which bade me welcome to Olde Tyme Scenes and Fantasies at 2.30 that afternoon. My train for London went at two. 'But I –'

'Sorry, girl. I know it's murder, but it's a living. I don't remember putting you down for it, because you've been a good girl lately and I thought I'd spare you, but I suppose there was no one else.'

I looked at the diary. The baseness of Victor. Not only had he altered his initials to mine, but he had done it with one of Mr Pellet's soft black pencils to look more genuine. He knew I could not say anything, since we were in league against the boss. One always is, however much one likes the boss and hates one's fellow workers.

When the boss had gone, I got my own back by rubbing out my name from opposite the elocution competition and substituting Victor's. He could not say anything either, and had to suffer eighty children between the ages of seven and twelve reciting 'Milk for the Cat', and 'Incident in a French Camp'.

He retaliated by coming in early one day and putting me down for the Grantley Village Drama Circle in 'Quality Street', and so we went merrily on.

Wednesday was the worst day of each week. We went to press, or, as we liked to say in our nonchalant Fleet Street jargon, we put the paper to bed. Each page was built up in a 'forme', a heavy metal frame with screws round the sides to hold the type in place. The feature pages and the small ads page and some of the news pages were completed as the week went on, but two pages were left open until the last moment to take late reports and advertisements, and the stop press news of people dying or running into each other on motor cycles and anything else that was inconsiderate enough to happen on a Wednesday.

Harold, the foreman comp, never got these pages finished until seven o'clock or later. Two of us reporters had to hang about, playing cards or reading or nagging Harold. When he got to the end of his material, there was always either too much or too little to fit into the last page, so we either had to take something out of a paragraph already in type, or fish out of the wastepaper basket the notes of some rejected function, and write that up. With the presses champing at the bit and the whole paper waiting on us, it seemed incongruous to be filling in that all-important gap with a parish council meeting from a village of two hundred inhabitants, or the birth of a fine boy to some woman of whom no one had ever heard.

'Surely you're not going to waste good space putting in *this*?' I used to ask when I was new to the paper and still thought I was part of a vital news service, but I would be told: 'Just you try and find enough news in Downingham to fill a sixteen-page paper.'

It was nearly always I who had to stay on and help put the paper to bed, because Mr Pellet said it was good experience for me to see it to its completed form. No one wanted to stay on late, so the others agreed with him.

When we had written our last paragraph and Ernie or Ricky had turned it into type, we then had to read a proof of it, recheck the corrected proof, and finally correct a proof of the whole page. There were always one or two mistakes which had been missed before, and Harold would bend over the forme and pick out a line with a pair of eyebrow tweezers It was then reset and dropped delicately back into place again and the forme screwed up.

We were supposed to look through all the page proofs

again before they started printing, in case any mistakes had got through. No one bothered except Murray, who was always in a fever of anxiety lest the eyes of Downingham should be shocked by the smallest misprint. If he found one on a page whose forme was already in place on the machine downstairs, Harold would take a hammer and knock the offending type, so that it would print blurred, and no one would ever know that we did not know how to spell Appellant.

The paper's bedtime had now arrived. With groans and cries of Hup, Harold and Maurice, the apprentice, would lift the almost unliftable formes from the steel table and stagger with them to the lift. It was hand-operated, pulled up and down by a rope, like a service lift in an old-fashioned restaurant. One always expected Harold to shout down for two tomato soups and a spaghetti, but when he put his head into the hatch, it was to shout at Bob, the old man who swept the floor, whose job it was on Wednesdays to pull the lift up and down.

Like everything else in the *Post* office, the lift was very old. One day, the rope would break and the lift would crash into the basement and the type would fall out of the formes and we should have printer's pie. We had had it once when Maurice was away and Bob had come upstairs to help Harold carry the last forme to the lift. Just as they were hoisting it in, Bob dropped his end with a hoarse cry and the forme fell through the gap between the lift and scattered its type all over the basement.

Harold was never put out of temper by anything. It would have been better if he was. He whistled and sang cheerily as he tried to salvage as many paragraphs as possible from the printer's pie, and then bounced upstairs on his toes to break the glad news to Ernie and Ricky, who were putting on their coats, that they would have to stay on and reset the rest of the page.

Ricky had a nerve storm and had to go home. Ernie lit the gas which melted the metal for his machine and sat tapping away there for an hour with a face like the end of the world. They had to keep Bob away from him in case he might do the old man harm. Maurice, who had a date with his girl, had to stay on and pull proofs of the reset type, and Vic and I had to stay on and read the proofs. They were full of mistakes, because Ernie was so cross, and we hardly dared hand him back the proofs so covered with our corrections.

There were still a few mistakes the next time, but they were not important, so we let them pass. Ernie had the kind of spare dark face and glittering eye that made you think of a knife at the belt and dark Sicilian alleyways. It was a good thing Murray was not on that night.

The press, which squatted in the basement like a monster waiting for its weekly feed, was an old-fashioned machine of the rotary type. Archaic, they told me, but it seemed the latest miracle of science. The machine minder pressed a button and away it went, roaring and clanking, the endless paper rolling and passing and crossing and folding back so that you could not follow the progress of any one page until it turned up at the end neatly in place among its fellows. I loved to stand at the vomiting end of the machine and see the pages slide down together open, have the middle fold knocked into them by a rod and then another fold, to be spat out exactly as they would appear on anyone's doormat.

The machine minder's mate, who wore a seaman's jersey winter and summer, carelessly threw aside the first few dozens because the ink did not mark so well until the monster got going, and then we had to grab a paper and take it upstairs to look through it yet once more for mistakes before the edition started printing in earnest.

The boys downstairs were supposed to wait until we gave them the all clear, but when neither Murray nor Mr Pellet was there they sometimes did not bother. Although we dutifully skimmed through the paper, and sometimes found a few mistakes which could have been blurred out with Harold's hammer, we knew that if we went downstairs we would probably find the press already rolling and the piles of copies being made into bundles for Mrs Hogg, the Post Office, Insham, and J. Jacks, Corner Stores, Marking Green.

We went downstairs and said O.K. just for the look of it, and then we shouted Good night above the voice of the machine and let ourselves out by a side door into the Downingham night, grumbling about not being paid overtime.

At home, Mrs Goff would not have kept my supper. You had to be on the dot if you wanted to be fed, so I usually went with one of the others to have cheese rolls and beer.

I was in the Plough one night with Joe. He would never go to the White Lion, except for darts matches, because in the evening, there were apt to be women with corduroy slacks and clotted make-up, who laughed like jackals. Joe liked peace and quiet when he was drinking. He got it in the Plough, which was too squalid to attract more than a few morose men, who would rather be there than at home, and an old lady stunted by gin, who lived on the corner bench in a collapsed hat, surrounded by all her possessions in oilcloth bags.

This night, Joe had been eating pickled onions with his cheese, which always made him sad, because they gave him indigestion. Later on, when he had had a lot more to drink, he would get sad anyway, but he was starting early tonight. He told me about his wife who had gone away years ago and taken their child with her. He had told me on other occasions that he was well rid of her, and if his description of her was true, I agreed, but tonight he chose to think of her as Circe.

'Fascinating devil she was, Poppy,' he kept telling me. 'Fascinating little devil. Never been the same man since she went away.'

I did not remind him that he had previously told me that it was because he was the man he was now that she had gone away. He was low tonight, and would probably get very drunk. I would go home soon and leave him to it. He was just in the mood to be upset, and when a man in a pullover came in and started insulting the *Downingham Post*, Joe sublimated his uxorious sorrowing into anger.

What the man was saying about the paper was the kind of thing I had heard Joe say about it many times. He always maintained that it was the foulest rag on earth, but no outsider might say so. Not tonight, anyway. He growled and his bald head began to sweat, which was a bad sign.

The newcomer, who was quite sober and thought he was being funny, laughed at him. 'Can't think how you can stand to work for a set-up like that,' he mocked. 'Reading it is enough to drive me round the bend, so that writing for it must be –'

'Oh look,' I said, before Joe could answer. 'It's not as bad as all that. After all, thirteen thousand people read it.'

'*Buy* it, you mean,' he corrected me. 'Of course, everyone takes their local paper, but that's not saying they read it. Oh, I daresay they look at the small ads, but if you could take a census of all the unread copies of the *Post* that go to light fires the day after it comes out –'

I agreed with him up to a point, but one has one's loyalties. He had a silly smile. He was beginning to annoy me. 'It's a better paper than the *Messenger*, anyway,' I said. 'They can't even write journalese, let alone English.'

'Yerrs,' said Joe, on a horrible note that was half a word, half an animal noise. 'You read the *Mess . . . enger*?' he asked the pullover threateningly, belching in the middle of the word. 'You would.'

'Of course I read the *Messenger*,' said the pullover, proudly, his smile growing even sillier. 'My young lady is one of their reporters.'

So this was the famous Len, about whom Nancy, the girl with the orange lipstick, was always talking. When I sat next

36

to her on the press bench in court, she would invariably whisper to me one of her 'Len thinks' or 'Len always says' just when a witness's name and address were being announced. I can't think how she ever got any of her stories right, for she always seemed to be in a dream of Len and the caravan home they were to share together next summer. She probably did not get them right, and as I had to copy a lot of her work, mine were probably wrong too.

I was so intrigued to see that the famed Adonis was only a man with hair on the backs of his hands and ill-fitting false teeth, that I forgot we were having a row. Joe did not. He said something really very rude about Nancy (though possibly true) and pullover stuck out his negligible jaw at him.

'Don't you square up at me, sir,' said Joe. 'If you want to fight, I'll –'

Still sitting down, he took a tremendous swipe at the man, fell off his stool, and landed on the floor still clutching his glass, which was empty, but intact.

'A fight, a fight!' yelled Len hysterically, backing off. 'Take him away!'

'Now, now,' said the landlord, oozing calmly through from the public bar. 'No harm done gentlemen, and let's have a drink on the house. Get up off the floor, Joe. You'll do no good there.'

Joe was sad again now. He hitched himself to his feet, hand over hand up the rungs of a stool, and leaned morosely over the bar in a little puddle of beer.

'Shake,' he said to the man in the pullover, making no effort to hold out his hand; but Len had gone, making a great windy swish with the door.

'Are you all right?' I asked Joe.

'I expect so.'

'Then I think I'll go home, if you don't mind.' A farmer had just come in, whom I knew to be one of his enemies. I did not want to go through the whole thing again.

'Leave me,' he said. 'I would grieve alone.'

Outside the Plough, the man in the pullover was waiting for the bus that I wanted. I stood on the other side of the post.

'All the same,' he said, 'what I said in there about your paper –'

'Oh, shut up,' I said. It had been a long day, and tomorrow morning I had to get up at crack of dawn and travel twelve miles to interview a woman who had lost two children in the current flu epidemic. I was fed up with local journalism.

'Shut up, is it?' he asked, and I remembered that Nancy had burbled about his getting his eyes from an Irish grandmother.

'It is,' I said, and decided to walk home.

Chapter Four

WHEN I first came to work on the *Post*, I lived with some friends in Downingham. We thought we were friends, but when I had been there a few weeks, we discovered that we were not. The Munts were quite different from what they had been on that cruise to Jamaica, and I suppose I was different too.

You can like almost anyone when the sun is shining and you have nothing to do but eat. There was not much sun in Downingham that winter, and all the Munts' meals tasted of gravy powder, so it was a relief when they went abroad again and gave me a polite excuse to leave.

I had made one or two attempts before, but although they thought my conversation silly, and were always making veiled references to footmarks on the hearthstoned doorstep

– was one supposed to jump over it? – if I ever hinted at a change, the Munts would not hear of it.

'We should never forgive ourselves,' they said, 'if we left you on your own in Downingham. It can be a lonely place. I always say one can never be so lonely as in a crowd. Lawrence dear, on your way out, just ask Mary to do over the step before the Fishers come, will you? No, my dear girl, we should never forgive ourselves if we thought we weren't looking after you.'

However, they suddenly announced one day that they were going to let their house and go to Switzerland. Whether they managed to forgive themselves, or whether they ate their hearts out with remorse in Neuchâtel, I do not know, because I never saw them again.

I had not very long to find a new home. I scanned the small advertisements in the *Post* and put in an 'Accommodation Wanted' myself. Gladys told me I could have it at Reporters' Rates, which sounded grand, but cost only threepence less.

I was pleased at the idea of no more gravy powder and no more of that chilly room, where the light hung in the one place where you could neither see to read in bed nor do your face, but soon I began to be worried. I could not find anywhere else to go.

To look at Downingham, you would not think that it was the Mecca of all the world. It had few factories, indifferent shops, an incurable bottleneck at the traffic lights, and no more antique charms than any other market town, yet there seemed to be nowhere left to live in it. The best hotels were much too expensive, the next best were too expensive and full of sad old ladies, and the next were still too expensive for a reporter's pay, and full of men with samples. I could have had a room at the White Lion, but it was separated only by a curtain from someone else's room, and I did not know who the someone else was.

I only had two answers to my advertisement. One was from a family who would take me as a paying guest, but when I got there, I found it meant sharing a room with the eldest daughter – and I saw the eldest daughter. The other was from a man, who wanted me to stoke the boiler, clean out rabbit hutches, and help to sell his herbal tea, in return for my lodging.

A few days before the Munts were leaving their house, I still had nowhere to go. I talked about nothing else in the office, and took time off when I should have been working to tramp the streets looking for notices in fanlights. Mike said that his mother would put me up in her sitting-room, but when he approached her, she said it would be asking too much of that poor old sofa, and anyway, Dad would not like to find me there when he came down to do the grate. I put another advertisement in the *Post*, and Doris told me with her boiled stare, that Reporters' Rates only lasted for one week. I paid the extra threepence, but I got no more answers, and trunks were already beginning to stand in the hall of the Munts' house, and the curtains were down in my room.

The curtains were also down between the Munts and me now that we were going to part, but I was now thinking desperately in terms of a caravan or the agricultural hostel, and although we were barely civil to each other and the meals had degenerated into picnics, their house seemed like home, sweet home, and I would have welcomed a change in their plans. I almost made up my mind to go back to the man with the herbal tea. I got as far as his gate once, but the wind was blowing from the back garden, and I got the scent of the rabbits. I even ventured to ask Mr Pellet, although I was still rather afraid of him then. He seemed to know everything about Downingham, but when I offered him that as flattery, he told me that he was trying to run a newspaper, not an advice column for distressed women.

How did he expect me to work for him if I had nowhere to

live? I was furious with him, but that was no use. He never noticed if you were cross, even if you were deliberately rude to him. I banged his door, crashed down the wooden stairs, ran into Joe in the passage and made him stagger, and went out with my notebook to get the details of all last Saturday's nuptials.

I had just been honoured with the job of writing the lesser wedding reports, but I felt far too worried and irritable to care who had married whom, and encased in what, and where. When a bride's mother, whose complexion looked as if she had had more port last Saturday than the doctor allowed her, sat me down and held forth to me about peplum waists and burgundy accessories, my mind wandered, and she pulled it back, accusing me of not taking full notes. 'And the report will be wrong, and then no one will be pleased, least of all Sonia's Dad. He's a marvel like that. Off like a flash at anything he doesn't like the look of,' she said, as if boasting about a watchdog.

The next house on my list was empty. It rang void to knockings on front or back door, and all the curtains were drawn. A neighbour put her head out of a top window and called to me that Thompsons were gone. All together on the honeymoon?

The next house was guarded by a snap-jawed woman with her hair tied up in a scarf, who was still clearing up after the wedding reception. She had her drawing-room furniture out in the hall, and there were mats and cushions in the garden, as if she were fumigating the place after disease. When I asked her if she would like to give me some details, she said: 'A piece in the papers? Oh no, we don't want anything like *that*.'

She tried to slam the door, but the mat was rucked up at one corner, and as it bounced open again, I handed her one of our wedding forms, which had a space for everything, including 'Presents to bride and/or bridegroom from employer', and suggested that she might fill it in at her leisure. She recoiled from it as if it were subversive propaganda, and I went away. We were supposed to do at least a paragraph about everyone who got married, even if nobody had ever heard of them, but I did not feel like being insistent. If I could not find anywhere to live, I would not be on the *Post* next week, anyway. I should have to go back to being a cook.

I had one more house on my list. Rain was falling through the dusk and I wanted my tea. I had half a mind to drop a wedding form through the lettter box and catch a bus back to the office, but I hardly liked to return with only the trophy of the peplum waist and burgundy accessories. I was supposed to have a ten-inch column of bridal news to be written up and set in type tomorrow morning.

Miss Marjorie Goff, before she became Mrs Cecil Salmon, had lived at the Victorian end of the town, in a tall, flaking house with a flight of draughtboard steps spanning a basement area full of overflowing dustbins. Into the riser of each step was set a slit of opaque glass, to bring a gleam of hope to whatever dungeon lay beneath.

There was a small front garden of mossy earth and old iris corms, screened from the street by a high brown wall, in which a spiked gate hung at the warp and grated the ground as you opened it. From gate to front door, over the path and the steps ran a curious glass roof, supported by pillars of cast-iron barley sugar. Some of the panes of glass were broken, and where the arcade joined the house above the front door, it had pulled away and left a large gap, through which the rain fell on to me as I waited for someone to answer the bell.

The bell was a knob shaped like a pineapple. Above it were three electric buttons with stamp-paper labels, which said: 'LING', 'HAWKINS' and 'CASUBON'. The pineapple did not say anything. I pulled it, and hours afterwards, something jangled miles away. I waited. I did not like to pull the pineapple again, because it had felt as if it might come right out of the wall into my hand. I could hear people moving about, and voices, so I tapped on the glass panel that was let into the door behind a curly grille, and presently a large flat face like a turbot looked at me through the glass and the door was opened.

The hall smelled of shoes and soup. Mrs Goff, mother of the bride, took me into the untidiest sitting-room I have ever seen. It was glutted with papers, books, handbags, teacups, dog collars, bits of clothing, and everything that anyone had put down and never bothered to take away. The piano stool was stacked so high with music that you would not be able to reach the pedals if you sat on top of it, but if you removed the pile, there would be nowhere else to put it. The top of the piano was loaded with dead potted plants and tobacco tins. The mantelpiece was a welter of photographs, vases, spectacles, a bottle of vinegar, a pile of coppers, and a jack-in-the-box hanging head down out of its box on the end of a broken spring. In the mirror above, which you could see had once been gilt, were stuck curling snapshots and grocers' invoices. The curtains were coming off their rings, in a picture high up was a piece of holly from last year's Christmas, and someone had had a meal of unfilleted fish and bottled sauce, perhaps today, perhaps a week ago.

Mrs Goff, who was slightly less untidy than the room, was a short, wide woman, not exactly fat, for her bulk was more sideways than from back to front, like a drawing in a child's picture book of the unpopular nanny run over by a tram. She wore a black openwork cardigan and a brown home-knitted dress, which had never been designed for shapes like this, and appeared to have been miscalculated in the casting on. Her grey hair, stained at the front with nicotine, was bundled insecurely into a hair-net. Her fingers were not stained, for when she smoked, which was from the moment she banged at her alarm clock in the morning to the moment she set it again at night, she held the cigarette in her mouth, shifting and

43

rolling it about and chewing on it until the last wet brown half inch was surrendered reluctantly to the brimming ashtray, or a flowerpot, or misfiring into the grate.

She lit a cigarette now, from the packet in the sagging pocket of her cardigan, cleared two leather chairs on to the floor, poked at her leaking hair-net, spread an infatuated smile over the spaces of her face and settled down to tell me about her darling daughter's wedding to *that man*. Fascinating though it was, I had to keep steering her away from the subject of Cecil Salmon in order to get the details I wanted. I could not print in the *Downingham Post* that Cicil was not good enough for Marjorie, never had been from the day they met at the Outing, and never would be, for all his reckoning to be chief buyer, thank you very much. I could not tell my readers that Cicil was common, and his mother, who was she? and that the ring he had bought Marjorie was nothing but paste, dear, and she so fond of gems, and that although the wedding had been a beautiful occasion mind, at the Coach and Horses, with everything as it should be and a cake they would still be eating a twelve-month hence, it had been the saddest day in Mrs Goff's life.

Her stays were too high in the front, and she had to push them down when she wanted to raise her bosom in a sigh. She was doing this when the door burst open and two tufted airedales came in on a double leash, pulling Mr Goff. If he had gone on all fours, he would have been about their size. Upright, one of them standing on its hindlegs could easily put its paws on his shoulders, which it did, and pushed him backwards on to the piano stool, scattering the music. The other dog slipped its collar over its head and went under the table with a yellowing copy of 'Chili-Bom-Bom'. Mr Goff was a bald, puckered man with a large Irish mouth and a whistle in his speech. He would have looked like an old jockey, if his face had not been innocent of a jockey's bitter history of striving to keep himself that size.

'Here's the Press, Waldo,' his wife told him, 'come to put Marjorie in the *Post*. We always take the *Messenger*, dear,' she told me kindly.

'Yes, indeed,' said Mr Goff, taking the airedale's front legs on his knee and crunching the back of its ear, which made it grunt.

'There's to be all about the ceremony,' said his wife, 'and what Marjorie wore, and that Cicil's sister too, with her awkward shape.'

'Yes, of course,' whistled Waldo, 'and who's to pay?'

Mrs Goff shook her head at him and made a shushing face. She pointed to my notebook, which after nearly half an hour had hardly anything in it.

It appeared that there was a mouse in the dresser. 'It's the biscuits, dear.' The airedales kept leaping towards it and backing away stiffly with little moans. One of them got its front half under the dresser and stayed there with its bottom half in the air and its stump of tail quivering. The other one put its front paws on the table and polished off the fish bones.

Mrs Goff jammed another cigarette into her mouth and talked on, but I could not pin her down to the details I wanted. The clock on the mantelpiece, which was propped up one side with a matchbox, said five o'clock; I did not think it was going, but I knew it must be getting late, and I had to get back to the office before Mr Pellet put on the black Homburg and locked up. I showed her a form and suggested that she should fill it in and I would call for it next day. She shook her head. 'I've lost my glasses.'

'Perhaps your husband –?'

'He can't write.' She pushed down her stays and laughed, hanging the cigarette on her lower lip and screwing up her eyes against the smoke, while Waldo grinned and looked coyly proud, as if he had done something clever. 'He's a lovely man, but he never could write.'

'Not a syllable,' Mr Goff said. 'Marjorie used to do the

necessary for me, and now she . . .' His rubber mouth dropped and his eyes pinkened and grew triangular.

Down must go the stays. You would have thought Marjorie was dead. 'And there's her room, you know, at the top of the house with all her bits and pieces, where she used to dream her girlhood dreams. . . .' The bride's mother was off on a long quote from a magazine story, but I was not listening. Remembering the three bells and the stamp-paper, I had an idea.

The Goffs cheered up a little when I suggested it, especially when we talked about the rent. 'A press reporter,' Mrs Goff said once or twice, as if trying out the sound of it. 'Well, I'm sure.' She inspected me, and I could not tell if she was impressed or disapproving. I thought she was impressed, until she took her eyes off me with, 'Oh well, it takes all sorts.'

We climbed up to see the chamber of girlhood dreams. I hardly looked at it, because it was a room, and it was empty, and it meant that I should not be on the street in two days' time when Rogerson's Rentacar came to take the Munts to the station. Mrs Goff would feed me, as she fed Ling and Casubon, though not Hawkins.

'They're difficult folk.' She gathered her mouth into an elaborate smockwork round the cigarette. 'They prefer a gas-ring. A great mistake. You can't feed a man on a gas-ring, say what you will. We have the meters, of course.'

'Not in *her* room,' put in Mr Goff, nodding his bald dome down at me. We were on the stairs then, discussing the other lodgers at the tops of our voices. A door on the landing below opened and a woman in a bath cap and a kimono looked out. She looked at me for a full minute without blinking or moving a muscle. She couldn't, because she had a mud pack on her face.

'Are you much on gas?' Mrs Goff quizzed me from the stair below.

'Have to have the meter put in *her* room,' Mr Goff re-

46

peated. For a long time, he never called me anything but Her and She, not disparagingly, as his wife spoke of Cicil as That Man, but as if I were a thing in a zoo that had not been classified: amorphous, not quite real.

The following evening after work, I moved from *chez* Munt to *chez* Goff. There was a slight dissonance with the Munts over a towel of mine that had got in with their laundry, but Mrs Munt said we must live and let live – she having got the towel – and gave me a Toby jug with a broken nose as a memento of my happy stay.

I put it on the mantelpiece in my new room, where it was not alone, for Marjorie had left some of her girlhood bric-à-brac behind, including a pot full of hairpins, a mug full of black hair and a photograph of Tyrone Power. Her books were on the window-sill. She appeared not to have read anything since she left school. There were some of her underclothes and a bag full of damp knitting in the chest of drawers, and a mackintosh and a hot pink dress in the cupboard.

When I asked Mrs Goff if these could be removed, the look that I was soon to know so well came over her wide face. It was a completely blank look, the mouth hanging a little and eyes half closed against the rising smoke, and it meant No. It was a face against which there could be no argument, for there was no one behind it. Mrs Goff had gone away out of reach of opposition, and would not return until the coast was clear.

First, the look said to me wordlessly that it was sure I had not as many clothes as all that, and then it said to me with words, many words, that Marjorie's things could not be moved, because Mrs Goff had it in her bones that one day Marjorie would come home again. I was beginning to feel sorry for Cecil Salmon. I did not know that next week his conversational value would be lowered in favour of something else. Mrs Goff would run a subject to death for seven days, and then suddenly switch over at Sunday dinner and start hounding something else, which would last her all the next week.

My room was narrow but adequate, with a window which looked out on back gardens, a wooden bed with a slipping green eiderdown and a gas fire which screamed for two minutes after you turned it on. The bed was too near the fire. It kept the heat away from the rest of the room, and if you wanted to dress before the stove, you had to sit or kneel on the bed. I would probably have to do all my writing on or in the bed until the warmer weather came. In any case, there was nowhere else in the room to sit.

I put away my things and tried not to feel bleak. The first night in that room stretched before me with too many hours, and I found that I was looking forward to going to work tomorrow. At the Munts', I had often craved solitude, and dreaded hearing the creak of the stair and the whimsical tattoo on my door that meant Mrs Munt had come up for a pow-wow, but up here on the top floor, a stranger to the rest of the house, I felt unwanted and alone. I wrote a letter home and that made me feel worse.

All my life, ever since I was old enough to realize the un-limited possibilities of the inside of one's own head, I had never got enough of being alone. I had loved to be with people, but I had loved, too, to be away from them. I had treasured the release of my own room as a monk treasures the spiritual liberty of his cell. That was when I did not have to be alone. I had only to open a door and there were the voices and the familiar jokes and the feet going about their small, predict-able affairs.

This kind of solitude was different. I was alone whether I wanted it or not, and nobody in the house cared whether I opened my door or kept it shut. I desperately wanted to talk to somebody. I felt that if I did not at least see someone before the night sealed me into that narrow room, I should be shut away in myself for ever and never make contact with the world again. People went mad like that. One had heard of it.

I went out on to the landing, and cautiously down the stairs, hoping that one of the chipped chocolate doors would open, yet ready to scuttle if they did. In the front room on the first floor, a wireless was playing: low, throbbing music, tuned down so that it sounded far away, like dance music in the Palm Court heard from a hotel bedroom above. In the first-floor back, which was below mine, two people were having a murmured, spasmodic conversation. The woman would say something in a light, rather lifeless voice. After a long pause, the man would answer. Another pause, and she would murmur again. It sounded as if they were busy with something else while they talked: she doing her hair or her nails, he perhaps mending something, or cleaning a pipe, or sticking stamps in his album. I could not tell, not knowing what he was like, and their seclusion deterred me, as did the intimate throb of the dance music in the front room.

I hesitated on the landing, which was stacked about with chairs and chests and other unwanted articles, such as a doll's pram and a mottled tin sea trunk, with 'L/COM. D. B. K. RINGWOOD, R.N.' painted in white on the top. There was also a bamboo table with a frayed rush top. Not the ideal writing surface, but I could do with it in my room, and I decided to ask Mrs Goff for it. I did not know her so well then.

I leaned against a knobless chest of drawers, which smelled of maids' bedrooms in old country houses, and wondered whether I could knock on one of the doors and ask for a stamp, or the time. Could one, in lodgings, call on people whose front doors were their bedroom doors as well?

The man in the back room coughed nearer the door, and I fled on down the stairs, afraid that he might come out with his braces hanging down, and share my embarrassment.

I did not know whether anyone lived on the ground floor except the Goffs. I did not think anyone would want to, for the congestion on the upper landing was nothing to this. Their untidiness had flowed out of the rooms into the hall and garden passage, and you could hardly move for all the coats and shoes and cardboard boxes, brooms, a tin of paraffin, a bucket of coal, two hat-stands, a vacuum cleaner without a bag, and pictures with broken glass and trailing wires leaning against the wall. It looked like one of those junk shops where nobody ever goes, and where it would take an hour to get at what they wanted if they did.

Casubon lived in the basement, whatever Casubon was. If I went down those dark, narrow stairs in the hope of meeting it, I could not casually appear to be just passing by. It would seem even more like intrusion than on the first floor. Stamps? The time? I wavered on the top step, looking down. I thought of my home upstairs that was not yet a home, and hated the idea of climbing back to it without a word or two of contact with someone. But Casubon might be doing something down there. Might be forging bank notes, or entertaining a lover, or practising Yoga.

As the kitchen door opened, I jumped towards the garden door, and pretended to be looking out into the blackness. A very small boy in square knickers and a congealed bib hanging back to front round his neck came round the door and stood clinging to the edge of it, a hand on either knob. At sight of me, his eyes contracted and his stained mouth dropped, but just before he could yell, a woman's voice remarked, without emotion, 'Barry, come back in here, you little sod.'

Barry suddenly gave me a beautiful smile, let go of the outer door handle and slid back into the kitchen. I went up the stairs, which were linoleum after the first flight, wondering about the Goff family and what they were doing in the kitchen, and who were Barry and the cold, unmotherly voice, in the fruitless way that one does tease one's fancy over people one is bound to know all about sooner or later.

The gas fire roared in my room, but the air was thick with silence. Now I really did want to know the time, for my clock had stopped. I did not think there was anyone in the front room, but I went across to look. It was a larger room than mine, but with less furniture. On the unmade bed was a piece of paper, which said, 'Mr Z. No money, no room. Pay tonight or never.' There were no clothes or possessions about, so I concluded it was never.

When I returned to my room, I traced the curious atmosphere in there. Marjorie's mackintosh smelled of fish. I hung it on the door in the bathroom, which was a mere slit, presumably once part of my room, for it was separated from it only by a wooden partition with misted glass at the top. When someone was in there, you could see the silhouette of their head and neck, unless it was little Mr Goff, but I don't think he ever went into the bathroom. He had tremendous washing sessions at the kitchen sink, sometimes while we were having a meal in there.

As well as the door into the passage, there was another door in the bathroom, oddly situated behind the side of the bath. I did not see where it could lead to, for there was no other room on that floor. When I looked at the house from without, there was only a blank wall on that side, with no windows above the ground floor, and certainly no trace of the other side of the bathroom door. When I lay in the bath unable to get out of the lukewarm water, I used to watch it all the time, for I dreamed on my second night there that the brass handle turned and the door opened, on to – what?

The next day, I was woken by sounds from behind the wooden partition, and I lay and watched the dim shadow of a man shaving himself in the bathroom. I could see that he was going carefully round a moustache. The church clock, which had been striking every quarter all night long, as dramatically as if anyone cared, told me that it was only seven o'clock. Was the moustache going to wake me at this hour every morning? No wonder Marjorie had left home.

I went to sleep again. I was in no hurry, because it was Petty Sessions today, and the magistrates did not sit until ten-thirty. There was nothing I ought to do in the office before that, except rewrite one of the stories for Murray, which I did not intend to do. It was about an Old Folks' Tea, and it played on the heartstrings. Murray did not like too much of the human touch. He had been brought up in a news agency, and liked his news straight and cold.

He had thrown my copy back at me and said that people in Downingham did not want to read stuff like that. I said that people in Downingham did not want to read any of the stuff we wrote, only there was nothing else, except the *Messenger*. Murray asked: Who did I think I was? That was a favourite question of his. I sometimes tried to think up funny answers to it, but they amused nobody, least of all Murray, who would slide away with his oblique walk and pretend that he was going up to a conference with Mr Pellet.

It was after nine o'clock when I woke again. Mrs Goff had told me that breakfast was at eight sharp, or earlier if desired. I believe she would have provided breakfast at five a.m. if necessary, for she never seemed to go to bed. However late one came home at night, there was always a light under one of the doors on the ground floor, and the sound of Mrs Goff's voice. If her husband was asleep and she had not managed to keep any of her family or friends as long as she wanted, you might meet her on the stairs, prowling about with her great ginger cat in her arms, looking for someone to talk to.

I tried the water in the bathroom. It was cold. I dressed quickly, with several jerseys, for the police court was one of the oldest in England, and full of draughts. I went downstairs. There was no one about. The front door and the door which led down a flight of iron steps into the chicken-soured garden were both open, and half a gale was blowing through the hall.

I went into the kitchen, where the small boy was sitting in a puddle in the middle of the floor. His mother came in from the scullery, said: 'Look at the little bastard,' in that same unemotional tone, picked him up, and carried him out, holding him well away from her.

'Good morning,' I said, but she had gone.

I stood in the kitchen and looked at the littered table, which looked as if many people had all eaten different meals on it at the same time. There was a faint smell of haddock on the air.

Mrs Goff came in from the scullery, holding a wooden spoon as if it were a sceptre. She was tautly polite to me, as if she had never seen me before. 'What can I do for you?' she asked. 'Breakfast is over, and everyone off and gone about their business hours ago, except Mrs Ling, of course.'

'Of course,' I agreed, for she said this confidently, as if I ought to know.

'Porridge there was,' said Mrs Goff, 'but porridge there isn't now. I clear my table at eight-thirty sharp.' It did not look as if it would be cleared until the next mealtime, and perhaps not even then, if room could be made by pushing the dirty plates aside.

'Oh, that's quite all right,' I said. 'I never eat porridge. If I might just have a cup of tea or coffee –'

'Everyone eats my porridge,' said Mrs Goff. 'I'm afraid the kettle is off the boil and coffee I don't make, except sometimes, after supper if we have company. You'll have to come down punctually to breakfast or not at all. I'm not running a cafeteria here you know, whatever some people seem to think. Eat, eat, eat, meals at any old time and all day long and this wanted, and that wanted, and please, Mrs Goff, may I have another bulb for my light? I tell you, dear, it's murder, letting rooms. It's keep on all day long, work, work, work, and no time to call your own. It will kill me at the finish.' She pushed down her corsets.

I longed to say, 'Well, nobody asked you to let rooms,' but I did not dare, any more than one dares say, 'Nobody asked you to be a butcher', or 'Why be a grocer then?' when shop-keepers complain about The Public.

'Anyway,' said Mrs Goff, 'shouldn't you be at work?'

'Well, you see, in a newspaper office, you don't keep regular hours. It just depends what's on. This morning, for instance, there's –'

'I know,' she interrupted. She was always doing this before you could finish what you were saying, although she could not possibly know. It grew to be very irritating. 'Lunch at one-fifteen punct.,' she said. 'My Kedigree today.' Of course. Always kedgeree when there had been haddock.

She ate a toast crust off somebody's plate, and waited for me to go, her face blank. Barry's mother came in again. She was a tall flat girl, with a bad-tempered face, which was made devilish by eyebrows plucked into a slant and greasy black hair parted in the middle and curled on either side like horns. She stared at me. 'Who's this?' she asked quite rudely.

Mrs Goff introduced us. The devil girl was Alice, Marjorie's elder sister, separated from an unsatisfactory husband and now living at home again, as Mrs Goff hoped that Marjorie soon would be. It seemed to me that it would have saved a lot of trouble if the girls had not got married in the first place.

Alice picked at her nails and listened dispassionately, while her mother expounded to me the sins of her husband. I did not want to hear about Hubert and his so-called cashier, and I edged towards the door. I did not dare ask again for tea, or even a bit of bread and butter. I would get something in a café on the way to the court. It was monstrous, when I was paying for bed and board, but I was not strong eough to fight it out now. Mrs Goff had a sapping effect on you, particularly when she had breakfasted on porridge and haddock and you had not.

As I went out, Mr Goff and the dogs came through the

back door like a chariot race, and I heard Mrs Goff greeting the dogs with high-pitched screams, promising them din-dins, and fondly begging her husband to 'Sit in, lovely, and I'll bring you something hot.'

It was somewhere to live, however. It would do until I could find something else.

Vic and Joe were already in court when I arrived. I was only there as a student, to watch and listen and learn how to report a case, and perhaps, as a great treat, to write two or three lines about a maintenance order. Ronnie, the callow youth from the *Messenger*, was also on the press bench, and a dumpy female from the *Moreton Advertiser*, who had been sent over because one of her residents had shoplifted in our town.

I slid on the hard seat next to Vic, and put my notebook on the scarred old table, which was as mutilated as a school desk. It was made of some very soft wood, so that you could do initials and drawings on it with a pencil, if you had not got a penknife. Victor was finishing off a female profile that he had started last week. He grunted. Joe was dozing.

While we were waiting for the magistrates to come in, I told Victor about finding somewhere to live, and about the Goffs. He displayed slack interest, but I was used to the morning torpor of everyone in the newspaper world. If it did not come naturally, it had to be assumed, like a bedside manner, or the tight-lipped smile of a bank clerk. He became a little animated when I mentioned the name of the road.

'That was where the murder was a couple of years ago, wasn't it, Joe?'

'Search me,' said Joe, without opening his eyes.

'Ronnie,' said Victor, leaning across, 'wasn't it Bury Road where they had that bread-knife murder?'

'That's right,' said Ronnie. 'Lots of blood. Bury Road. Number five.'

'Number five,' I said. 'But that's the house where I am. It can't have been.'

'Well, it might have been six,' said Victor. 'I only know I got a peach of a story there. A gift, it was, because it happened on press day, so we had it as soon as the London papers.'

'Number five,' said Ronnie, nodding as to a happy memory. 'I remember it well.'

My spine crept. I thought of that bathroom with the sinister door to nowhere. Anything might have happened there. 'Which room was it?' I asked.

Nancy came busily into the court with a rattle of her heels, and leaned over the bench behind Ronnie. 'There are half a dozen cases in the children's court,' she said. 'One's that Martin boy with the airgun. Shall I do them?'

'O.K. dear,' said Ronnie, knowing that she would anyway, if she wanted to. Nancy was very bossy, and always knew everything. Often, she knew it wrong, but she still went on bossing.

'You going then, Joe?' asked Victor

Joe groaned. 'I suppose so.' He picked up his untidy bundle of notebooks and copy paper and lumbered out past our knees.

'Victor, which *room* was it?' I repeated. 'Ronnie, do you know? Which room was the murder in?'

'One of the top rooms, wasn't it?'

'Which one?'

'Oh, Lord, I don't know. Don't make such a row. You'll get turned out. There's old Nobby looking at you now.'

'But which –'

'Silence !' yelled Police Sergeant Clarke, unnecessarily loud in the small room, and we all stood up as the high door behind the Bench opened and the magistrates trooped in.

There were four of them, an unprepossessing bunch by any standards, and I have often thought, here as in other country courts, that if I were a malefactor, I should wonder what gave these humdrum characters the right to judge over me. They would be harmless enough in their own homes, no doubt – the chairman a gruff but kindly father, the lady in the black hat a popular hostess. If you met all four of them on a bus together, you would not be disturbed about them; but here, stuck up in majesty on the Bench, they seemed too ordinary, too like the rest of us facing them in the body of the court, to be set thus in judgement on their fellows.

The chairman was a well-known local character, who had once been lord of a large mansion and park. He now lived in a villa just outside its gates, from where he could watch the heedless schoolboys rampaging in and out of the lovely old stone house, and churning up the park with football boots.

Like the one old deer, which escaped when the rest of the herd were rounded up for sale and still ranged the park, suspicious and aloof, Colonel Burrows would not move away from his family home, nor accept the new régime. Although he lived in a little creeper-snug house with a peaked roof and lattice windows and a lawn that took only half an hour to mow, he still dressed and behaved as if he were lord of the cold old manor, with bow-legged men touching their caps in the stable yard and a booted donkey pulling the mower all day over the slopes and swards.

The two elderly maids who had remained with him were still called by their surnames, still smelled of linen cupboards, and were treated as if they were a whole servants' hall in themselves. When the Colonel dined alone, they both had to come in with the port decanter, and stand behind his chair while he drank The King.

They were used to him and they understood, and the jobbing gardener, who came once a week from the village, was so deaf that he never knew that Colonel Burrows shouted at him as if he were a fool or a damn foreigner.

The Colonel's clothes had also outlasted the change, for

their cloth had been the best that Harris could weave. In stifling plus fours and green socks with yellow tassels under the turn-ups, he stumbled about the small rooms of his villa, bumping his head. When he shopped in Downingham for household articles he once had never heard of, he wore breeches and gaiters and a yellow waistcoat, and hectored his way round the ironmonger's, as if small boys were holding his horse outside, instead of tracing irreverence in the dust of his car.

In court this morning, he wore the plus fours, with a fox-patterned silk scarf tied like a hunting-stock, and a general air of having left a tweed deer-stalker and a knobbly stick hanging on the pegs outside. The front of the Bench was solid, so you could not see his feet, but when he took the children's court, where the magistrates sat behind an ordinary table, juvenile delinquents were fascinated by the sight of enormous ankle boots, well dubbined and studded on the soles, inanimate at the end of surprisingly thin and shapely legs.

Next to the Colonel, the top of his head on a level with the bristly tweed shoulder, sat a neat old man in a wing collar, who never contributed anything to the proceedings, and seemed not quite to know why he was there. His hair was parted in the centre and eked carefully over his clean pink head, and his eyes were round and mild. He looked lost, but patient, as if his wife had sent him there to be out of the way until lunchtime.

On the Colonel's other side were two women, who took the whole business more seriously than anyone else, and did not like witnesses to make jokes. One was flushed and heavy, with a jaw like a boxer. She always wore the same felt hat, punched into shape and held on by an elastic that made her bun stick oddly up and out behind. She looked like a Socialist M.P. about to ask a question in the House about fish prices.

The other lady was much younger than her colleagues, and had only recently been sworn in. The weekly Sessions were still quite an occasion to her, so she dressed for them in smart town clothes and a careful make-up, although there was nobody to fascinate among the joyless collection of bareheaded policemen, bored solicitors, and witnesses and relations of defendants, who were scattered on the public benches with mackintoshes and large, misshapen handbags. Everyone dozed from time to time in the magistrates' court, because none of the windows would open, but Mrs Chance, being a new girl, kept brightly awake all the time, and kept raising minor quibbles, or saying things the other way round, to show that she was not just the chairman's yes-woman.

Police Sergeant Nobby Clarke, his grizzled head rising massively from the numbered collar which identified him like a dog, opened the proceedings with various requests for extensions of licences for dances, for Christmas was approaching and Downingham was putting on the motley. Nobby had been running the magistrates' court for years, but it had not improved his diction. He read in a monotonous drone that ran the end of a phrase, and often of a sentence, into the beginning of the next. When he came to the extension of licensing hours for the Police Ball, he paused for the expected shifting and murmur of laughter. The old chestnut never failed, although the police had been holding dances twice a year for as long as anyone in Downingham could remember. The magistrates smiled graciously, and even the woman in the pummelled hat relaxed her jaw perceptibly.

Colonel Burrows said, as he had been saying twice a year ever since he had been made chairman fifteen years ago: 'Well – mph, mph –' (He could not speak without constantly clearing some imaginary strangulation.) 'Well, I suppose we need not ask the police whether they approve of that extension – mph?' He glanced round blinking, to receive the polite laughter. A very young constable, who had not heard the quip before, laughed a little too loud, and Nobby turned slowly round and looked at him. The young constable suddenly remembered urgent duties outside the courtroom and took his red ears away through the swing door.

After this jollity, we settled down to serious business. Maintenance orders and applications for legal custody of children came first, and the witness box saw the usual dispiriting procession of bedraggled wives and shiftless husbands. Whether the women looked bedraggled because they were deserted, or whether their husbands had deserted them because they had been bedraggled all along, one did not know, but the fact was that the women in these cases were mostly so unpalatable that one wondered why the husbands had taken them on in the first place, and felt a sneaking sympathy with them for having walked out. Until one saw the husbands. Then it seemed that they had been pretty lucky to get a wife at all, even one like this chewed-up little viper, who was whining out her dreary story in the witness box now.

Victor was putting a body on his female profile. Ronnie was cleaning the nails of one hand with the thumbnail of the other. The magistrates may or may not have been listening, but the large woman looked as though she were planning her menus for the week. I felt depressed. I had not yet been to enough Petty Sessions to become immune to their bitterness. Hearing only about the marriages that went wrong, and never about the ones that went right made one think that all marriage was a hopeless proposition doomed to rancorous failure.

The viper's story held all the unloveliness in creation. You could write a shelf full of existentialist novels without ever seeing more of the world than the inside of a magistrates' court. Stupidly, ineptly, she told it, contradicting herself and leaving out the most important details, but you could see behind it all those years of bitter life in the grey, degraded street, where the main-line trains threw soot at your back windows and drowned your voice a hundred times a day.

You could imagine the wife with her spiteful mouth still moving unheard while the train thundered past, the galling nag going on day after day, until the husband heeded it as little as the noises of the railway. You could imagine him coming home drunk, and the smell of him in the airless passage. You could imagine what he looked like on the mornings when he refused to get up and shave and go to work. You could imagine her and her mother, who lived with them, talking, talking about him with the same sunken mouths, and the paralysed father crying when they cursed him for wetting his bed. . . .

Victor dug me in the ribs. 'You're supposed to be taking notes, Poppy. You can write this one up if you like.'

I scribbled madly, filling the pages of my notebook. I would write a moving, shocking story, a slashing indictment of the housing conditions that lurked unheeded at the back of our town.

'Not all that,' muttered Vic, leaning back and yawning. 'You've only got a few lines, not the whole mucking column. Just the name and address and that.'

I asked Ronnie if he had got those details. He pushed his notebook across with a superior smile, and in trying to decipher his writing, I missed the magistrates' verdict. Ronnie took his notebook back and scribbled something, and before I could see what it was, he had closed the book and gone out for a coffee, as he did not want the next case. I would have to ask one of the policemen, which was a pity, because they called me the New Girl and did not take me seriously, and I was trying to show them that I was a seasoned reporter.

At last the matrimonial cases were finished. The magistrates were holding out well. Colonel Burrows had had his eyes closed some of the time, but that did not prove he was asleep.

The lady in the felt hat looked at the clock and asked the usher for a glass of hot water. She took two tablets with it, and settled down again to frown on the raw youth with the shifting Adam's apple who stood accused of riding a pedal cycle without lights at Marking Green.

'Mph – this is – mph – a very serious offence,' Colonel Burrows said, leaning his stomach on the Bench and pointing his wiry brows at the defendant, who chased his Adam's apple more feverishly up and down his neck, not knowing that this was one of the few remarks in the Colonel's magisterial repertoire.

The girl from the *Moreton Advertiser*, who had so far been sitting looking down her nose as if she were slumming, set herself in motion for the next case. It was a theft from a café by a 'foreigner' from her town – as if we had not enough thieves of our own, without importing them from pottery-shadowed Moreton.

The poor man had gone to endless trouble to break in, and then all he had taken was two threepenny ice-creams and a tin of baked beans. It did not seem worth it. The tin of beans appeared as an exhibit, but not the ice-creams.

The little story took a long time to tell, with policemen and detective constables and several witnesses all saying the same thing in different ways, which confused the magistrates. It took a long time to settle too, because even after they had stopped the Colonel talking at cross-purposes, Mrs Chance felt it was about time she made her presence felt, and quibbled about the fine.

The old gentleman in the wing collar sighed and took out his Albert, but it was not nearly lunchtime.

When the thief in the frayed brown coat had finally been disposed of, with Mrs Chance victorious, the girl from the *Moreton Advertiser* shut her notebook with a plop, shut her handbag with a loud click, and left to catch her bus. It seemed a long way to come for half an hour of ice-cream and baked beans.

'Must want a job,' Vic said. 'Doing us out of our lineage.

I might have got three bob for sending them that story. Here, you do the next case, Pop. I'll die if I don't go out for a beer.'

At lunchtime I went to a café, instead of going home to Mrs Goff's kedgeree. After what I had heard about the murder, I did not feel like going back to the house sooner than necessary.

I went back to the office early, because I thought that the case which Vic had given me would take me all afternoon to write up. It was an order for possession of one of a row of cottages, in which the tenant's wife had been registering her dislike of the neighbours by such practices as spitting on the ground when she saw them and trampling in her spittle, calling names out of top windows for all the road to hear, and directing a garden hose at them over the back fence. Victor had told me when I joined him in the White Lion that it was worth a lead story of half a column, and I was as nervous as if I had been told to write a leader for *The Times*.

The problem was how to keep the full flavour of the story without putting in the operative words? Or could one? Alone in the office with the morning's dirty ashtrays, I searched through old files of the *Post* to see if such words had ever got past Mr Pellet before, or whether one put the first letter and a dash, or only a dash, or just: 'Defendant used insulting language,' which took all the life out of the story.

I found nothing to help me. I sat down at the table, cleared a space, found some copy paper, and started to sketch out a story. The others could sit right down, flip through their notebooks, and skim off a finished report, without having to copy it out and alter it again and again, but I laboured painfully. I wished that we had a typewriter in the office. There was only one in the building. That was Mr Pellet's and no one was allowed to use it, except occasionally Murray, who would bring it downstairs like a high priest carrying the sacred calf, tap its keys reverently, and lock it up ostentatiously if he had to leave the room for a moment.

It was a relief to be in the office alone for a change, but I wished that someone would come and help me with my opening sentence, which would be printed conspicuously in bold type. I had tried ten, but each one looked less like journalism than the last. In the comp room next door, I heard them come back from their lunch. Maurice the apprentice was whistling 'The Mountains of Mourne' and presently the others took it up in song, dragging the slurs. I threw an empty ink bottle at the dividing wall. They threw back what sounded like a lump of type, and went on singing. The lino-type machines began their hysterical chattering, and outside the grimy windows a dog fight started, a woman screamed, and several cars hooted in the traffic jam at the crossroads.

I took off my jacket, ran my hands through my hair, and felt like a typical battered journalist. I should have had a green eyeshade and elastic bands to hold up my sleeves. Joe came in, looking cold and old.

'Joe,' I said. 'Good. Look, when you want to write Bloody, do you put B dash Y, or what? But actually, it wasn't Bloody.'

Joe went over to the corner where the gas ring was. 'God, girl,' he said, 'haven't you even got the kettle on yet? I thought you'd have the tea made by now.'

'You make it,' I said. 'I'm in the middle of something frightfully important.'

'Not my turn.' Joe sat down with his overcoat on, took out half a bent cigarette, looked at it glumly, and started to roll another. The comps next door began to sing 'I'm Dreaming of a White Christmas.' Joe threw a book at the wall.

Murray came in, rubbing his hands with a dry sound. 'Come along then, Poppy,' he said, like a kindergarten teacher. 'Your turn to make the tea today. I should have thought you would have had it brewed for us by now.'

It was not my turn. I went on writing.

Victor came in, banging the door. He blew on his hands,

stamped his feet, slammed some chairs and books about, and yelled: 'Shut up!' at the comps.

'Tea up?' he asked me. 'Come on, girl. Get cracking.'

'It's not my turn.'

'It's always your turn. You'll have to get up, anyway. I want that phone book you're sitting on.' He pulled it out from underneath me.

I turned my copy upside down so that no one could see what I had written, took the kettle, and went downstairs to fill it in the lavatory. The little room was ice-cold, because nobody had been able to shut the window for five years. There was only a cold tap in the basin, and while the kettle was boiling, I washed the cups under this, dried them on the towel that we used for our hands, and went upstairs with my fingers blue.

While I was trying to warm them at the fire, which was as sulky as a waiting-room grate, Mr Pellet came in.

'Got nothing to do?' he asked me. 'Didn't you go to Sessions this morning? There's no reason why you shouldn't write up some of the smaller cases now. By the way,' he said to Victor, 'that possession case came up this morning, didn't it? Woman with the foul mouth. Leave it alone. Major Back, friend of mine who made the application, asked me to keep off it. Says there's been too much talk about it already.'

'Oh, but,' I said, 'it was the best case of the lot. It would make a wonderful story, and anyway the *Messenger* will run it.'

'Blast them,' said Mr Pellet. 'We won't. A friend's a friend. I want you to come up to my office and go through that school concert report. It's time you learned how to do the damn things properly.'

He passed by the kettle, which lifted its lid at him. 'What's this?' he asked. 'Tea again? I don't know. Women. There never was all this tea drinking before you came to the office.'

I spent the rest of the afternoon correcting proofs with

Victor. He read out the original copy, while I made mysterious signs in the margins of the galleys, indicating where the type was wrong. I had never been shown how to correct proofs properly. They had all been doing it for so long that they could not imagine anyone not knowing, so I had to pick it up as I went along, inventing symbols where necessary. The comps were getting to know what I meant.

Victor read very badly, with no inflections, running one sentence into the next and making it duller than it was already. After columns and columns of sits. vac. and wanted and second-hand car advertisements, we were both nearly asleep and ready to go home. Harold came in with 'just the one more roll dears,' and we sat down again, reviling him as he tripped out of the room. He always walked on his toes, as if the floor was hot. Joe said he was in the first stages of locomotor ataxy.

' "On Tuesday last week," ' gabbled Vic, ' "the St Mary's group of Boy Scouts held their annual sale of work and exhibition of" – what's this? – "handcarts." ' He never could read people's handwriting, often not even his own.

'Handicrafts.' I was thinking about going back to Mrs Goff's. 'Vic,' I said, 'are you sure it was number five Bury Road where the murder was?'

'What murder? "The stalls were well stocked with all manner of useful and ornamental articles. The organizing committee consisted of Mrs Morris, Mrs Bagley – Budget – Rickey" – what the hell?'

'The bread-knife murder. What was the house like?'

'Oh that. I don't know. Tall thin house with – ah, I've got it! Rigley. Mrs Rigley. Got that? "Mrs Rigley, Mr Stott, Mr T. F. Mannering. A. Buffer" – no, hold it – "a buffet tea was provided by" – hm – hm – God! Why can't people learn to write?'

'It was number five though?'

'Might have been. I forget. It was ages ago. Why are you all steamed up about it, anyway? Shut up, and let's finish.'

'I've just taken a room there. I *told* you.'

' "... by Troop Leader – caps there – Dwight and Patrol Leader – caps ditto – Perks, ably assisted by –" Oh yes, so you have – "by T. E. Smart and F. Tonks." Might have been fifteen. No, I shouldn't think it was number five.'

'But Ronnie said he knew it was.'

'Ronnie never knows anything. He wouldn't be on the *Messenger* if he did. "The sale realized the grand total of seven pounds three shillings." Done, thank the Lord!' He jabbed the sheets of copy on to the spike where we filed them, and went home.

Not reassured, I walked slowly down Bury Road towards my new home, which rose up out of the dusk behind its high garden wall with what seemed to me a secret in its lighted eyes. The top floor was dark, since there was no one in Mr Z's room. I half expected to see a spectral face loom at one of the windows.

I went up the steps under the arcade, looking out for blood-stains. Mrs Goff had not given me a key, and I waited for a long time before the bell was answered. When it was, the opening door took me by surprise, for it was Mr Goff, and he was not tall enough to show through the glass behind the grille. He greeted me cheerily, but suddenly hiccoughed and dashed out past me, as one of the airedales hurtled between his legs into the garden.

When I was going upstairs the door of the room below mine opened and a watery-looking girl with limp hair and no make-up came out, carrying a kettle. She smiled with just a twitch of her mouth and began an embarrassed retreat as if the kettle were an indecency. She was probably going up to the bathroom, and I was glad of someone to go up to that top floor with me, so I introduced myself and we went up together.

She was Mrs Hawkins. She was so shy that it was almost an affectation. You had to drag conversation out of her, but

67

she was company, and I asked her if she would like to see my room, because the light switch was not by the door, and I did not want to go into the dark alone. I was getting very silly. I thought I should probably have to go to sleep with the light on, and there would be trouble with Mrs Goff, and I should find myself homeless once more.

When I switched on the light, Mrs Hawkins stood in the doorway and looked round without comment. 'Quite nice, isn't it?' I said, hoping that she would persuade me of its charms. It still smelled a little fishy. I opened the window and saw her light shining from below. 'I suppose yours is about the same size.'

'Well, a little bigger, but of course, it takes up more space with the two of us.' She looked embarrassed at the mention of being in the same room as her husband.

I asked her what he did. She looked at the empty kettle in her hand and then towards the bathroom, as if longing to get away.

'He's a fitter at the White Star Garage,' she whispered, and started to back out.

I remembered that I had not asked Mrs Goff what time supper was. I did not want to miss it, as I had missed breakfast, but I did not like to go down to the kitchen to ask. I felt it would sound greedy, and they might not call it supper. It might be high tea.

I asked Mrs Hawkins, but of course she fed herself and the fitter, so she did not know.

'You could ask Mrs Ling,' she ventured, 'on the first floor front.'

'Go and knock at her door? Would she mind?'

'Oh no.' Again the twitch of a smile. 'She's lovely. If it wasn't for her, I don't know what I'd do.'

Did the fitter beat her then?

'She's ever so nice,' whispered Mrs Hawkins, and finally got herself away to the bathroom.

I took off my coat and went downstairs to call on lovely Mrs Ling.

I knocked on the door of the first floor front, but the wireless was playing a rumba that sounded like gravel being shaken in a canvas bag, and no one heard me. When the music grew more stealthy, I knocked again, and a muffled shout told me to come in.

The first thing I saw, and it nearly sent me straight out again, was a neat round bottom in a pair of white cotton trunks. It was lying on a table opposite the door, and from it two well-muscled legs rose into the air, ending in ankle socks and tennis shoes, on the soles of which a parasol was being juggled and spun and bounced in time to the rumba music. For a minute I watched fascinated, as the strong, fleshy legs rippled their dance in the air, and the *dégagé* feet tossed and caught and twirled the parasol like a ball on top of a fountain. The hips were raised on a bolster, so that the body was invisible, except for a pair of hands clutching the sides of the table.

In an armchair in front of the gas fire, which, like mine, fluttered yellow behind broken asbestos, a man sat reading with his back to me. I could see only his newspaper and the patent leather top of his head. The music stopped. I moved my foot with a squeak on the linoleum, and although the legs did not stop dancing, the prone head on the table screwed round to squint at me over a naked shoulder.

'Hi, there!' it said. The parasol came to rest on one foot. The other foot came up to steady it, and then with the tiniest movement of the knees, the parasol was tossed across the room to the man in the chair, who put up one hand to catch it without looking up from his paper. The legs swept down over the edge of the table to the floor, and with a little bounce and a skip, the juggler was on her feet, smiling at me with long, uneven teeth.

She was a not very young girl with a firm, squat athlete's

body clad only in the white trunks and a rather grubby brassière. The top part of her bright chestnut hair was set in curling pins, and the rest swung loose on her shoulders. She had a long, genial face, full lipped, broad under the eyes, tracked with much movement of expression, and glistening now with cold cream.

'Hullo!' she cried, as if I were the one person in the world she wanted to see. 'Excuse the jinks. Got to keep the old hinges from seizing up,' she shouted, for the wireless was now playing one of those jolly thumping tunes beloved of English dance bands.

'Turn that bloody noise off!' The man in the chair did so. 'How do you like the act?' she asked me.

'It's wonderful,' I said. 'I can't think how you –'

'Oh gosh,' she said, shaking her hair about round her short neck. 'You ain't seen nothing. That's just routine stuff. We open next week in the Empire panto – Mother blinking Goose, if you can believe it. You'll see then what we can do. Double uppers, tip-tops, over and unders, and with the balls and the rings, of course – all the works – don't we dear?'

The man looked round the back of the chair and grinned. He was a Japanese, wearing the inevitable Westernizing horn-rimmed spectacles.

'Your husband juggles too?' I asked, for she had said we.

'Oh, no, but he catches and throws for me. Matters a lot – the timing. And of course he does flip-flaps and fancy stuff on the way on and off. It's a double act, you know,' she said defensively, as if used to having this disputed.

'You're the new one upstairs, aren't you?' she asked. 'Mrs G. told me all about you, and what she didn't know, I guess she made up. Press, isn't it?' She leaned forward anxiously, and relaxed with her open, toothy smile when I nodded. 'Oh, smashing,' she said. 'We've never got to know the Press before, that's to say, not what you might call intimately, have we, dear? Do you cover the shows?'

70

'Some of them,' I lied, although Murray jealously guarded all the tickets and I had not been allowed the smell of a theatre yet. I was going to tell Mr Pellet soon that I needed the experience. I was sure that I could write better reviews than Murray, who wrote long sycophantic essays, calling everyone Mr and Mesdames So-and-So, like *The Times* when it tries to disassociate itself from the vulgar world of the cinema.

'Oh, look,' said the girl, who looked sometimes a girl, and sometimes quite old, 'you must come and meet my old man. I'm Maimie Ling. I expect you only know my stage name. Mimi del Robbio and partner. My name before I was married was Robb. del Robbio. Artistic, you see.'

I told her my name, and she introduced her husband. When he stood up, I saw that he was shorter than she and looked much younger.

'He's a Jap,' she said with pride, as Mr Ling grinned and bobbed a bow. 'But naturalized American. You can't get your tongue round his real name, so I always call him Tick. Tick Ling – get it?' She dug me in the ribs and gave a little scream of laughter. 'And doesn't he too? My dear, these Japs. He's naughty as a hat-stand.'

She was much given to these inapt similes – lively adjectives coupled to inanimate household objects. She put on a torn cotton kimono, told me that she was thrilled as a bedstead that I had come, and offered me a drink.

I accepted a toothglass of beer from a crate under the bed. 'God bless,' said Tick, and drank at his like a bird, licking the froth neatly off his flat upper lip. He was a trim, pleasing little man, more like a polite brother to Maimie than a husband. I could not imagine him doing anything so virile as tickling her. He did not speak much, for she did most of the talking, and when he did, his voice was a clipped, lighter version of a New Yorker's.

I sat on Mimi del Robbio's practice table and she sat on the bed and cut her scarlet toenails and told me scandalous things about people in the house, and why Alice's husband had left her, and that I must lock up anything valuable, because Mrs Goff had a skeleton key to all the rooms and went through your drawers when you were out.

'Now, honey,' said Tick. 'You shouldn't talk that way. I still think you'd used those shillings for the meter.'

'O.K. then, it was the old man who took them. There – you see he won't have that. He and the old gent are as thick as sofa cushions. Mr G.'s getting to be his contact man, like. Tick's in the jewellery business on the side. Get you anything you want, Tick can.'

'Only the best stuff,' Tick said, moving his hands at me with a salesman's gesture. 'Strictly on the up and up. Why pay fancy prices in shops? What do you want – art, pearls, diamonté, slave bangles? What you want, I get. You've only to ask, remember.' I promised to remember.

A terrible noise sounded from downstairs, like the Fall of the House of Ussher. It was Mrs Goff beating the supper gong.

'Cripes!' Maimie slipped off the bed, picked up the eiderdown and shook her toenail cuttings out of the window. 'Better get buzzing. Doesn't pay to be late, because the old cow puts all the food out willy-nilly and them that aren't there gets theirs even colder than when she puts it on the table. No don't go dear. You've seen me in my scanties, anyway. Have a little quickie while Madame del Robbio slips into a hostess gown.'

I drank more beer, while Tick put on a tie and combed his unreal-looking hair carefully, with a geometrical centre parting. Maimie pulled on a pair of stockings, which she rolled below the knees, stepped into a bright green woollen dress, wiped off the cold cream with a few slick, professional movements, and slapped on some make-up. She took the pins out of her hair, combed the top part into a high swoop, flipped the rest out with her hand and a shake of her head, and we went down to the kitchen.

'Ah and aha!' said Mrs Goff. She had her social manner on for the evening meal. 'So you have introduced yourselves already. So well and good.' We seated ourselves at the table, which had pickle jars, sauce bottles, mustard pots, vinegar, sugar and a large bottle of soda mints placed at strategic intervals to cover the stains on the tablecloth. Little Barry was with us, sitting on three cushions and banging the table with a spoon, until his mother took it away from him and banged his own hand with it.

While Mrs Goff went out to the scullery, a furtive young man in a tight suit sidled into the room making an embarrassed face, nodded to the Lings, and sat down next to me. I smiled politely, and after one desperate sideways glance, he shifted a little away as if I wore a knife at my belt.

'Ah! Mr Casubon you don't know,' said Mrs Goff, coming back with a big cracked soup tureen which she put in front of her place at the head of the table. She introduced us, and the young man whispered how did I do, his grey, hungry face registering distress. He looked as if he had just suffered some tragedy which was still colouring all his actions and his attitude to the world. Maimie had merely told me that he was a crackpot. She had also said loosely that he was an abortionist, because he lived in a basement, which was where all abortionists lived, and Tick had clicked his gold-filled teeth at her and told her not to talk that way.

Mrs Goff served out the soup. It was interesting to see who got the biggest helpings. 'Come along, dear!' she called, and Mr Goff took his face and dripping arms out of the sink, towelled himself vigorously on a dishcloth, and came to join us, greeting 'the ladies' jauntily.

While we ate brown Windsor soup, which I have fortunately never discovered how to make, but which seems to be a tribal art with people like Mrs Goff, she told us some more

73

about Cecil Salmon. The subject was evidently not exhausted yet. I had brought her home a proof of the wedding report I had written, because I thought it would be better to have objections now than after the paper was printed. It was passed round the table, collecting soup and butter stains, and to my surprise, was voted to be a fine piece of writing. Mrs Goff's bosom rose, but she did not push the corsets down. They stayed there, gratified, while she read the report out again for her husband, who apparently could read very little better than he could write.

I gathered that the Goffs had never had anything about them in the paper before, except that time when Dad took a highly commended at the dog show. Alice's wedding had been a hush-hush affair. 'At short notice, you know,' said Mrs Goff, making a funny mouth and nodding at little Barry, who was having soup poured into him from a teaspoon. Neither she nor Alice seemed at all abashed at this, because it was obviously all the fault of 'that Hubert'.

Mrs Goff was pleased because either Ricky or I had got Cecil's middle initial wrong. 'That'll take him down a peg, with his Cicil Watkins Salmon.' I felt that my entry into the household was favourable.

This emboldened me to ask, while Mrs Goff was measuring out the slices of meat loaf, and there was much passing round of potatoes and beetroot, whether I might have a small table in my room on which to construct further journalistic gems. Maimie looked at me, winked with the whole of one side of her face, and shook her head. Alice removed soup from little Barry's chin with a vicious swipe and made a slight hissing sound through her thin, cyclamen-coloured lips. Mr Goff, who was a slow eater, and always a course behind, imbibed brown Windsor like a gurgling drain. Mrs Goff either did not, or pretended not to, hear.

'Mr Casubon, I'll trouble your kindness to fetch the gravy,' she said, and the young man stumbled to his feet and went

74

out to the scullery, catching his toe on a piece of torn lino-leum. He could be heard crashing about in there, before he returned with a jug with a broken spout, which made another stain on the tablecloth as he put it down. He pulled out his chair with a grating noise, trod on one of the airedales, which yelped and went to Mr Goff, who fed it with bread, and sat down awkwardly, jogging my elbow as I was drinking water.

'So I thought,' I ventured on, when I had recovered, and we were all served and eating rather suspiciously, for it was that kind of meat roll, 'if I might just perhaps have that little bamboo table which seems not to be in use on the first floor landing –'

Mrs Goff gave me her drooping-eyelid look, a loaded fork half-way to her mouth. 'Your room,' she said, 'is let furnished, and that means it is furnished. It wants for no more.'

Everyone was silent, surprised that I had dared. 'I'm sorry,' I said, 'I only thought –'

'If we all said what we *thought*,' said Mrs Goff, 'the world would be a very funny place. I'll trouble you for the pickled beetroot, Alice.'

Dear Maimie came to my aid, as I felt she always would against people like Mrs Goff. 'But you know, Mrs G.,' she said, in her easy, generous tone of someone who does not expect snubs and seldom sees when they are given, 'there's such a heck of a lot of stuff standing about unused in this house, it does seem a pity –'

'It will all come to its use in good time, no doubt, my dear,' said Mrs Goff. Surprisingly, Maimie was one of the people to whom she gave big helpings.

I tried to curry my way back into favour. 'That tin chest there,' I said. 'There is someone naval in your family then?' Since it was marked Lieutenant-Commander, she would surely be proud to talk about him.

Alice gave what passed for a laugh with her. It came down

her nose, which was long, but cut back sharply at the end, with wide red nostrils. 'Some people,' she said.

'She wasn't to know,' said Mr Goff. 'One of my best bargains, but she wasn't here when I brought it home in triumph like the spoils of war.' He seldom spoke directly to me.

'Mr Goff is a great one for the sales,' his wife told me. 'There's hardly a Monday goes by but what he doesn't come home with some nice piece or other.'

'But he'll never sell,' said Tick. 'I tell him that's his trouble. If he'd only let me help him catch the markets at the right time –'

'He has his reasons,' said Mrs Goff, who sometimes treated her husband to a tempest of abuse, but would allow no one else to criticize him. 'There's untold riches in this house. Alice and Marjorie will be thankful when we are dead and gone.'

'I'll sell the lot for junk and be glad to get rid of it,' muttered Alice, but no one heeded, for little Barry chose to tip his plate of food into his lap and was hustled out with routine revilings and gravy running down his bare legs.

After supper, Mrs Goff suddenly felt mellow, even towards me, and announced that there would be tea for all. I gathered that it was the usual custom for the lodgers to make it on the gas rings in their own rooms. I would have to ask her to do something about mine, which stood on the floor detached, with a broken pipe leading to nowhere.

I had something else to ask her first. I dared not do it without her consent, after what she had said about the bamboo table. I despised myself for toadying to her, since I was paying – and had paid in advance too – but it was a question of anything for a quiet life.

'I was wondering,' I said, when she had poured out magnanimously and we were all stirring and sipping appreciatively, as if her tea were a special nectar, which it was not, 'I was wondering if you'd mind if I moved my bed over a little, against the wall. It's rather awkward having it so near the gas fire.'

Mrs Goff, who was just going to pour tea into saucers for the dogs, put the teapot down with a thump and stared at me, her cigarette hanging straight down and dropping ash on to her front.

'Mind?' she said, with an umbrage out of proportion to my request. 'And why should I not mind? You come into my house, and the very first day think you can turn everything upside down to suit your own whims and fancies. If you wanted an unfurnished room, you should have taken it. With a furnished, where the furniture is it stays, as I should have expected anyone to know.'

She glared at me. I felt myself blushing with anger, and hoped it did not look like shame. Mr Casubon, whose general distress about life embraced other people's troubles as well as his own, looked as if he would have blushed, too, if he had enough blood. He finished his tea with an unfortunate sucking sound, scraped back his chair, and mumbled that he must go and work.

Mrs Goff took no notice of him, even when he fell over the dog again. She was still looking at me, and she muttered something to her husband about 'knew we should have trouble taking on the Press', which I suppose I was meant to hear. I was afraid that I was going to supersede Cecil Salmon as a conversational issue.

Maimie got me out of the room. The Goffs sat on, a dour family party among the debris of supper. They looked as if they would stay there a long time discussing me, and never get round to the washing-up.

'You are a dope,' Maimie said, as we went upstairs. 'Why fly against the old bag? She's perfectly O.K. as long as she thinks she's got it all her own way, but she'll devil you now like she did poor Mr Zenobia, and these aren't bad rooms really, as they go. My dear, you should see some of the places we've been in, eh Tick? I could show you some, even in this town. Last time we played the Empire here, I got typhoid from the water, honest.'

'Now, Maim,' said Tick. 'Now, honey. You know that was only a little colic. Never mind, kid,' he told me, patting my arm. 'Come and have a drink.'

We went back into the litter of their room, which smelled of stale scent and American cigarettes. Maimie threw the bolster off the table and moved it in front of the fire, and Tick told my fortune with cards. They said that I should be rich and famous.

'He'll tell them again for you tomorrow and they'll say something different,' Maimie said. 'He knows all the tricks, Tick does.'

She took off her dress, and I thought that I ought to go, but I was not anxious to get upstairs to my bogey.

'No, don't go, darling,' Maimie said. 'The night is young and there's four more bottles. I'll go and ask the Jacksons in. Do 'em good, poor mutts.'

She put on the kimono and went out on to the landing. Mrs Goff was there, and I wondered if she had been listening to what we said about her. I heard her voice running on, and Maimie's cackle of a laugh. Presently, her heavy tread went downstairs, her hand squeaking along the banister, and Maimie returned with Mr Jackson, who looked worried. He said his wife would not come, as she did not feel quite the thing.

'*That* sort of thing?' asked Maimie inquisitively.

Mr Jackson said 'Oh *no*,' and licked his forefinger, and drew it nervously along his moustache. He was a slight man with short stiff hair and dangling hands. He looked as indeterminate as his wife.

'Oh well, dear, it happens to the best of us, you know,' said Maimie cheerfully. 'I thought I was caught that way myself once, but it was a false alarm, thank God, and me with my living to earn. However,' she giggled, 'there's always Mr Casubon in the basement.'

'Maim – please,' said Tick.

Mr Jackson looked at her over his tumbler, which seemed too big for his meagre face. Her kimono was coming apart in front, and he lowered his eyes quickly and coughed into his beer.

'You want Tick to read the cards for you?' Maimie asked him. 'Oh no, perhaps better not, after last time. Well, come on, what shall we do? You're not very jolly any of you.' She roamed about the room, fiddling with her hair, picking up underclothes with a mind to put them away and then dropping them where they were, turning the wireless on and off. She never sat still for long.

I did not want any more beer, and I would have to go soon. I voiced the thought that was foremost in my mind.

'Murder!' Maimie swung round from the mirror. 'But, darling, no! Tell us *all* about it!' When she was excited, her voice had a husky catch, which was probably too many cigarettes, but was attractive. She leaped on to one of the beds and cuddled the brass knob eagerly, showing the whole of a muscular leg. Mr Jackson, who was listening to me, stared at it without seeing it. Tick leaned forward with his face unruffled but his ears sticking farther out than ever.

I told them what I knew and what I feared, and they believed every word of it.

'I knew there was something about this house,' Maimie breathed, awed by the thought of herself psychic. 'Didn't I say so, Tick, when we came? I wonder you didn't see it in the cards.'

'There's one thing I must ask,' said Mr Jackson, 'that you don't mention it before my wife. It would upset her dreadfully.' We nodded. Mrs Jackson should not be upset. He looked pretty upset himself, and I wondered if he would now give up shaving in the bathroom at that ungodly hour.

Maimie insisted on coming up to see my bedroom. Tick was coming as well, to smell out murder with his oriental sixth sense, but when we were on the landing, Mrs Goff hooted at him from below.

'Mr Ling! Could you spare a moment? Alice has blown the fuse again with her iron.'

'Tick's the only one who can fix it,' said Maimie, so we went up alone.

She manufactured a shudder as we stood outside my door. She was behaving like a child trying to frighten itself for the sake of a thrill. Hand in hand, we tiptoed across the dark room to turn on the light. I found the switch but nothing happened when I clicked it down. Maimie gave a little scream.

'Of course –' I said. 'The fuse.'

'But ours was on. And the radio.'

'Different circuit perhaps.'

'Could be. This house is mad enough for anything.'

'Let's light the fire.'

We found that we were both whispering, but when the gas had stopped roaring and settled down to its fitful flames, the room looked more friendly, and we talked normally again.

'All nonsense, of course,' Maimie said. 'I expect your friend did get the number wrong. I do hope so, dear. I wouldn't like to think of you as good as alone in the room with a corpse. They never rest, you know, when there's been violence done. And what about us below? Blood dripping through the ceiling and that. Oh no, it would be on to the Jacksons.' She giggled. 'That wouldn't half upset the little woman.'

She went about in the half light, peering at my photographs and my make-up and asking me why I had so many books. 'I see what you mean about the bed though. It is daft to have it there so near the fire. Let's move it over.'

'But Mrs Goff –'

'Oh, b— her. It's your room, isn't it? I don't suppose she ever comes up to clean it, and if she does, she can bloody well move the bed back if she doesn't like it. Come on. You take the bottom end. I'm stronger than you. Last year, when we were doing the coast towns, I used to lift Tick on my feet, but he didn't like it really. He thought it was unwomanly. So we – oopsadaisy!'

We lifted the bed over to the wall. As we put it down, the lights came on, and Maimie gave one loud scream and stood staring at the floor with her mouth open.

Where the bed had been was a large, irregular, dark brown stain matting the pile of the green carpet. No wonder Mrs Goff had not wanted me to move the bed.

'She *knew*!' breathed Maimie, and we fled downstairs.

I spent that night with her in her bed. She snored and Tick clicked in his nose and the church clock told me all the hours I did not sleep.

Chapter Five

'WHAT'S the matter with you?' Victor asked me the next morning. 'You look as if you'd seen a ghost.'

'I have,' I said. 'Or as good as.' I told him about the stain on the carpet.

'Looks as if Ronnie was right for once after all,' he said. 'And yes, you know, now I come to give my mind to it again, it was number five Bury Road. Dead sure. I say, you have got yourself in pretty, haven't you?'

He was suitably impressed. He looked at me with a new respect. So did Mike. We were supposed to be checking corrected proofs and filling in last-minute football and darts results ready to go to press that evening, but we did not do much work. We made our morning tea half an hour earlier than usual and discussed the bread-knife murder. Vic and Joe told me what they remembered, or thought they remembered, and Murray, who was trying to write his notice of last night's performance of A *Damsel in Distress* by the Co-Op. Drama Circle, put his lean head in his hands, shuffled his feet, refused tea, and eventually removed himself pointedly to a small table by the window, where his papers kept dropping on to the floor.

Mr Pellet stumped through on his way to the comp room with the purposeful executive air he wore on Wednesdays, and asked how was it going.

Fine, we told him, and Vic took his feet off the table and said, 'Be on the rollers early tonight, sir.' He always called Mr Pellet Sir when he was telling him a lie. When the editor had gone, refusing tea with an impatient grunt, Vic put his feet up again and we went on hashing over the murder. Downingham was not a great spot for homicides, and this one, which had reached nation-wide interest, had made a breeze in the doldrums of the *Post* office, which had been remembered longer than most news stories.

Mike went down to the basement to look it up in the files, but some heavy bales of art paper for printing Christmas cards for the District Council had been put down there in front of the old copies of that year, so we never knew whether Joe was right about the wedding finger being cut off.

Everyone agreed that I could not stay on at number five. It was my nerves, we said. That was where it would get me. I felt despairing about starting the hunt for rooms again. I thought of going up to Mr Pellet then and there and turning in my job. I would go back to London and live with my family until Fleet Street realized my worth, but Vic said they would never do that in a million years, and Mike offered uncertainly to take me home until I found somewhere else to live.

'I don't say Mum will like it – but in a crisis. She always rises to a crisis, Mum does. Sylvia did promise to come round after supper tonight, so we might be using the sitting-room till late –'

'Oi, oi,' said Vic, as Mike's face went moony.

'But you won't mind that, perhaps.'

I said I would go to the cinema.

Harold came in from the comp room in his black alpaca overall and asked what the blazes we were doing with those proofs. He'd ought to have two page formes screwed down by now, but screwed or not screwed, he was going out to his dinner on the dot, and see how the old man liked it.

I went back early to number five at lunchtime, not to Mrs Goff's fishcakes (she always told us in the morning what was for lunch, whether or not as a deterrent, I don't know), but to pack up my things and tell her that I was going. I would have to write off the fortnight's rent. She would never give it me back, even if I dared to ask her.

Maimie was just getting up. They had finished rehearsing for her pantomime, and she had nothing to do all day but eat sweets and read magazines and do her exercises on the table. She finished dressing and came up to my room with me to help me pack. The bed had been moved back to its original position.

'There, you see! Talk about a guilty conscience! I wouldn't say no to it being the old girl herself who done the deed.' She lifted the counterpane and peeped under the bed at the stain to make her flesh creep.

I told her that it could not have been Mrs Goff who murdered the crippled woman, because the family had not been there five years ago, and then I told her the things that Vic and Joe had remembered about the murder. It did not seem possible, standing there in that ordinary, ugly room, with a pale winter sun giving substance to the dust on the chest of drawers, to imagine that it had seen such horrors. However, there was the stain, and there, when I went into the bathroom to get my sponge, was the unwholesome atmosphere, which was partly the meaningless door, and partly the bow-legged claws of the bath and the eternal gurgle in the wastepipe.

Maimie and I packed slowly. She had to examine all my clothes and try some of them on and pry into all my possessions. She was the most stubbornly inquisitive person I had ever met, but somehow one did not mind, for it was an open, not a sneaking curiosity. If she had wanted to read one of your letters, she would have opened it while you were watching, and said, 'May I, dear?' when she was already half-way through it.

'I'll miss you,' she said, trying on my only hat. 'It's been a short, sweet friendship, but I like you. You're about the only human being around this joint.'

I felt warmed. 'I'll miss you too,' I said. I would. Mike's home did not promise much welcome, and I did not expect to make a friendship so quickly when I found other rooms. People in rooms tend to creep about and keep themselves to themselves, and look at you like guests in a hotel dining-room when you come in on the first day of your holiday.

We had nearly finished packing, and were planning what I should nerve myself to say to Mrs Goff, when there was a knock on the door.

'It's her!' said Maimie, with instinctive guilt, and we faced the door together.

A plump girl with a stiff new coat and a badly-set perm came in and stood looking as surprised as we were. 'Excuse *me*,' she said. 'I didn't think – mother didn't think you were in. Dinner's on the table.'

I told her that I was just leaving. She said, 'Oh, fancy,' and her eye travelled to the mantelpiece, checking over the mugs and the photograph of Tyrone Power.

This was Marjorie Salmon, *née* Goff, back from her three days' honeymoon to fetch the rest of her things. She was not like the rest of the family. She would be large one day, like her mother, but rounded, not spread out sideways like a trodden bun. Her eyes had not her father's pebbly look, and she was milder, more gentle-voiced than her sister Alice. She seemed a little shy of Maimie, who greeted her like an old friend, and asked her rather coarsely how she liked married life.

She took her pink dress out of the cupboard, and turned it round distrustfully as if she thought I might have worn it, which God forbid. I fetched her mackintosh from the bathroom.

'It's a pity you're going,' she said, looking round the room. 'This is a nice little room, really. I should have thought you'd have liked it. I was always very happy here, I'm sure.' Her eyes lifted in their sockets and she gave the trace of a sigh, an implication of life with Salmon which her mother would have loved.

'Well, I don't know how you could,' said Maimie, 'with the hand of death on it, and the atmosphere enough to freeze the strings off rhubarb. Even to be up here like this in the day-time gives me the staggers, let alone spend a night in it.'

'What's the joke?' asked Marjorie. 'You're a great one for jokes, I know.'

'No joke,' said Maimie grimly, and we told her what we knew. It seemed inconceivable that she did not know about the murder. Surely she had seen the stain? 'Didn't you ever move the bed?' I asked.

'Move it? Well, I put it where it is now. At least, mother and me did.'

'Then you knew?'

'About the stain? Well, I ought to, seeing I made it myself. I wasn't going to tell mother about the hair tint, but of course, when I spilled the bottle, I had to and – well, you know how mother is. She did create that time. It didn't work, anyway, the hair tint. Fancy you thinking –' she giggled,

85

sucking in her lower lip. 'That old murder! That was down the end of the street, where the music school is.'

'Why didn't it work?' asked Maimie, recovering enough to switch to her usual interest in someone else's appearance. 'What make was it?'

Marjorie told her. 'It was soft of me really to try it –'

'Nonsense, kid. I use it myself. Finest thing out. Didn't it do you? I expect you didn't mix it strong enough. I'll show you how to do it. It would suit you, a bit of copper would.'

'I don't think Cecil –'

'Oh, shucks. He'd be thrilled as a bedstead. Come on, let's go and have a bite before the dogs get it all, and I'll do it for you after.' She linked her arm in Marjorie's and they started downstairs. I opened my case, took out a few things to make the room look homey, glanced round it with a brightening pleasure, and went downstairs to fishcakes.

When I told them about it in the office, they were not particularly excited. Their interest of the morning had worn off. Victor and Joe had had too much to drink at lunchtime, and were embarking sourly on the afternoon pile of work. It did not look as if the paper would ever get to press, but then it never did, until one actually saw the formes of type going down in the lift to the machine room.

Mike said it was a good thing he had not asked his mother yet as there would have been no sense upsetting her for nothing.

Murray, who was poring over the first page proof of the paper, which had just been run off, looked up from the long columns of property advertisements and Council notices, which were the *Post's* idea of an arresting front page, and said, 'I could have told you all along it wasn't number five.'

'Why didn't you?'

'You never asked me.'

'Well, really –' I got up to go over and quarrel with him, but he said, 'Let's have a little quiet, *please*. Who do you

86

think you are, upsetting the office like this on press day?' He hunched his shoulders over the wide shelf where the page proofs were spread out for him to fuss over for hours, and for Mr Pellet to skim through, picking up the mistakes that Murray had missed.

Mike and Sylvia had a satisfactory session in the sitting-room that evening, knowing that I would not be wanting the sofa. He was very happy the next day and could not stop whistling, which caused protests to be hurled against the wall by the comps, who always had a hangover after press day, and did not like the look of another week's work. Mike had washed his hair and it stood up in a fluffy brown crest. He wore a clean white shirt and his cricket-club tie, and looked like an illustration of the honest prefect in a boy's magazine. He told Vic that Sylvia was a girl in a million.

'Don't kid yourself,' said Vic. 'Just because she lets you. There's millions of 'em do. The odd thing, I always think, is when they don't.' He scratched his hair with the end of his pen.

Mike and I were going to the Licensed Victuallers' ball that evening. The office had been sent two tickets, and Mike had wanted them both, so that he could take Sylvia, but Mr Pellet had said that I must go, for the experience.

I did not know what to wear. I had no evening dress in Downingham. Maimie offered to lend me one, but it was too short, and I did not think even the Licensed Victuallers could have stood that colour on me. I supposed that as I was The Press it would not matter what I looked like. I would go in a suit and look professional and importantly aloof from the frivolous throng.

I met Mike in the Green Man, which was just round the corner from the Downingham Arms Hotel, where the dance was being held. He was wearing a dark suit and a light matrimonial tie, and his hair was slicked down, which did not suit him so well as when it was standing up and fluffy.

We fortified ourselves a little at the public bar. Mike did not usually drink very much, but the Licensed Victuallers' routs apparently lived up to their name, and he looked forward with misgiving to an evening of having to accept drinks from everyone who wanted to get their names in next week's paper.

We did not hurry to the dance. In fact, we stayed in the Green Man until we were thrown out, because Mike got talking about Sylvia. When we went into the ballroom, I thought that we were still too early, for although the dance was supposed to have started two hours ago, the long narrow room with the flag-hung picture of Edward VII was almost empty. A small band in royal blue dinner jackets was playing to itself in a bemused strict tempo. A blue-and-gold shield in front of each man's knees announced that they were Don Donald's Commodores. I had seen them often before, but I missed the maestro himself, a vast, moon-faced man with a tight collar who usually kept the party going with industrious hilarity. A few dejected women were sitting round the walls. An old man in a braided waistcoat thumped out the time with his foot. Two women in thick lace hissed confidences under the gallery, and three very young girls in unsuitable summery dresses were being very gay and giggly to show they did not mind.

Where were the Victuallers? Mike led me across the floor, which seemed endlessly empty, and we crossed a passage into another room, where gaiety burst upon us. There were chairs and tables here, and a long bar across one end, and the Licensed Victuallers and their wives were all hard at work victualling. They appeared to have been at it ever since the dance started. They were very smart, mostly in white ties and tails, the women in low-cut dresses, wearing jewels and silver fox furs, with more silver in them than seemed natural to any fox. I had not seen such a resplendent gathering since I came to Downingham. I felt very drab, and brought out my notebook to show why I was drab.

The crowd round the bar was so thick that Mike had difficulty in getting through it to buy me a drink. Several men greeted him, and one of them slapped him on the back and asked him what he was taking. I saw him look uncertainly at me, and then he was swallowed up by the crowd and I saw him no more for some time.

'Hullo!' an orange-nailed hand clutched my arm, pinching the flesh. It was Nancy from the *Messenger*, bunchy in a green taffeta dance dress with dangling ear-rings that looked as if she had taken them off a chandelier. She shook them against her neck and kept fluttering her hands about as she talked. If she had had a fan, she would have flirted her eyes at me over it.

'Here on business?' I asked.

'Of course. A woman's work is never done, I always tell Len. Lennie! Come here, dear. Look, here's the girl from the *Post* I was telling you about.' I wondered what she had told him. He looked me over unenthusiastically, and did not seem to remember that we had already met in the Plough.

Nancy twisted her arm through Len's and leaned heavily against him. She had had too much to drink. She was holding a glass of gin and every time she sipped at it, she shivered and snuggled closer.

'Put your arm round Nancy,' she said. 'Nancy's cold.' She did not notice when I moved away from them to the other side of the room. I fended off a man who could only walk backwards, and stood watching the crowd for a while, longing for something to eat or drink, and hoping that I was getting the experience that Mr Pellet had wished for me.

A balding man in an evening suit that must have been made for him some years before he got his middle-aged spread bore down on me from the bar with a whisky in either hand.

'The Press, isn't it?' he said. 'Oh – the *Post*. I thought so. I think I've seen you with the boys in the Lion. That's my brother-in-law's place. Allow me to introduce myself. I'm

M.C. of this do. Anything you want to know – be only too happy to tell you.'

I did not know whether Mike or I was supposed to be taking notes. I could not see Mike anywhere, so I thought I had better take something down, in case he let me write the story. I flipped open my notebook, with a casual air I was cultivating, and licked my pencil.

'There you are, for Christ's sake.' A minute woman with hair like thin straw and a blue satin dress that would have been revealing if her bosom had been in the right place, came up under the M.C.'s arm and took one of the whiskies from him. 'I've been waiting for my drink,' she complained.

Her collar bones, sternum, and top ribs were as visible as a chicken's that has been carved and left for soup. Her face was painted in primary colours, and her hoarse voice scarified her larynx on the way out.

'You naughty Dadda,' she said to the bald man. 'Who's the girl friend?' Her husband introduced us.

'I call him Dadda,' she told me, 'because we haven't got any kiddies, so he has to be Dadda to me.'

He beamed on her, and then introduced me to some of the right people. I wrote down as many names as I could hear. They all seemed fairly well victualled up, and none of them noticed that I had not got a drink. I needed one. I was finding it difficult to keep a foothold in the merry backchat that ebbed and flowed round me as the Licensed Victuallers milled about, toasted each other, slapped each other on the back, complimented the ladies and brayed at anything that could possibly pass for a joke. I could hear the band still throbbing away across the passage, but no one seemed to have come here to dance. Perhaps they couldn't by this time. A waiter passed by with a plate of ham sandwiches and my soul went with them.

At last I saw Mike. He swam through the crowd towards me with his tie a little crooked and his face pale and desperate.

He seized my arm and dragged me to the wall behind a potted fern.

'Poppy,' he gasped. 'It's terrible. What do you think?' I did not think anything by now.

'Syl's here. She told me she was going to the pictures with her mother, but she's here with that George Deakin. You know. Oh, yes you do. Everyone knows George Deakin, but I didn't think Syl did.'

'Go and knock him down,' I suggested.

'Oh don't.' He pushed back his glasses. 'How could I? They haven't seen me yet, and Syl mustn't. I didn't tell her I was coming, see, because I knew she wouldn't like me coming with you instead of her, even in the line of work. She wouldn't see that.'

'Well, as she's come with someone else,' I said, 'it doesn't matter. Do her good. I'll pretend to be awfully chummy with you if you like. Let's go and dance cheek to cheek.'

He drew away from me in horror. 'You don't understand,' he said, 'it would spoil everything, just when we were getting on so well last night. I must go, that's all there is for it. I must go before she sees me.'

I thought he was the silliest thing ever, and told him so, but his methods of conducting a difficult love affair were not mine. He left me, begging me to get all the names that mattered and to write the story, and disappeared, with his hair rebelling against the macassar, through the gents' cloakroom.

I went to find the M.C. He was sitting at a table eating sandwiches with two hands and talking to Don Donald, who did not look like conducting the band that night. They did not offer me a seat, so I stood up and made the M.C. spell out for me the names of all the officials and as many of the guests as he could think of. Mr Pellet had drummed well into me that the only thing that mattered in reporting a local function was to get as many names into it as possible, and to get the names right. 'You think I fuss,' he said, 'but I tell you, girl, a wrong initial here, or a Mrs there when it should be Miss can cost you readers.'

While I was writing the M.C.'s wife came up, holding a cigarette in one of her claws. 'Dadda dear,' she waved it at him. 'Set me on fire, for Christ's sake.'

He laughed and gave her the eye of alcoholic lechery. 'I'll set you on fire later on, all right, all right,' he crowed.

'Isn't he dreadful?' She sat on his knee, took a light from his cigarette, and blew clouds of smoke round his glistening head.

I turned away. A very small man surprisingly came up and asked me to dance. I did not want to, because I was in the wrong clothes, there was hardly anyone on the dance floor, he was half my height, and I wanted to go home. He told me that he was running a concert and gymnastic display at the Youth Centre next week, and wanted me to ask Mr Pellet to send someone along and give them a good write up, as they needed money.

He had not wanted to dance with me at all. It was just the Power of The Press.

The Power of The Press took itself home after that, jaded. Mrs Goff let me in, wearing a brown woollen shawl and felt slippers and grumbling because I was late. She threatened to come upstairs with me, but I told her that I must get straight down to work.

'Work?' she said. 'At this hour? I don't like it. I don't like it at all. There's the light, you know. We shall have to think about a separate charge if there's going to be all this turning night into day.'

I had to write up the dance that night, because I would be in court all day on Friday. Maimie and Tick were out, so there was no chance of getting any tea. I found a bottle of beer under the bed and two stale sponge fingers on the wash-stand in their room, and took them upstairs with me. My room seemed quite different now that I knew that its history had not been blotched by blood. I did not mind groping across it to find the switch, and when I had turned on the light and lit the fire and drawn the short curtains, it began to feel to me quite like the friendly little refuge it had been to Marjorie.

I took off my shoes and sat on the floor by the fire with the bottle of beer and the toothmug out of the bathroom. Really that had been a horrid dance. It was wonderful to be home. A horrid dance.

'Last Thursday evening', I wrote, 'saw the joyful occasion of the annual ball of the Downingham and District Licensed Victuallers' Association at the Downingham Arms Hotel. It was a memorable evening of gaiety and good cheer, at which a splendid time was had by all.

'To the melodious strains of Don Donald's Commodores, led by the popular Mr Donald himself, some hundred smartly dressed ladies and their partners danced the night away and kept up the revels until the town was long asleep.'

The door opened and Maimie came in. 'I saw your light under the door,' she said. 'Have a good time?'

'So-so,' I said, stricken, as one is sometimes, with that odd unwillingness to admit that one has not enjoyed oneself. 'I took your sponge cakes, and some beer. I hope you didn't mind.'

'That's good, dear. I'd left the cakes out for the dogs. What are you doing – *writing*?' she asked in wonder. 'Let's see.'

She bent down to look over my shoulder. 'Organizing secretary,' I wrote, 'was Mr William (Bill) Parkhurst of the Crown. Master of Ceremonies was that well-known figure Mr Gilbert Wagstaffe of the Flowers Hotel, who spared no effort to see that everything went with a swing and that all enjoyed themselves to the hilt.'

'That's beautiful,' said Maimie. 'I've always thought I'd like to write myself. I think that's lovely.'

So did I, all things considered. I only hoped that Mr Pellet would think so too.

Chapter Six

WHEN the Press ticket for the first performance of *Mother Goose* at the Empire came into the office, Mr Pellet put Murray's initials down against it in the diary. I wanted very much to see Maimie's act, and she had convinced herself that I was the star reporter on the *Post*, and would be going along to write her up as grand as glory. However, it was no use altering Murray's initials to mine, for no one would believe it.

I asked Murray if he would give Maimie a good write-up. He blew his long nose and said that the integrity of a dramatic critic must never be attacked and that he disliked acrobatics anyway, so I wished I had not mentioned it.

I prepared Maimie for the worst. She was anxious to get good notices, as she had no other engagement after the panto-mime, and she would not understand that I was only the sweepings of the office floor and could not do as I liked. She seemed to think that I was letting her down. She was prac-tising on the table at the time, and her head, screwed round to look over her shoulder, carried on an acrimonious conver-sation, while her legs danced and bounced the parasol with smooth unconcern, as if they belonged to someone else. I asked her if she could get me a ticket for the first perform-ance, and she said no, and kicked the parasol at my head.

I was in for a dull time that week. There was a catch in Downingham's breath, before it let itself go in the gust of Christmas festivities. I was only down for a school prize-giving, a round of the shops to report on Christmas buying and the price of turkeys, a lecture on 'Bird Species and Be-haviour in the Outer Islands', and a demonstration of gas stoves. I could see myself spending most of the week in the office reading proofs and rewriting pick-ups about village dances and bazaars. A night out at the Empire would have brightened things up.

Murray was late in on Monday morning, which was unusual, for he was generally there before any of us, to do his big weekly tidy. He had lately taken to blacking round the grate of our narrow arched fireplace. Heaven knows why, but if he expected me to do it, he would just have to be disappointed.

A pile of wedding reports had come through the post. Vic, Mike, and I each took one with a sigh and settled down with our coats on to turn the information on the forms, which was always either too much or too little, into paragraphs of prose. When Joe came in, Victor pointed silently to the pile of forms, but Joe turned his back and stood hunched over the fire, which was burning extravagantly for once since Murray had not lit it, rubbing his hands and blowing his nose with a sad, hollow sound.

'Where's the head boy?' he asked. 'He owes me seven and six.'

'That's why he's not in, I suppose,' Vic said. 'Here, Joe, remember that girl who used to work at Filbert's? Here she is – bridesmaid to old Goldie's daughter. Not *bad*. Look, they've sent a picture.'

He propped the photograph up against 'Revised Guide to the Law of Libel, 1908'. Joe would not come over. He stood by the fire, snuffling and grumbling in his chest and knocking the fire irons with his foot. His overcoat, which was a long green raglan like a tent, wanted cleaning and darning. Both his socks had holes in the heels, and his shoe laces had been broken and knotted so many times that they would not reach to the end holes and were tied half-way down the shoe. His landlady was not good to him. She did not remind him to send shirts to the laundry, so that when he had worn all he had, he had to start on the dirty ones again.

Mr Pellet shouted down the stairs for Murray, and Joe

winced as Vic shouted back: 'Not in yet!' Our manners towards the editor were casual, but he liked it that way. Once, when I held a door open for him, he pushed me through it quite roughly and said he wasn't in his dotage yet, blast you, girl.

He came down presently to look for Murray and to ask Joe to go and see the Town Clerk about a rubbish dump that had come up at the last Council meeting. Joe kicked the fender, put his head on the mantelpiece, and muttered that he had a lot of work to get through and would go when he could.

'I've drafted out the story,' said Mr Pellet. 'It just wants some details filling in. Here.' He handed Joe some half sheets of copy paper each covered with a few lines of his overgrown handwriting. He was very wasteful with paper. We always used the paper torn in half, because that was supposed to be economical, but it defeated its own object, because there were twice as many margins.

'I could have done this,' said Joe. 'You're always trying to do my work for me. I wonder you won't let me be the editor and you be the hack. What's this?' He looked at the paper despondently. ' "Daneshill and Brocket Refuse." Refuse what?'

'Not *refuse* anything. *Refuse*. Garbage. Muck. Can't you read?'

'I can, but our readers can't. Ambiguous headline. No good.' He took a stump of pencil out of his pocket, licked it, and started crossing out on the mantelpiece.

'All right,' said Mr Pellet. 'Write the bloody thing yourself.'

A stout woman with heavy cheeks and a bold manner pushed through the swing door. 'Morning, Mr Pellet,' she said commandingly, as if he were the grocer. 'Bitter out.'

'I hadn't noticed. Anything wrong?' he asked, for the woman was Murray's wife, and she never came to the office

96

except for the annual tea party. Last year, they told me, she had refused to sit down, because she thought the chairs were dusty, although Murray had spent all day cleaning the place up.

'He's got flu,' she said, with some exasperation. 'Wanted to get out of his bed and come out this morning, if you please, but I don't want to have to nurse a pneumonia case, thank you very much.'

'Aspirin and hot whisky,' said Joe. 'You give him that.'

'Thank you,' said Murray's wife. 'When you've had three children and a husband who's silly about his health, you'll know how to deal with influenza.'

'Poor old Murray,' said Joe, wiping his nose on his sleeve.

'Caught cold from you, I shouldn't wonder,' said the woman, 'by the look of it.' She nodded to Mr Pellet and went out. The swing door rocked gustily after her.

'Nuisance,' said the editor. He looked at the diary. 'Joe, you'll have to go to Quarter Sessions tomorrow, and I'll do the Conservative dinner. Victor, you come up with me, and we'll settle up the letters. I want you to write one about the Sunday trains. It's time we stirred up that old subject again. And there's Burton's week-end speech. I've got the script of that. Let's see, what else was Murray down for? That Empire show tonight. Who wants to go to that?'

'Oh, please,' I said quickly, 'can I?'

'No, girl,' said Mr Pellet. 'The Empire panto is one of the few things people want to read about. You can't do it yet.'

I begged him to let me try. I even promised to copy almost word for word what Murray had written about it last year, but he said, why should I, when Joe or Victor or Mike were longing to go?

They displayed no enthusiasm. 'Let her,' said Vic. 'It can be her Christmas present.'

'She'll make a hash of it, like she did that dancing school show.'

'Well, I'm sorry,' I said. 'I couldn't help it if I didn't know which was Sir Alfred's daughter. I've said I was sorry.'

'On a newspaper, it's too late to be sorry,' snapped Mr Pellet, suddenly not genial any more, and cowing me. 'I've told you that hundreds of times. I never knew a girl be so sorry so often, and do the same damn fool thing so many times over. Joe, you can go to this brannigan tonight. The ticket's in my desk, and for Christ's sake give it a bit of Yuletide spirit. This paper's getting like the *Undertakers' Gazette.*' He went to the door. 'Come *on*,' he said to Victor, jerking his grizzly bear head. 'I told you to come upstairs.'

'Right away, sir !' Vic jumped smartly to his feet. 'Looks as if the widow didn't come up to scratch again this week-end,' he said as he followed the editor out.

'What widow?' I asked.

'Red-haired and squishy,' said Mike. 'There isn't one. Vic made her up.'

'Pity there isn't,' I said. 'She might make him less uncouth.'

'He's all right,' said Joe. 'He's only trying to make a journalist of you. You'll be grateful to him in twenty years' time when you're chief reporter on the *Downingham Post* and allowed to write a précis of the sub-postmaster's speech at the sorters' benefit, and sub it yourself. Tell you what, you can come to the show with me tonight if you like and we'll write it up together afterwards in the Plough. I'll get Abrahams to keep me another ticket.' He reached for the telephone.

'Save it,' he said, as I began to thank him. 'You've never seen panto at the Empire.'

It was all I could do to get him there at all. The show began at half-past six, and at twenty-five past he was dragging me into the Feathers to give us courage. By the time I had got him out of there and across the road to the Empire, the foyer was empty, except for the manager in a greenish dinner jacket refurbished with new silk lapels for the season. This was Joe's friend Mr Abrahams, so we had to go into his office for another drink, and by the time we found our seats, the pantomime was well under way.

We pushed past dozens of knees and laps, whose owners said: 'Some people,' and 'It's not good enough.' Others added to the commotion by shushing. We sorted out a small child who was standing up and would not move, tripped over a rolled-up coat and a suitcase, and Joe kicked a woman's hat two rows forward under the seats.

The long-faced comedian who was on the stage dressed as a schoolboy and doing some kind of business with a blackboard was able to brighten up his act by calling attention to us. He wrote on the blackboard: 'SO GLAD YOU'VE COME,' and got an easy laugh. Joe did not see this. He was having a coughing fit, and soon afterwards he was taken with a succession of volcanic sneezes. It was worse than taking a small child to the theatre.

We had missed the opening scene of the Village Market-place (Song: *All on a Summer's Day*). When the scenery had been changed, the comedian with the blackboard removed his ambiguous presence from in front of the drop curtain, which represented a Scottish glen, and we were now in Mother Goose's kitchen, and here was Mother Goose herself in the person of a thin but padded man with a lascivious mouth and bolting eyes, wearing the voluminous oft-lifted skirts, striped football jersey, and red topknot which showed he was the Dame. I had last seen him singing dirty songs in a London night club, and now here he was to bring joy to the hearts of the kiddies, and the best one could hope for the little dears was that they would not understand his jokes.

He sang one of his night club songs, with a few topical and local alterations, and then did a dance with twelve of Jackson's Juveniles, who were dressed as tots, but looked as if they *could* understand him and a lot of other things besides.

At last the goose came on, with spindling legs in wrinkled tights and a vast feathered body, with movable jaw and a winking eye. It appeared to be under-rehearsed, for it managed the body awkwardly and knocked over one of Jackson's Juveniles who came to stroke it. The tot picked itself up, clutching a large handful of feathers. The goose was moulting all over the stage. By the end of the run, it would look as if it were plucked for the table.

With a skip and a jump and a merry laugh, here came the heroine, none other than Mother Goose's daughter, bursting out of the top of her simple cotton frock. She had fat bare legs, high heels, and a lot of black hair which she surely should have washed before the first night. However, she had taken a lot of trouble to arrange it in ridges and sausage curls, with long iron hair grips clearly visible from where we sat.

The Prince, when she arrived striding on even higher heels, was equally buxom. A front to front embrace between the two was going to be quite a sight. She had better legs than the other girl, or perhaps it was the silk tights, but when she turned round, there was a hole the size of a halfpenny in the seam behind one thigh.

She was struck all of a heap by the heroine, and curried favour by stroking the goose and calling it the dee-ar oh-erld crea-tewer. She was probably wont to say Creacher, and had been taught to be careful. Before the young folk could get together, the village lads and lasses, who had been standing round smiling when they remembered, but looking a bit slumped in the background, leaped forward into a Scottish dance, with shrill cries.

This quaint Scottish motif appeared all through the panto-mime, which, according to the programme, was set in a vil-lage of Merrie England on the road to York. That was so we could get Dick Turpin in later on (Song: *My Bold Black Bess*). In the Grand Finale, Mother Goose herself appeared in the full dress tartan of the Royal Stuarts, dirk, claymore, and a' and a'.

In the first interval, Joe wanted to go out to the bar, but no one else was getting up in our row. I could not face those knees and the coat and suitcase again. The woman's hat had not been found yet, and the small boy's family were settling down to a good meal out of paper bags, so I persuaded him to sit still. He dozed. Joe always nodded off when nothing was doing, and often when something was. He called it cat naps and said that all great men did it to nourish their vitality. Once, with me, he had slept right through a Council meeting, and fallen off his chair while the Borough Engineer was paying a moving tribute to the memory of Councillor Dutt, so sadly passed on.

'Aren't you going to take any notes?' I asked.

He laughed and put the programme in his pocket. 'This is all I need. I could write the notice without seeing the show.'

'But you must write something good about Maimie – my friend. She's wonderful.'

'She'd better be.'

I took the programme out of his pocket. There she was: 'Speciality Act in Act II by Mimi del Robbio and Partner.' I wondered if she and Tick were still pursuing the quarrel that had started that morning about making toast, and was still going when I went back at lunchtime. Maimie would not speak to Tick, and would hardly eat any stew. When Mrs Goff asked if there was anything wrong with it, Tick said: 'First night nerves.'

'Nerves my foot,' said Maimie, glowering at him. 'When you've played as many first nights as I have in hick towns like this –'

'Well!' said Mrs Goff, who was always telling us that she had lived in better places than Downingham, but would not have it belittled by Maimie. 'You don't disdain to come here and take our money, I notice.'

'Now, Letitia,' said Mr Goff, putting a whole boiled potato into his mouth. 'You mustn't be sharp with the young lady. We artists, you know, we have our temperament.'

'Mr Goff was quite a figure in amateur dramatics,' Mrs Goff explained to me, helping herself to the last bit of meat in the stew. 'Before his operation. After that, he took up dogs.'

Mr Goff's operation was often mentioned, but never specified, so that one imagined something quite indecorous.

'Yes, indeed,' he said. 'Remember my duet in *Maid of Mystery*? Now dawns the day' – he burst out, with his mouth wide open. He had not quite finished the potato – 'when all the flowers shall bloom!' His top note was like a factory siren, and one of the dogs howled and slunk to the door.

Mrs Goff smiled on him and lifted a ladleful of carrots and gravy to ask if anyone wanted seconds. Maimie got up.

'No sweet?' asked Mrs Goff.

'No sweet.'

Tick rose politely, but she pushed him back into his chair. 'Where are you going?' he asked.

'Never you mind.'

'Oh, don't think I care. I only thought –'

'Don't strain yourself.'

'Ha, ha. Funny, aren't you?'

'Oh, shut up.'

When they quarrelled, they were like children, with futile repartee, and sometimes slaps and pinches.

They were on at the beginning of the second act, for no reason at all in the middle of Mother Goose's kitchen, before the brokers' men came to smash it up. The kitchen table was placed endways to the audience, with a red velvet cushion on it. One of the village lasses, now disguised as a toy soldier and still panting from the dance in which they all fell over in a line, brought on the parasols and rings and rubber balls, and the band began a drum roll.

The crescendo grew like thunder, and then – crash! went the cymbals, and Tick leaped on to the stage wearing tight bolero trousers flared below the knee and a white silk shirt with billowing sleeves. A red cummerbund clipped his neat waist. He looked like something that bounds with a troupe into the circus ring, looking very small from where you sit high up in the tent. He executed a few backsprings and cartwheels quite featly, but without over-doing it, and finished up by the pile of props, with his hand outstretched to bring on Maimie.

She skipped in, bowed, flashed her teeth, and tossed her head with strenuous joy. I began to clap, praying that the audience would respond, and not maroon her high and dry with her *éclat*. There was a dribble of applause. In Downingham, you wait to see what people can do before you commit yourself.

Maimie was wearing a silk blouse like Tick's, with a short white skirt and ruffled panties. The panties were very important, for when she was on the table they were the only part of her that could be seen. I felt proud to think that I had put the elastic in them last night. She wore suntan make-up on legs and arms as well as face, and her hair, piled high on top and swinging round her shoulders, was a dazzling advertisement for the tint with which Marjorie Salmon, *née* Goff, had stained my bedroom carpet.

The band stopped doing rolls and chords, had a small hiatus while it turned its music, and then was off on an unassuming background version of the Destiny Waltz. Maimie lay on the table, settled the cushion, raised her legs smoothly and flicked a finger at Tick, who threw a parasol deftly to her feet from a much greater distance than in the bedroom.

The act went on for about a quarter of an hour, and although it was skilful enough, it was rather a solemn affair. You could not have done it yourself, but then, would you want to? One never saw Maimie's face, only the panties and the legs, endlessly treading and dancing on the air, while the parasols and the rings and the rubber balls, getting bigger and bigger, were thrown to her, juggled and returned to Tick, who received them with a jump and a little cry. Half-way through, the band speeded up the tempo with the Donkey Serenade – that was when the rings were whirling round Maimie's ankles – but otherwise the act went smoothly on with a mesmeric, almost soporific effect.

Then suddenly, when you were thinking that you would almost rather Maimie dropped something than went on like this for ever and ever, the band crashed into a chord, Maimie leaped to the ground in a graceful arc, sprang into the air and poised, receiving the applause open-armed and joyful, as if she were running to meet a lover.

She got quite a good reception. I clapped until my hands stung, and kept nudging Joe. He was sitting like a real dramatic critic, who will not give away tomorrow's notices by either clapping or booing. Tick did a few defiant acrobatics on his own, like a child in the corner of a drawing-room where an infant prodigy has been reciting, and then Maimie ran off the stage with her hair like fire in the wind, he bowling after in a series of somersaults. When she returned to take her call, she looked towards the wings, but he did not follow her. Perhaps the manager would not let him. I understood now why Maimie carried on a losing battle to get the salary due to a double act.

Having seen Mimi del Robbio and Partner, I took no more interest in the pantomime. Joe and I climbed out for a drink in the interval, and in the bar upstairs, he met a man called Captain Warwick, who looked like a newspaper picture of a bogus military man, taken outside the Old Bailey. Long after the curtain had gone up, I still could not get Joe away, so I went down myself to stand at the back, in time to applaud Maimie and Tick as they came down the palace steps in the grand finale.

Maimie said that the worst thing about pantomime was having to wait about in your costume and make-up in order to come on at the end and sing 'Land of Hope and Glory'. In variety, you could go home as soon as your act was over, and have your shoes off and something frying by half-past nine, as like as not, but panto could not be wound up without the whole crowd of muggers on stage.

After the show, I collected Joe and took him round to see Maimie and Tick. He had been drinking all through the last act with the bogus captain, and when we went down the cat alley to the stage door, he decided to become a stagedoor Johnny. He curled his atrocious felt hat up at the sides, threw the green raglan coat over his shoulders like a cape and gave saucy looks at chorus girls when we passed them in the passages. I was afraid he was going to pinch a Jackson's Juvenile with hard rouged cheeks and Dutch-cut hair, so I hurried him on through the rabbit warren.

We found Maimie in a tiny room like a cupboard, littered with other people's costumes and abandoned ends of make-up and old good luck telegrams. Joe and I had to stand pressed against the wall in order to get in there at all. He was still in his masher role. He had kissed her hand on being introduced, and when she offered us some beer from a suitcase under the make-up shelf, I half expected him to try and drink it from her shoe.

We were all going out to supper together, but Maimie and Tick, still in dressing-gowns, were in no hurry to get away. There was a certain amount of first night coming and going in and out of dressing-rooms, and laughter and excited chatter in the passages. Several people came in for beer, and Joe had to stand outside. Presently we lost him, and he was found later in the dressing-room of some of the chorus who had discovered that he was The Press and were trying to force their names on him.

The demon king, in red tights, a grubby vest, one false

eyebrow off and the other on looked in to say the show would run for ever. Mother Goose's daughter, surprisingly small and squat in a tight grey suit, with the sausage curls and hair grips wrapped up in a turban scarf, came in to say had they ever known such a flop, and this was the lousiest town since Barnstaple. The Dame, still with his make-up on, was even more terrifying close to than he had been on the stage. His nose was like ill-shapen wax, and the paint and powder were clogged with the sweat of his coarse-pored skin. His revolting mouth, the top lip painted in points up to his nostrils, was like a carnivorous sea anemone. His hoarse voice filled the cupboard with asinine remarks. He was even less funny off stage than on. Maimie took off her dressing-gown while he was there and began to change her clothes, for he was not at all interested in her. It was Tick he was after.

Joe came back while she was greasing her face, and drank whisky until she and Tick were ready. When we went out of the theatre, he put his arm round Maimie's waist and said she was a lovely little butterfly, too good for all this.

'Going to give me a good notice?' she asked.

'Of course,' said Joe thickly, tripping over the kerb. 'Write it yourself if you like. We'll do it at supper.' But in the Dover restaurant, which was one of the places where people went for celebrations, heaven knows why, Joe suddenly put his head down on the table among the lobster shells and slept.

'Before the trifle too,' said Maimie. 'What a shame.' We finished our supper, but the waitress did not like us much, because the Dover restaurant was not the kind of place where people slept, so we woke Joe and dragged him outside.

There was just time to go to the Plough. He was able to drink a double whisky, but his sadness was on him now, and he could hardly keep awake. He told me that he had not slept for three nights, and although Joe was just a joke, and we always laughed at him for being a disreputable old man, I could believe this, for he did now look really ill. His dry cough sucked at his stomach, and although he was by no means drunk by his standards, his dead fingers could hardly hold his glass.

Maimie was growing fond of him. She was one of those rare finds in life who took to the unlikely people that one liked oneself. She wanted to take him to the hospital, because she said that he was looking just the way her mother started with her kidneys, but Joe, with chattering teeth, said God forbid, because they would say in Casualty that he was drunk. Maimie, who was full of homely medical lore, put her hand on the back of his neck and said he had a fever. She sent Tick out to find a taxi, and insisted on taking Joe all the way home. She would have gone up to his room as well and probably helped him into bed had not Joe's landlady slid out of a downstairs room like a figure on the Stockholm clock and barred the stairs.

Joe crawled on up, dragging himself by the banisters.

'He's not well,' Maimie told the landlady. 'Will you get the doctor to him tomorrow?'

'No doctor can cure what's wrong with *him*,' said the land-lady with a thin smile, folding her arms.

'That's libel,' said Mamie. 'How dare you?'

'It's not,' said the woman. 'You don't know what I meant.'

'I do,' said Maimie, 'and you'd better be careful and look after that poor old man properly, or you'll find yourself in court for wilful neglect.' Maimie's knowledge of the law was about as homely as her knowledge of medicine.

When he reached the top of the stairs, Joe turned and stood crouched forward like a beetle in his green coat, as if he were going to throw himself down again. He called to me that he would not be in tomorrow, and I would have to write the notice, and say that he had done it.

When we were outside the front door, I remembered that he had got the programme, so we had to ring the bell. The landlady had secured the door, and she opened it on the chain and put half her face to the crack. She refused to let us in. She said that we were turning her house into a Babel, making such a noise at this time of night, and Maimie said that she could have her up for unlawfully refusing entry. Tick, who did not like scenes and loud voices as Maimie did, held out two half crowns. 'For your trouble,' he said, with his quick, nodding smile.

I thought the landlady would be offended, but surprisingly, she took the money, unchained the door with far more noise than we had yet made, and let Tick go upstairs.

When we got home, Mrs Goff was in the hall with her monstrous cat on her bosom. She did not ask how the performance had gone, so Maimie told her.

'You left your gas fire on,' she said. 'It's been burning all evening.'

'I meant to,' said Maimie. 'That room's as cold as an outside privy to come home to. Anyway, we've got the meter.'

Mrs Goff murmured something about wear and tear on the fire, and dropped ash on to the ginger cat, which had a broad empty face and derogatory eyes like hers. She was cross about something, but we did not know what. It might not be anything to do with us, because when somebody annoyed her, she took it out of everyone else.

Maimie offered to get her free tickets for the pantomime any night she liked. That was the least that Mrs Goff expected, and she was not mollified.

'We'll have to see,' she said. 'It's not everyone can spare the time, you know, to go jaunting off to the theatre like some.' She looked at me.

'It's my work,' I said grandly, and went upstairs, while she was saying that she did not approve of working at night and never had.

I lingered on the landing, and when I heard her shut the kitchen door, I went into the Lings' room. The fire had been turned off, and Maimie, putting money into the meter, swore that the lock had been tampered with and Mrs Goff trying to get at the shillings. Tick said: 'Now, Maim,' and we made tea and settled down to write the review of *Mother Goose*.

Next morning I took it in to Mr Pellet and said that Joe was not coming in today, but had written it last night and given it to me to copy out. I hung round while Mr Pellet glanced through it, hoping that he would say: 'There! That's the way to write a review. You can learn a lot from Old Joe.'

Maimie and Tick and I had taken endless trouble over it. We had sat up half the night rewriting it, but the editor got out his soft black pencil before he had read the first two sentences.

'Poor old Joe's going off,' he said. 'He can do good stuff, but he doesn't bother any more. This is all wrong for a paper like this. People don't want to know what we think of a show. They want to know who's in it, who played the triangle, and whether it was raining. Take a lesson from this. How not to do it. Oh, no, no.' The pencil moved. 'Terrible. What the devil's Joe been up to? Was he tight?' I saw the pencil striking through the paragraph which sang Maimie's praises. I thought her remark about Unequalled on any stage would not get by, but I did not expect him to kill the whole thing.

When the paper came out, her name was simply down among the 'many diverting and varied acts'. I could have shot Mr Pellet. Maimie could never understand that he was not completely under my thumb. She said she would never work in an office where she could not do what she liked with the boss, and I felt that I had failed her.

We soon found out why Mrs Goff was cross. When I got up one morning, the bathroom door was locked. This was unusual, for I knew everyone's bathroom habits by now, and timed my getting up to miss them. It was too late to be Mr Hawkins or Mrs Goff or Alice. Mr Goff, like a Paris concierge, never came upstairs, and Casubon only took a bath once a fortnight. No one knew where he washed at other times, but he looked quite clean. His greyness was constitutional.

It was too early to be Maimie or Tick, so it must be Mrs Hawkins. I tapped on the door and called: 'How long will you be, Margaret?' It was Christian names by now, and the fitter was William. Just one great big happy family at Five, Bury Road.

There was no answer from the bathroom, and the taps were turned on to drown my voice. Margaret would never do that. Though timorous, she was the kindest soul and obsessed by a desire not to hurt anyone. She was always the one who said: 'You're *not* !' when Maimie teased me about getting fat on Mrs Goff's carbohydrates. She had once been out all afternoon trying to get some brains for William, who, when he came home, was queasy and could not fancy them, but being as kind as she, had eaten them and been sick afterwards in the bathroom.

I left my door open, so as to see who came out. It was a tall, middle-aged lady, making a face to herself, with her hair in a net worn low on the forehead and a woollen dressing-gown clutched desperately round her angular bones. She saw me and scuttled for her life into the front room.

I had given up going down for breakfast. It was too early for me, and I didn't like Mrs Goff's porridge. I had seen it being made without cleaning out the saucepan from the day before, but if you refused porridge, there were looks given, and sometimes things said.

I had coffee and rolls in a snack bar on the way to the office, so I did not see the new lodger until lunchtime. As I came up the road in the rain, I met Mr Goff being pulled home by the airedales.

'Out in this weather?' I said. 'I thought you had a cold.'

'I have.' He remembered it and sniffed. 'Got fed up with being indoors, though. Between you and me, the wife's a bit upset.'

'I thought she hadn't seemed her usual cheerful self just lately.' I quickened my stride to keep up with the airedales.

'It's Vera. Miss Martlett, you know.' I looked blank. 'Of course,' he said, 'you wouldn't have seen her. She came last night while you were out. She's in the top front – and there !' He would have thrown out his arms despairingly if they had not been held down by straining dog leads. 'There's a likely let gone for goodness knows how long, for she can't or won't pay the full rent. Besides the aggravation of her.'

We paused at the high wooden door in the wall and had the usual difficulty in lifting and opening it.

'She suffers, you see,' he told me, 'with her nerves. And when a woman suffers with her nerves, everyone else suffers too.' Mr Goff knew a thing or two about life.

As we went up the leaky arcade, he told me briefly that Vera Martlett was the sister-in-law of Mrs Goff's brother, with whom she normally lived. The brother and his wife had gone away, and Vera had been foisted on to the Goffs, since there was nowhere else for her to go.

'Though an institution would be the proper thing,' he said.

When I met Vera, she did not seem to qualify for that. She was timid and awkward, as if she were sixteen instead of something nearer sixty, but she seemed in possession of all her faculties, and packed away a good lunch, saying briskly: 'Yes, yes,' and 'That's right,' to remarks which were not addressed to her. She had a nervous condition of the epiglottis, which made her clear her throat tensely when there was nothing to clear.

When I apologized for having disturbed her in the bathroom, she blushed, or rather, at her age, flushed, and said : 'I didn't answer because I thought it was *a man.*'

She did not bother me much upstairs, apart from spending hours in the bathroom, scrubbing herself madly as if trying to purge the original sin of mankind. I hoped she would not stay too long, for when Mrs Goff was not about, I had taken to working in that empty front room, since it had a table, and a much better light than mine.

I had to work on Christmas Day, so Mr Pellet let me go home for a long week-end before it, and I came back to Downingham with a second-hand typewriter, which I had bought with the money people gave me instead of presents. Since I was working on a local newspaper, they thought I must be badly in need of it. I was.

I took the typewriter to the office, and did not let Murray use it, to pay him back for not letting me use Mr Pellet's machine. His wife had chased him back to the office too soon after his flu, and he was feeling low and looking more than usually unloved. When he had to do a long article on the spirit of Christmas in Downingham, inevitably dragging in Tiny Tim, I took pity on him and asked him if he would like to use my typewriter.

'No, thank you,' he said stiffly. 'I can use the editor's if I want to.' He was like that. He was a difficult person to help.

Joe had gone to hospital with acute bronchitis, and Murray's doctor had overridden his wife and said he must not do any evening work yet, so Vic and Mike and I were busier than usual. I was sorry about Joe, but I was glad that it gave me the chance to do more on the paper. I was sent out alone quite often, and even allowed to cover Petty Sessions by myself, since there was no one else to send. This gave me great apprehension, for court reports were one of the major features of our newspaper, and allotted ample space, some of which the Women's Institutes would have liked. Didactic presidents were always ringing us up and complaining that they had been squeezed out. I took my Petty Sessions very seriously, sat alert even during the succession of Riding Without Lights cases, and sat up late at night anxiously composing my report. It was rather like being a hospital nurse. One day, you are not trusted to take temperatures, and the next you are suddenly left in charge of a ward full of dying men, because there is no one else.

With more to do in the daytime, I often had to write my stories up at night, and I could have done that in the front room, where every evening at nine o'clock Vera locked herself in against Men. There was nowhere to type in mine, except standing up at the chest of drawers, or with the machine on your knees in bed, where there was no light.

Vera was Mrs Goff's new subject. She had abandoned the topic of the gas-meter man, who had forced an entry with a penknife one day when everyone was out, and she talked about Vera all the time when she was not there, and sometimes when she was. She kept inventing people who would have liked to take her room, and tried to forget to serve her at meals, but we thwarted her by passing on our plates.

If poor Vera had never suffered with her nerves before, Mrs Goff would drive her to it now. Short of actually pushing her out of the front door and slamming it, she did all she could to get rid of the wretched woman. She even found a distant cousin in an isolated farmhouse who might take her, but when she mentioned this at supper Vera cried and choked on a rissole and said she would not go. She had stayed there once before, and they had all gone to the cinema and left her alone with not a house for miles, and she had heard footsteps round the house, and heavy breathing.

'Cattle,' said Mrs Goff. Vera hiccoughed and tried to put a forkful of rissole in among her tears. She was always ravenous.

In the end it was I who, quite inadvertently, got rid of her. One night after supper, when there had been a scene about Vera knocking over a glass of water, we went upstairs together and I asked her to come to my room for a cup of tea. She looked trapped, as if I were forcing her to a pipe of opium, but she did not know how to refuse. She would not sit on the bed, so she perched on the only chair and drank tea with so many fingers crooked that I was afraid she would drop the cup.

We talked of this and that, but conversation did not flow because Vera had on her party manners and would only agree with everything I said without vouchsafing anything of her own. Eventually, because I could think of nothing to say, and she did not look like being able to find the way out for some time, I told her about the murder scare.

Her face worked. She clutched the sides of the chair and looked as frightened as if I had said there was a man under the bed. Before I could reach the reassuring anticlimax of the story, she had risen to her feet, still clutching the chair like a life-preserver, dropped it half-way to the door and fled to her own room. I followed her, but she had locked herself in. I knocked on the door and tried to explain that if only she would listen to the end of the story, she would feel quite happy.

She would not answer. I could hear her banging about in there – she always knocked into the furniture when she moved about a room – and then I heard the strident window thrown up. Was she going to throw herself out, or let herself down on sheets?

'Miss Martlett!' I banged with the flat of my hand. 'Please open the door. I want to talk to you!'

'What's the Dutch concert for?' Maimie came up the stairs. 'Tick has a headache and is trying to lay down.'

'Vera's gone berserk.'

'Oh yes,' she said, 'we had one of those, but it died.'

I explained to her, and we both kept knocking on the door together. All that happened was that Alice came up to the bathroom with little Barry, who always went to bed too late, and said that we were a crying shame, teasing someone who was not quite, and why couldn't we leave the poor soul alone. She'd never done us any harm.

Vera's room was silent all night. We went down to the

garden, but there was no body. No body scrubbing itself in the bathroom next morning either, and when I looked out of my room, there was Vera's door open, her drawers tilting out, and herself gone, with all her hair slides and stockinette skirts and modesty fronts.

When I told Mrs Goff what had happened, she was quite pleased with me. She would never have thought it of me, but she supposed it came from all this making things up for the papers. I was quite pleased with myself too, when I had got over feeling sorry about Vera, surrounded by breathing cows in a lonely farmhouse, for I could now take my typewriter into the front room and work in comparative comfort. Vera seemed to have loaded the meter with money and forgotten to use the fire, for I went on burning it for hours without having to put any shillings in. I had all the tea and coffee I wanted, for I was basking in Mrs Goff's good favour, and she gave me jugs of milk.

It did not last. I was tapping away up there like mad one night, when the back of my neck froze and my spine contracted. I turned round. Mrs Goff had come in unheard and was standing nodding her head at me, as if waiting to see to just what excesses I would go.

I apologized. I explained about the light and the table.

'If you want the use of two rooms,' she said, 'then you must pay for the two. I have my living to earn the hard way, unlike some.'

'But I don't *use* the room. I only come in here occasionally.'

'Occasionally is too often. And the machine. I've never had anything like that in my house before, even when those Australians were here. Mr Goff and I were on the first floor putting away his new mirrors, and I said to Mr Goff: "Whatever is that noise?" I said. "Like a thousand crickets in the wainscot, and they're a thing we've never had here, whatever else we may have had." '

I scratched my head.

'In any case,' she went on, 'this room's let. A gentleman came after it today, so that will put an end to your carrying on.'

Let to a gentleman? I was not pleased at that. Apart from using the front room, I liked to have the top floor to myself. I could wander in and out of the bathroom in a towel, and it gave me the illusion of having a flat. I was planning to get Vic and Mike along to have a small party up there. A gentleman in the front room banging on the wall for silence and wanting to know why beer bottles were cooling in the bath would spoil everything.

I would scare him off, as I had scared off Vera, only more convincingly. The murder story should be true, and I might even make a dark brown stain under the bed in his room. I would get Maimie to lend me the hair tint.

Chapter Seven

ALTHOUGH Mrs Goff had stopped giving me milk after she found me in the front room, my stock went up a little when she heard that I was working on Christmas Day. When Mr Goff had been with the bus company, he had always been taken ill if they asked him to work at Christmas. I was held to be something of a martyr and treated to the mystified respect given to someone who elects to flog himself with a knotted cord. I did not say that I was not doing it from choice, but only because Victor and Mike said that they had had enough of spending their holiday trudging round the hospitals, so let Poppy do it.

There were five hospitals in the town, counting the maternity home and the Northgate Asylum. I had to go round them all and report on the festivities, and as they were spread out all over the town, with the asylum a mile outside, I asked Mr Casubon if I could borrow his bicycle. I had not made much progress with him yet. He was always agreeable for a 'Good morning' in the hall or a few seasonable remarks at meals, but he made some excuse to escape if you tried to go farther than that. He was still something of a man of mystery, and even Mrs Goff did not know exactly what his work was. She thought it was something to do with politics, which Maimie interpreted as either fascism or the I.R.A., and certainly the young men and women in mackintoshes who crept down the back stairs to visit him did not look as dedicated as if they were involved in a plot to overthrow the government.

When they left, he always came up the stairs with them and saw them to the front gate, guarding them off the premises. They would stand a long time talking under the lamp-post outside, as if they could not say all that they must inside. I watched them from Maimie's window, and they never laughed. They stood looking at their feet, never arm in arm or touching each other, like people exchanging good-bye banter. One talked at a time, earnestly, his white face pointed at the others, who listened until it was time for someone else to hold forth.

Casubon was holding one of these nocturnal conclaves when I tackled him about the bicycle. I had been to a dance with Vic. This time I had worn a long dress and mixed business with pleasure, and the only difference between being there as a reporter and as a reveller was that Vic knew me too well as an equal to bother to see me home. I walked along through the cat-haunted streets, and when I turned into Bury Road there was a little knot of conspirators under the lamp. They must have been there for quite some time, for Mrs Goff's rule was no visitors after ten-thirty, and she had her methods for getting rid of them if they were not gone by then.

The I.R.A. stopped talking as I approached, and watched me, waiting for me to pass by before they spoke again. Mr Casubon did not recognize me in my long dress and Maimie's pony-skin jacket, and when I slowed down and he saw who it was and greeted me, his friends, without waiting to be introduced, melted silently away down the street as if I were the Black and Tans.

Casubon did not call after them. He turned to lift the gate for me. 'Been on the spree?' he asked, screwing up his eyes commiseratingly.

'If you can call it that. Part of the job.'

'It must be very exciting – your job,' he ventured, pleating his forehead. People often thought that. I had thought so too, before I came to Downingham.

'Not half as exciting as yours, I'm sure,' I fished, trying to make him open up.

'Oh, well.' He looked down at the steps as we climbed them. 'It is pretty important, of course.'

Mrs Goff had shut the door while he was outside, and he had not got his key. While I was looking for mine, I said, 'You won't be working on Christmas day, I suppose, so I wonder –'

'Our work never stops,' he said darkly. What on earth was it? I did not dare ask him.

'You mean you'll be going to the office?'

'Oh, not that. I mean, it's not just a job. It's a way of life.'

Was it religion, then? That would account for the hats of some of his female friends. In the darkness of the porch, before I opened the door, I ventured to invade the privacy of his life by asking him if I could borrow his bicycle to do my self-conducted tour of the hospitals.

To my surprise, he said at once, 'Oh yes !' leaning towards me and looking much less distressed. 'I'd be delighted. Any time you like.' He seemed genuinely pleased at being asked for help. Perhaps he was really longing to be friendly, although he ran away. I must tell Maimie. She could cultivate him.

On Christmas morning, I went down the back stairs and knocked on his door in the dark passage. He could not use the door in the little area outside, ostensibly because it was blocked by dustbins, but really, I think, because Mrs Goff did not want anyone coming or going in the basement without her knowledge.

'Happy Christmas,' I said when he cautiously opened the door.

'Oh – er – the same to you.' He glanced into the room behind as if he had a mistress spread out on the bed in there. 'Look – er – you go back and I'll bring the cycle up for you.' Evidently he did not like my going down there among the bombs and printing presses.

When he staggered upstairs with the bicycle, I saw that he had cleaned it up for me and tried to scrape the rust off the handlebars. He took it out to the street, settled it by the kerb, gave its saddle a proud little pat, and stood by to see that I got safely off. I performed the undignified feat of mounting a man's bicycle in a skirt, and as I pedalled away I looked back to see him standing smiling after his bicycle, as if it were his horse going into the show-ring.

At the first hospital, the matron was sticky and told me more about the places I could not go into than the ones I could. At the second, she was charming, and took me all round the hospital herself and told me what to write. At the third, the patients were having their Christmas dinner. A doctor was on each ward, carving up a turkey and ham, which the nurses carried round with paper napkins over the battered tin trays. I looked into all the wards and made a few notes about bows in the women's hair, and the dear old men in red bed-jackets, and the dear little kiddies with their Christmas tree and paper hats, almost as happy as they would have been at home.

Joe was in the medical ward, and I went in to see him. He had no red bed-jacket, but was wearing an old brown cardigan and a scarf. There was a system in that ward of opening alternate windows to avoid draughts, but Joe's bed seemed to be placed in the direct current from any window that was open, and, judging by the costumes of the other patients, so were most of theirs. Joe looked very shrunken. He was holding a hard brussels sprout on the end of a fork and tapping it with his knife. I was telling him the story of Mr Pellet and the lady editor of the *Messenger*, when a small, jerky sister in much-laundered navy blue fussed up like a toy engine and said that if I was The Press, Matron had deputed her to show me round.

'I've been round, thank you,' I said. 'I think I've got all I want.'

'Matron said to take you round, so you had better come with me. If you want to talk to any of the patients –' She looked at Joe, who put the sprout into his mouth guiltily.

'I'm afraid I haven't time. This is a friend of mine, you see. If you wouldn't mind me staying a moment?'

She stayed too, so I had to promise Joe that I would come and tell him the rest of the story next visitors' day, and depart with the toy train on a second tour of the hospital.

When I got to the maternity home, pedalling Casubon's bicycle through a slight sleet, it was not feeding time for the patients but for the babies, so I could not go into any of the wards. I noted down Christmas ribbons tied on the empty cots in the baby-room, and the rest would have to come from last year's files.

My last call was at the Northgate Asylum, a mile or so outside the town. I was cold when I reached the gates, and quite frozen by the time I had pushed my bicycle all round the drives and coal yards and cowsheds and laundries, looking for the way in.

Detached from the world by its high grey wall, the asylum

was like a self-sufficient little town. It was reputed even to have its own gasworks, which somehow set the seal of horror on the place for those who had not been there. Seen from the road, the buildings looked grim enough, spires and pinnacles and crazy turrets in which one could imagine lunatics immured, chained and slavering. Seen close to, however, the buildings looked more reassuring. There were window-boxes and bright curtains, a wireless playing somewhere, and the sound of a piano thinly tinkling. The main entrance, when at last I found it, had a glassed-in porch full of potted plants, like the Grand Hotel at any seaside town. I half expected to see an elderly couple come tottering out in scarves and mufflers to lean against the wind along the promenade, but all that came out was a pair of jolly-looking fat nurses, with caps on the back of their heads, and arms folded inside red capes.

Behind the glass porch it was warmer, and my hands and feet began to come to as I talked to the porter and waited while he telephoned to distant regions. He had a friend with him in the office and they were grumbling about having to stay on duty on Christmas Day.

'It isn't as if I didn't do it last year,' the porter kept saying. 'It isn't as if I didn't do it last year. I mean, fair's fair, and I'm ready to do my trick the same as anyone, but they take advantage. I don't know. This place is enough to drive you balmy.' He did not mean this for a joke.

A nurse came through a high, heavy door, locked it behind her, spoke to me and took me through the door, locking it behind us again. We went down tiled corridors and through several more doors, each of which had to be unlocked and locked again, until at last the sound of music brought us to a large hall like a gymnasium, full of men and women dancing, or standing and sitting round the walls looking on. There were more women dancing than men, so several of them were dancing together. Some of them were quite old, in faded, waistless dresses. They took the dancing very seriously, holding each other far apart and moving with slow, high steps like horses working in a ploughed field.

A young boy with a Mongol brow and small, surprised eyes was fooling about among the dancers, throwing his arms and legs about and uttering occasional yelps, as if he were at the Caledonian Ball. When he saw me he roared with laughter, stood on his hands and threw himself flat on his back on the floor. No one paid any attention to him. He was a natural hazard and they danced round him.

'He's showing off because of you,' the nurse told me. 'He always does that with strangers.'

He was the only one among the patients who looked as if he should be in an asylum. Most of the men and women who were dancing looked quite normal, although when the music stopped they wandered away a little vaguely, abandoning their partners, lost until there was something else to do. Behind me, a tall, stooping man with an exaggeratedly cultured voice was carrying on an intricate conversation about something that was 'purely a question of applying the laws of dynamics, old chap'.

'No, *no*,' he said after a pause. 'That's mathematically absurd. You must see that.' He sniffed, with mouth drawn down and nostrils pinched. The only difference between him and a dryly arguing professor was that the man with whom he was arguing was not there.

I stayed to see the staff concert. I had read and imagined a lot about the horrors of asylums, but Sister Taylor singing *Bless this House* in a different key to the piano, wildly thumping to try and bring her into line, was the only horror I encountered at the Northgate.

Afterwards, there was old-fashioned dancing. I stood with the assistant matron and watched the patients dancing the barn dance and the Valeta and the Boston two-step. They seemed to enjoy these more than the ballroom dancing, and executed the various movements with concentration and grave skill. One woman, however, with basin-cut grey hair and a parakeet-coloured dress too short for her square figure, was very hysterical about the barn dance. She kept trying to order the other dancers about, and then going the wrong way herself and getting lost in the middle of the set, throwing it into chaos, and prancing about with her knees very high and her elbows stuck out. At the end of the dance, she panted: 'Lovely, lovely!' clapped her hands, grabbed a man who was walking away for a rest, and swung him abandonedly into the Valeta.

I knew that there were many insane women in this hall, but she was the only one who looked it.

'Er – that lady in the bright dress,' I asked the assistant matron. 'She seems – poor thing – I mean, I suppose she's one of the worst cases –?'

'She,' said the assistant matron, 'has been sent from the occupational therapy centre to teach the patients old-fashioned dancing.'

She turned away, so that I could not see whether she was smiling. In case she was not, I found a nurse and got myself let out of all the locked doors to where my bicycle waited in the cold beyond the potted plants.

Boxing Day found me still working. Someone had to go and write up the Boxing Day meet in the market square, and Victor had said: 'You're always talking about horses. You can jolly well go.'

I hoped it would freeze, but when I woke next morning the sleet had turned to rain, so hey for boot and saddle, a fine hunting morning, with the rain soaking down as if it would never leave off until it had us all in arks. Casubon was obliging again, so I hacked my mettlesome bicycle through the veiled streets to the market place, which was a dismal, steaming pit of horses with their tails tucked in against the rain, riders ditto, with white mackintoshes over habits, and spectators with their collars up.

Quite a crowd of townspeople had come to stare and try to stroke the hounds. They viewed the scene without envy, glad that they had not got to do it themselves, but glad that someone should uphold the old tradition, which they had been vaguely led to believe had made England what it was. Hunting, the rich man's sport, curiously inspired no anarchy. Out of the field, the hunting classes had had their day. They could not get servants, their homes were being sold for schools and institutions, no one called them Sir any more, and there were the *oddest* looking people nowadays in the Berkeley. But having achieved the bloodless revolution, the working man allowed them this small, picturesque pleasure, and rather liked to read in his paper in wartime that Major the Hon. Justin Ogilvy had gone into action blowing a hunting horn.

The other people on foot were the indefatigables, who had come in porkpie hats and indestructible clothes to dash about in cars to strategic points, and then wade over a ploughed field to stand in a gateway, waving to their mounted friends as they charged through and splashed them with mud, and telling the Master, who knew better, which way the fox had gone. They had brought friends who were staying with them over Christmas, because 'Everyone always goes to the Boxing Day meet.' No question of who wanted to and who did not, the friends had accepted the fate of their shoes and come partly to counteract last night's port, and partly because there was no fire lit in the drawing-room before lunch.

I wanted to speak to the Master, to get the Personal Touch, which was still my Mecca, whatever the others might say, or Mr Pellet's pencil might do. I found him struggling out of a small car, in a long camelhair coat, stamping about with his legs spread to get the feel of his boots.

I introduced myself and he said 'Morning' and started to walk away to where a rat-faced groom was trying to keep more than two legs of his horse on the ground at the same time.

I followed the Master. 'Excuse me, sir, er –' What on earth could I ask him? He stopped, surprised to find me still there. 'Er – do you expect a good hunt today?'

'Can't tell. Scent's tricky.' He walked on.

'Have you had a good season so far?'

'So-so.'

'How many couples have you out today?'

'Well, count for yourself,' he grunted, but then took pity on me and paused. 'Nineteen and a half. Bitch pack.' He walked on. I followed him like an insect, tickling him with questions, and he kept brushing me off with impatient answers. He reached his horse, exchanged sour nods with the groom, and put a foot in the stirrup, while the animal went round in mad circles on the slippery cobbles. When he was up, and his weight pressed the saddle on to its cold back, it became even madder, so I left him to his Goddams and went in search of further copy.

I was handicapped in Downingham by not having lived there long enough to know all the notables. Vic and Murray and Mr Pellet knew everyone, and knew how to spell their names and what letters came after. All these people in top hats and bowlers looked alike to me, except that some of the men looked more stupid than others, and some of the women were weathered and terrifying, with hair already at odds with the wind, and some were quite pleasing, with bright make-up and neat hair.

I found one of my constable friends from the magistrates' court and he pointed out to me the Joint Master, a moneyed type, who had been unwillingly co-opted to keep the hunt going. His vast white breeches squatted insecurely on a chest-nut cob with a behind like a great round orange, which rolled its eye backwards at him as if it feared he would fall off.

My policeman also showed me Lady Peppering, who had the lean, cold-eyed face of a greyhound and legs that looked as if they had been sewn into her breeches and then moulded on to her beautiful horse. I knew all about her. She was as much liked by men as she was disliked by women, and looking at some of them here today I wondered whether perhaps it was not the women's own fault.

When the hunt moved off, hooves clopping hollow on the wet tarmac, I asked a groom where they were going first. He told me Gibbet Wood. Of course he was wrong, but Mr Pellet, who uncannily knew everything, knew where they had gone, and altered my copy without comment.

When I got back from the meet, Casubon, who appeared to be spending Christmas in the basement, popped up the stairs to ask me how the bicycle had been, like a groom inquiring how the favourite hunter has performed.

'Of course, I don't approve of blood sports,' he said, as he carried the dripping bicycle through the hall, for fear of Mrs Goff's linoleum. 'I read a very interesting pamphlet on the subject. I'll lend it you if you like.' Pamphlets were the only things he read. He did not have time for books, but there was always a leaflet or two sticking out of his pockets, and he was often to be seen reading one as he tacked down the street. He had a slight weakness in his legs, more of a wobble than a limp. That was partly why he bicycled to work, to strengthen them.

Such few opinions as he expressed came from pamphlets. Whatever their subject, he took them for gospel truth, his argument being that if it was not true it would not be worth making a pamphlet of it. I found this out later, when I got to know him better, but at the moment I did not know that he was an inveterate pamphlet-sharer, so I accepted the tract on blood sports which, indeed, I found most convincing.

I condensed it next day into a Letter to the Editor, which I sent to Mr Pellet in the hope that he might print it. I signed it *Misericordia*. If it started a correspondence, I would write again under the pseudonym of *ex*-M.F.H. to say that the fox enjoyed being hunted, if no one else did so first.

Mr Pellet shouted down his belfry stairs for me. He had my letter on his desk. 'Think I don't know your typing by now, girl?' he asked. 'You always get a faint "8" under the apostrophe.'

'I'm sorry, I thought it –'

'Why be sorry? It's a good letter, though I suspect you cribbed it. We'll print it, and write the answers ourselves if the hunting mob are too illiterate. Ay, you're no sich a bad lass.' He looked on me with wondering approval. Scots mixed with Yorkshire meant mellowness indeed.

'Just for that, you can do the letters this week.' He handed me a bunch of unopened envelopes. 'Look through these, take at least one answer about last week's playground thing, and if there isn't one, write your own drip about kiddies playing in the streets. Cut your own a little. You can head it "This Cruelty Must Stop!" and then make up with road safety and housing – the usual thing.'

'Must be the widow,' Vic said, when I told them downstairs. 'She's always at her best, Christmas.'

'Of course,' said Murray, with his back to me, 'I usually do the letters, but naturally I shall be only too glad to have them taken off my hands. I'll help you, though.'

'Oh, no thanks. I'd like to try by myself. I'm going to make this a really super column for once – Oh, I'm sorry. I didn't mean that.'

To cover my confusion, I took the cups downstairs, filled the kettle and washed and dried the cups with extra care while the kettle boiled, hoping that Murray would have got over being offended by the time I came back.

When I did, he had gone out, so I had wasted my time over the cups. While we drank tea, laced with a little rum which Victor had saved from his home festivities, I read the letters. Some had no sense at all and went straight into the waste-paper basket, which had not been emptied since halfway through Advent. Others made too much sense but went the same way, since we never printed any criticism of the paper. Most of them were about politics or local council affairs and were terribly dull, but there was one from a woman who had got it into her head that Mr Pellet was Aunt Mabel and wrote to ask him how to get rid of a fine growth of hair on her upper lip.

'You see,' I said, when I had read it out. 'We *ought* to have a woman's column. Hundreds of them would write in like this, and they'd all buy the paper.'

'They do already. Shut up,' said Mike. 'If I've got to do Joe's confounded Kiddie's Korner, I must have peace.' Sylvia had spent Christmas Day with him and Boxing Day with someone else. He was a little rattled.

'Some of them read the *Messenger*,' I said, 'and they've only got Nancy's silly little thing about how to crochet hats and knit toy bunnies. They'd all come to us. It would shoot up the turnover like mad, and we could have new lino on the stairs. Joe will break his neck one day.'

'Might even give you a rise for thinking of it,' said Victor.

'They might. It's a good idea. I'm going to try it out in the letter column. Who wants to read all this about road safety and housing? The daily papers don't have letters about road safety and housing. They have letters from ordinary people, about ordinary things that matter, like – like divorce, and who's got the oldest cat, and whether men respect the girl who says No –'

'And hair on the upper lip,' said Vic.

'Yes, hair on the upper lip. Woman's angle stuff. That's what people want. I'm going to put some woman's angle into the letters this week, instead of road safety and housing.'

'Never get past Pelly.'

'We'll see. He may come round to it when he sees it in writing. After all, he liked my letter about blood sports.'

'All right,' Vic said, pouring rum into his teacup, 'we'll see.'

I composed the letters carefully, with the help of Maimie and Margaret Jackson. Nothing about moustaches or the girl who says No. The editor would have to be broken in gently, with more serious matters. I asked Maimie and Margaret what they would like to see discussed in a newspaper. Maimie said hair-styles, and Margaret said the cost of living. We kept the cost of living and invented a weekly budget for a mythical Mrs Salter, trying to keep house with two children on the wages of a railway linesman. I liked Mrs Salter. I worked over her so long that I almost believed in her. I admired her gallant effort to give up cigarettes so that her children could have new shoes to go to the school camp, and I felt that Mr S. should either cut down on beer or go less often to the pictures.

Maimie, who always said that she and Tick would never have a child until she was too rheumatic to juggle, suggested a letter saying that people ought to have big families. Margaret blushed. Even an indirect reference to the intimacies of marriage embarrassed her. I wondered how she and William had ever got through their first night.

'We'll put in a stinger about landladies like Ma Goff who won't take children,' Maimie said. 'She reads the *Post*.'

'She won't after that.'

'And why not one for Alice about children not being house-trained at the age of three. Don't tell me it's the dogs.'

Margaret was still looking uncomfortable. She was paler than ever these days and a little of her negative quality had been supplanted by an active depression. I thought it was because she went out so little. She did her shopping, and for the rest of the day she cleaned her room and waited for William to come home. One afternoon when I was free I asked her to come to the cinema with me, but she would not be persuaded. I think it was because she could not afford it, but when I hinted that I would pay, she refused even more vehemently. She was a sad little person with only half a life, and William was incomplete too, because he had no joy or

129

energy. Thank goodness they had each other. Even so, they had not much, but without each other they might be the quietly agonized kind who are found in the river, or in a gas-filled room, the surprisingly brave yet logical act of someone who sees no reason for living.

I liked my letters. If I had been an impartial reader, I should have paused in my idle turning of the pages and thought, Ah, good! The old *Post* is waking up at last. Page five was set early in the week, so I delivered the copy in good time to Mr Pellet. I put it on his desk before he came in, so that he could digest the innovation calmly and alone before he started shouting.

He came in at ten o'clock, and started shouting at half past.

'There you are,' said Vic. 'He likes it. What are you waiting for?'

'You go,' I said, 'and tell him I'm out,' but Mr Pellet was already coming down in search of me, his brows weighing down on his bright blue eyes.

I trailed up behind him, feeling as I had not felt since the headmistress summoned me for going out shopping during the individual study period.

Road safety and housing. Of course, it came up again. He had told me to put in road safety and housing, and I had put in tripe from silly women. 'But I suppose you wrote them.'

'Oh *no*. They're genuine. Readers really are interested in these things.'

'I'll see the letters later.' I would have to make Maimie and Margaret write them. He would recognize my writing, even disguised.

'When we want something new on the paper,' he said, 'I'll tell you. Otherwise, you'll do the job you're hired for.'

Then he suddenly became quite nice. He sat down and looked out of the window, so that I could not see whether his eyebrows had gone back into place again. 'Everyone who comes here', he said, 'starts off by thinking this is a lousy old rag and they must have been sent from Heaven to bring it up to date. Victor, Mike, even Murray – they all started like that. It didn't last, when they had rumbled what the job was. Do you know why people read this paper? Because they've been reading it for umpteen years, and it's still more or less the same as the first copy they ever read. It's safe. They know where they are. In Downingham, they've been eating meat pie and chips on Saturday nights since the world began, and if they were suddenly asked to eat their joint on Saturday and the pie on Sunday they'd think the bottom had dropped out of life. So they would if the *Post* started printing strip cartoons or life stories of sex murders. When they open the *Post*, they like to know what they're going to get. God knows there are shocks enough in this world already.'

'But you let me print my letter about blood sports. Isn't that a shock in a hunting county?'

'Lord, girl, we've been printing that letter at intervals for years,' he said. 'It's one of the old favourites.'

'Shall I do the letters again, then?' I asked, feeling crushed.

'Have you time? Harold wants the copy now. What have you got on?'

'Only to go and see a woman whose husband died in the coal shed.'

'The postman. That's page five too. Better get on with it. I'll do the letters, and you get on out and see the corpse.'

Which was truer than he knew. The postman's widow lived in a row of brown brick houses with bow windows, green paint, and a bit of stained glass in the front door. The road ran downhill so that the terrace of houses and privet-topped walls was built at the angle of a funicular railway. Some of the houses had numbers. Some had only names, and I walked right down the street and back up the hill again before I found 'Marengo'.

'I saw you go by,' said the postman's widow, as she opened the door. 'I thought you might be coming here. I saw you taking notes at the concert where my little grandchild sang.'

'I hope you don't mind me coming at a time like this?' It was a job I hated. I thought how furious I should be if someone came to make copy out of my bereavement, but most people were surprisingly agreeable.

The postman's widow was even pleased. 'Bless you, no,' she said. 'When mother went, in the big frost three years ago, I had ever such a nice young man from the papers come to see me. We had quite a chat.'

She sat me down and gave me a cup of cocoa with too much sugar in it and told me about the last hours of the postman. It seemed disrespectful to take notes. I felt I should have been sitting listening with nods and clucks, but the postman had been on this round for so long that he was a well-known figure, and Murray had told me to get a story, so out came the loose-leaved notebook.

'He should have retired two years ago,' his widow told me, 'when the doctor said it was his heart, but he wouldn't. They thought very highly of him at the post office, you see, but I didn't like it. Pant! I've seen him come home up this road sometimes and have to stop at the gate to draw his breath, though if I was at the window he'd always pretend he was tying his shoe. And then two nights ago, the fire was low, and he'd gone out the back to get me a scuttleful of coal. When he didn't come in, I thought perhaps he'd called over to his friend next door and gone out the side gate to go down the road with him. I never thought. But when I went later to get the coal myself, there he was, poor soul, laying forward on the heap, and I said to myself, "He's gone." Black, he was, from head to foot, but nurse has washed him and made him look really lovely. I expect you'd like to see him?'

'Oh no. No, thank you. That isn't necessary.'

She insisted, however, and I was taken up to a spotless bedroom. The widow drew back the curtains, and there on the high double bed was the postman, scrubbed and aloof, with his teeth prominently in, his hair plastered down, and his hands folded over the sheet. The nurse had not been able to remove the nicotine stains from his fingers, and although at first sight he had looked as reassuringly not there as all dead bodies, this small reminder of his living habits made me suddenly as afraid of him as if he had stirred and sat up.

'Doesn't he look beautiful?' the woman whispered, straightening a corner of the counterpane.

I took a step backwards, looking at his hands. He was laid out on one side of the wide bed, and the pillow on the other side was slightly creased with use. The thought came to me that the widow might be sleeping in the same bed as the corpse, and I left the room.

She came out after me, leaving the door ajar and taking a look back through it, as if a child had just been settled to sleep in there.

'I thought you'd like to see him,' she said, as we went downstairs. 'I wouldn't let them take him away. It's a great comfort to me to have him here and got up so lovely. I only hope someone will do the same for me when my time comes.'

When one outgrows the morbid visions of childhood, one does not think of oneself as a corpse, but she, already seeing herself laid out in that upstairs room, started me thinking about dying, and wondering what people would say and whether Mr Pellet would give me an obituary in the *Post* if I died while in his service.

Depressed but touched by my own tragedy, I went back to the office to write up the postman. Mike was still struggling with Joe's Kiddies' Korner. Joe had an intricate cross-reference system by which he could offer birthday wishes to members of the Korner Klub on the appropriate dates, but the files had got muddled and Mike was in despair. While I was trying to help him, Sylvia telephoned with what appeared to be a series of enigmatic remarks, for Mike's end of the conversation consisted chiefly of 'But what do you *mean*, Syl?'

He could not concentrate after that, so we left the birthdays and tried to think of a subject for the competition. The prizes for these were small, but it was surprising how many children entered. One imagined every week-end, the paint water spilled on the living-room table, the tongues between teeth, the hunched bodies, the flowers pressed under Pears' Cyclopedia, and every Thursday the tears, the bitter disappointment, the parents agreeing: 'Of course you ought to have won a prize dear. We ought to write to the paper.'

Joe knew the rule of all competitions: Never print the winning entry, so that no one can write in to claim that theirs was better than that.

Every subject we thought of had something against it. A model snowman, a poem about Christmas, a water-colour snow scene, had all been used recently by Joe. A story about 'What I got for Christmas' would be tedious for whoever had to read them, for we did Kiddies' Korner now as a syndicate, each tinkering with it when we had time. Victor wanted to have putting the last line to a limerick, but would not be serious about inventing four seemly first lines. We looked in the notebooks in which Joe kept his lists of subjects that could be used over and over again at decent intervals, but could not decipher his faint pencillings.

We thought we could have a Quiz – 'on your honour not to look up the answers, Klubbers!' – and let the little beasts cheat if they wanted. Harold came in for the copy while we were arguing about the capital of Brazil. We waved him away.

'Come back next month,' we told him. 'Not nearly ready.'

'Must have it by two,' he said. 'My deadline.'

'All right. What's the capital of Brazil, then?'

'And here's a little present for you,' he said, disregarding this and putting a fat roll of proofs into the broken-off tin suitcase lid that was our In Tray. 'Urgent.'

We ignored him. Mike was looking up dates of kings and queens of England in the encyclopedia, which went no further than the accession of Edward VII.

Victor could only think of racing questions. 'I'm fed up with this,' he said, going over to the coat hooks. 'Come on.'

'We'll never get done by two,' I said, 'and you know what Harold is. And all those proofs, and there'll be hundreds more this afternoon. They've been setting away in there like mad. I've got all the weddings to do, and some re-writes, and that man to see about the chicken killings. I'll have to stay in and miss lunch, I think.'

'Come off it,' said Victor. 'You're poison. When you've been here as long as I have –'

We went out to the Lion and played darts until a quarter to two, so I neither had my lunch nor did any extra work.

Chapter Eight

AFTER the success of his bicycle, which he now kept pressing on me, even when I knew he wanted it, Casubon quite came out of his shell. He still did not speak at meals, because Mrs Goff paralysed his throat muscles. Sometimes, when she was having a carry-on, he could hardly swallow, but he would now exchange more than two words with me in the hall, and once I saw him walking down the road with Margaret, carrying her shopping bag. They were not speaking, but for two such shy people even to be walking together was good progress.

Casubon was also fired by the discovery that Maimie and Tick were not so terrifying as the label 'theatricals' had stamped them in his mind. He came up to their room for tea, 'just for five minutes', and stayed for hours, because the basement seemed a lonely place after their room, which had the chaotic, casual welcome of a theatre dressing-room. Everywhere they lived would be like that, a room where no one ever knocked on the door.

One Sunday, he asked us all down to tea with him. He found that his tea tin was empty, so we had coffee made from dark brown syrup in a bottle. As with all Mrs Goff's rooms, the light in the basement hung in the wrong place, in the corner away from the gas fire, where no one would want to sit. On the table by the window, which was half below ground level, stood a rusted metal lamp with a green shade connected to the light by a long cord looped across the ceiling. It was a wonder Mrs Goff allowed this, for she was usually against anyone tampering with The Electric. The table was covered with papers and pamphlets, and a cracked leather suitcase and a music case bursting with more documents, for this was where Casubon worked.

He slept on a narrow divan bed by the wall, which was now covered by a green cloth, with flaccid cushions propped against the wall. Maimie and Tick and I sat there in a row, with aching backs and cricked necks, trying to foster the old illusion that a bed and a wall are a satisfactory substitute for a sofa.

There was a cane-seated bathroom chair by the table, with a newspaper over the broken canes, and by the fire, one of those sloping wooden chairs with square velvet cushions, which are called easy, and are very difficult to get comfortable in. The pile was rubbed off the velvet, and also off the rug of indefinite pattern which covered part of the floor boards.

Off the sitting-room, there was a little stone-floored cell, with a naked light and a gas ring and a shallow brown sink. This had once been the scullery, when the house was all one and the front room a kitchen. When Maimie and I were washing up the coffee cups, two of which had G.W.R. on them, we saw Casubon's moulting toothbrush and ragged sponge and a variety of medicines and digestive powders on a shelf over the sink. Two cloths hung on a nail, and we could not tell which was his towel and which was for drying up. In the cupboard, we found a heel of cheese growing mushrooms, and a lump of bread like stone. Mice had knocked off the top of the Bovril bottle, and eaten through a packet of soup powder. Maimie determined to find Casubon a wife.

His little underground home was depressing, but he did not seem to mind. He was too busy being eager about whatever it was he and his furtive friends were up to. One imagined him working down here under the green lamp night after night, with a cup of mouse-tainted Bovril growing cold at his elbow, then at last dousing his head under the cold tap at the sink, throwing off the green cover and falling asleep at once, with the blankets churned and his awkward young limbs sprawling over the edge of the narrow bed.

We still did not know what his work was. We might have asked him, but in the course of the rather leaden conversation, he had said something like, 'You understand, of course, that my work being what it is . . .' and we, sitting like a row of puppets on the bed, half hypnotized by the dullness of our visit, had nodded and said, 'Of course,' before we realized that we had lost our chance. We could never ask now.

After that evening, there was no holding Casubon. We were friends now, and he could come and go upstairs as he liked, and Maimie had elicited from him that his Christian name was Neil. Nothing would satisfy him but that he should give a party, not only for the conspirators, but for his fellow lodgers as well. The new gentleman in the top floor front was invited, but was gone before the party. I had not had to scare him away. Mrs Goff had done it for him, because he did not pay the rent. She had been enthusiastic about him at first, often mentioning his reputed connexions with some titled family of whom no one had ever heard, but now it was, 'There's a gentleman for you! You may all have been taken in, but I knew from the minute he set foot in this house that he would give trouble.'

Although my imaginings had been disproved, the top floor front did indeed seem to be haunted by a jinx. No one had ever stayed there long, and it was Mr Goff's favourite joke that when he wanted to get rid of me, he would ask me to move across into it. Then I would know. This jest called for loud laughter from me, a sudden hoot and cackle from Mr Goff, and wild barking from the airedales.

Because of Maimie's evening performance, Neil Casubon's party started late. I saw some of the Mafia arrive, and heard the Jacksons go downstairs, but I waited for Maimie and Tick, because I could not face going down to the basement alone. I thought they might be playing parlour games.

They were. When we went downstairs, we found William, with a handkerchief round his eyes, trying to stick the tail on to a paper donkey which was pinned on to the wardrobe. The small low room was full of people and empty of air. The gas fire roared, hesitated and roared again, and two of Casubon's friends were already sitting in the velvet chair, squashed in together, hip to hip. There was no funny business going on. Holding each other round the waist seemed to be the summit of their desires and, apart from them, the party was most refined.

We were introduced to half a dozen people who only had Christian names, and a girl called Bunch, who was cross about something, and sat by the table pretending to read a book. Margaret, in her best green, sat on the edge of a hard chair looking worried. Casubon looked even more worried. He had been tortured by the dilemma of whether or not to wait supper until we came. He had decided to wait. That was why the party was so refined, but now, with two girls coming in from the scullery with a loaded tray, Tick helping Casubon to open the beer, and Maimie finding a gramophone, which played 'What'll I do?', things livened up considerably.

There was not enough furniture for us all to sit down, so some of us sat on the floor, which lent the gay, Bohemian air. There were sausage rolls, hard-boiled eggs, potato salad, beetroot, and all the toothglasses in the house had been pressed into service for the beer. Bunch had brought the cutlery, but that was not what she was cross about, for she had volunteered herself to bring it.

'Good old Bunch,' said John, who wore his jacket open, with a white shirt loose over his long waist, and a wide, unpinned tie that trailed into the potato salad as he bent to offer it round. 'Good old Bunch, always turning up trumps in case of need.' But Bunch sat on at the table, reading moodily while she ate.

We ate off plates balanced in our laps, and the two in the easy chair shared one plate, and giggled when they both stabbed for the same bit of beetroot. Margaret hardly ate anything. Neil kept going to her with plates, but she always shook her head. She looked distressed, and kept glancing across the room into the shadows where William sat marooned on a stool, unable to get to her, because he had been put there and did not know how to change his place. He sank his moustache in the beer, and it came up rimed like a hedge at dawn.

Maimie sat on the floor next to Neil Casubon, and when it came to the jam tarts and fruit salad, again fetched by the girls, for the very young men had not the gumption to go and help them, she picked out the cherries she did not like and put them on to Neil's plate. When he had finished, she played 'This year, next year,' with his stones.

He called out excitedly, for he was not used to beer, 'Next year! I say, everybody, I'm going to be married next year!'

Bunch humped her shoulders and would not look round.

So that was why she was cross. She was busy being jealous with Casubon.

After supper, Tick went upstairs and fetched some more beer and half a bottle of whisky from the cornucopian store under Maimie's bed. He also brought down their portable wireless, and he and Maimie and another couple threw back the rug and danced, shifting on a few feet of floor. Neil went over and spoke to Bunch, but she shook her head and ran her propped hand through her hair, making it stick out at a funny angle. She wore no make-up and the collar of her blouse was not clean. I wanted to tell her that it was not much good being jealous with Neil, if she was not prepared to make a small effort herself. If only I had a woman's column in the *Post*, I could tell her so in print.

Later, when more people wanted to dance, and even the couple in the chair had prised themselves out and taken to the floor, moistly cheek to cheek, like two blancmanges meeting, the table was moved into a corner and Bunch had to get up. She went into the scullery to martyr herself over the washing-up. Neil went after her. I was dancing with John, and we got jammed near the door, so I heard Bunch say above the clatter of china, 'Well, who wouldn't be? Nothing but talk, talk, talk about her before she came, how wonderful she was, and then making a fool of yourself there on the floor for all to see. Anyway, she's not wonderful. She's thirty-five if she's a day. The –'

There was a gasp. Something breakable clattered into the sink and there came the sound of a wet smacking kiss. Well done, Casubon! If you had read my woman's column, you could not have done better.

'Move along there,' said John, pushing against the couple in front. 'Let the dog see the rabbit.' He jiggled me round the room, compensating in upward movement for what he could not achieve lengthways.

Sausage rolls, kisses in the scullery, dancing in a ridiculous space – it was exactly like a hundred other parties in basements or top flats. I don't know what I had expected – secret signs, or whispering in corners – but certainly these were the most normal lot of revolutionaries I had ever met.

John and I were getting on rather well. He had taken off the wide tie, and we were sharing beer in a corner, because we could only find one glass. We watched the dancers. Maimie was teaching the rumba to a spotted youth in a state of high excitement. Tick was politely letting himself be steered by a girl twice his height. William had been forced to his feet by a frog-like girl called Betty, to whom Tick had been giving whisky, while Margaret sat on, tacitly left alone because she looked so unwilling. Casubon, who had come out of the kitchen with a trace of lipstick under his ear, dutifully asked her to dance, but she only gave him a frightened look, and Bunch pulled his jacket from behind and took him away.

Every time William jogged slowly by, he bent and spoke to her, but she shook her head, and smiled until he had gone by.

John squeezed my arm absently and said he was glad that such a nice young lady as myself was a member of the Party. Communists then! I had feared as much when I saw the lean voracious girl who was steering Tick.

'What do you think I am?' I asked, finishing the beer. 'I wouldn't go within a mile of it.'

'But my dear,' he said with burning eyes, 'you're hiding something. You write for the *Post*, don't you? Well then, you always give us a good press. Say what you like about its being non-political, we know which way the wind blows.'

I was aghast. Communism in the *Post*? I knew Mr Pellet was a diehard Tory, and old Mrs Murchison, the owner, was reputed to wear blue garters and to fast, in weeds, on the anniversary of Disraeli's death. Had someone then been insinuating Red propaganda unnoticed, a party rally, disguised perhaps as a Women's Institute tea? Murray? Mike? Victor? You never knew these days, with the enemies of the old order always at your door, and Central Europe a place where you could not go for a holiday without getting involved in a war.

Now was my chance to find out. 'Of course I'm with you really,' I whispered, taking hold of the arm that was squeezing mine, so that we stood there like two people about to give a bandy chair. 'All *sub-rosa*, but I'm glad you can spot the propaganda. I do some of it.'

'Then it was you who gave us that write-up last week about the dinner. Good, good. Have some more beer.'

He went across the room to get some. Dinner, dinner? I puzzled my brains. There had been no dinners last week, except the pensioners and the Young Conservatives. The Young . . .

I looked at Neil, dove-grey with semi-asphyxiation and beer. I looked at Bunch, with her uncalculated hair and face; at Betty, with her young skin patching through the places where the whisky had sweated off her cheap make-up; at Nigel, whose voice had only just broken and had gone back to adolescence now that he was singing with Maimie. I saw John, whose pleased, open face prophesied that he would early learn to wear a waistcoat and support a family, coming seriously towards me with an open bottle of beer in each hand dribbling a twin wake across the floor.

'The dinner at the Dover, you mean?' I asked casually. He nodded eagerly, trying to pour both bottles of beer into our one glass and flooding a pile of Casubon's pamphlets. 'No, I wasn't there. Our junior reporter covered that.' I de-ranked Murray.

'Never mind. Junior or not, it was all right. One day, they'll send the editor himself. We're going places. You'll see. They can't keep us down. All of us here –' He swept out an arm and knocked over the table lamp, which sputtered and went out. 'It's those like us who make the future. Your children will thank us.'

'I'm not going to have any children. Tick saw it in the

cards,' I put in, but he was carried away now, and talked on with his face straining forward and shining as I had seen it so often under the street lamp. He talked as if the Conservative party was an embryo and persecuted cause and he the crusader sent by providence to slash its way into history. He was wasted on the Tory party, but I suppose he and the others shut their eyes to its prosperous complacency, because there was no fun in being a Young Conservative if you could not have intrigues and flaming speeches and the hint of knives in dark alleyways.

Mrs Goff had been strangely quiet. Usually, if there were more than the right number of people in any of her rooms, she would hang about outside, or make some excuse to knock on the door, to see what was going on. Casubon, of course, had asked her about the party, and she had consented, subject to the usual curfew, with a possible half hour extension for good behaviour.

It was now after eleven, and Maimie and Tick were embarking on an acrobatic display in the middle of the room. Tick had his coat off, and Maimie whipped off her skirt and stood on his shoulders, bowed under the ceiling, with her blouse tucked into a pair of green trunks. A larger space was cleared, and Tick, who was incredibly strong for his size, whirled her about until her foot caught William in the teeth, and he retired to the scullery.

He came back, mumbling through a handkerchief, 'It's really time we went.' Margaret was still sitting transfixed on her chair, and Maimie, hanging wrong side up down Tick's back, called out, 'Don't break up the party!'

Neil gave William some beer, and he rinsed his bleeding tooth in that, still unable to get across the room to Margaret, because Maimie was whizzing round again like a chair-o-plane.

She landed on her feet with a bounce, quite unruffled. Tick shook back his plaited hair and spat neatly on his hands.

'Oh, let me try! Do let me try!' shrilled Betty, darting forward. 'It looks such fun.'

Tick smiled and shook his head.

'I toud. I'se only a ickle one.' She pouted and pranced before him, taking his hands and trying to put her foot up on his thigh.

'No dear,' said Maimie, pinning up her hair. 'You've got the wrong sort of knickers on.' But too late. Tick suddenly grasped Betty's wrists and swung her screaming into the air, where she teetered, more frog-like than ever, upside down on his shoulders, kicking the ceiling. Maimie was right about her knickers.

The door opened, and Mrs Goff stepped in, cigarette, drooping eyelids, and bosom charged with air. We were all in an instant silent, like children caught out by the dreaded nanny. Betty could not see her and went on screaming.

Tick lowered her to the ground in a heap. Sitting up, she saw Mrs Goff, and kept her mouth open on the unuttered scream.

'So!' Mrs Goff let half the air out of her bosom and kept the rest in reserve. 'So this is how you repay my latitude. It'll be out for you, Mr Casubon, whether you've a roof to put over your head or no.'

'Oh, come on, Mrs Goff,' said Maimie, going to her. 'It isn't his fault. We're just having a good time. No harm in that. Come and have some beer.'

'Mrs Ling!' She shook off Maimie's hand. 'I never thought to hear you bandy words with me like that. No harm, indeed, with young women naked to the waist in my basement! I'll give you No harm, with my decent place turned into a bawdy house for rabble. I'm calling the police, that's what I'm doing.' She turned towards the door.

Casubon cowered. John, tousled and excited, and looking like a boy who has just kicked the winning goal for the school, rushed forward and shut the door.

144

'Come on, Mrs G.,' he said, standing against it. 'Be a sport. All good clean fun. Take back them words, and I'll let you out.'

I thought she was going to hit him. She lifted her hand, and he jerked his arm up. We instinctively pressed forward, as if a fight was brewing, when suddenly there was a little cry behind us and a shout from William. We turned to see Margaret lying flat on the floor in a dead faint, with her arms to her sides and her toes turned up.

William carried her upstairs, and the party broke up, with shocked whisperings and guilty good nights. Casubon was left amidst the wreckage, not knowing whether he had a roof over his head or not.

Mrs Goff, having achieved more than she hoped for, went to her ground floor room, where her voice could be heard all through the house, waking up Mr Goff to tell him about it. Presently he got up and went into the garden in his pyjamas, with the airedales on a double leash, as if he thought there might be remnants of the party hiding in the bushes.

When we had brought Margaret round and made her comfortable, Maimie and I went out of the Jacksons' room. Mrs Goff was waiting for us on the landing. She stood as if she were nailed to the floor.

'Well, now you know,' she said. 'Now you know.'

'I suppose you think she was drunk,' said Maimie truculently, 'but let me tell you –'

'Drunk?' Mrs Goff's eyebrows shot up like gables. 'Oh dear me no. If that were all, I'd say no more.'

'You *would*,' muttered Maimie.

'I've suspected for quite a time what was wrong with that young lady,' said Mrs Goff, watching us carefully. 'You must all be blind, or else you've never seen a pregnant woman before.'

We gasped and looked at each other. 'God,' said Maimie. 'Poor kid.'

William came out of his room on tiptoe. 'She's asleep,' he whispered. 'Could you please –' His voice trailed away before Mrs Goff's expression.

'I suppose she hasn't told *you* either,' she exulted, feeling the oats of her triumph. Her voice rose.

'Told me what?'

'That she's going to have a baby.' The words dropped on to him like darts.

His face fell. 'Oh no,' he said helplessly.

It was so miserably wrong, all of us receiving such news like this, but Mrs Goff had announced it as a calamity, and calamity it seemed. We ought to have been pleased, and deflated her, but we just stood round in silence, while she watched us, gloating. Then William snapped himself out of her spell, mumbled something, and turned back into his room, looking less like a prospective father than a man condemned to the electric chair.

Mrs Goff said that they must go. There could be no argument about it. No children, she had said when the room was let, so with young madam four months gone, they had better set about finding somewhere else, for she was not going to have them leaving it too late, and then coming to her with a new-born baby and trying to impose on her charity.

Presently she announced that they must go in a month's time. The room was let to someone else from that date, and she would get the magistrates in if necessary to see fair play on her own property.

Margaret was too ill to go out looking for rooms. She was supposed to stay in bed, but she got up once when we were all out, and went searching desperately round the town. She was brought back in a taxi by a policeman who had found her in the street half fainting against some railings.

Casubon's dismissal had blown over in the excitement about Margaret. Mrs Goff could only run one subject at a time, and at the moment she had the Jacksons, so he stayed on in the basement, although the conspirators never came there again. They used to meet in teashops. I saw them once in an A.B.C., eating filling buns and making little puddles with their umbrellas and looking as dejected as if the Conservative Party had lost every seat in the House.

Anxious to help, Neil kept creeping upstairs with little gifts for Margaret: a pamphlet, an orange, or a bag of toffees. One day he came home in a state of ecstasy and announced that a girl at the office knew of a furnished room. We were all very excited, until it turned out that he had forgotten to ask the rent, and it was much more than the Jacksons could afford.

William spent all his lunchtimes and some of his working hours looking for a room within their means. Soon, this cost him his job at the garage. He could not find another. He spent his days waiting in queues at house agencies and the labour exchange, and trekking all over the town and sometimes out into the country on Casubon's bicycle, in pursuit of jobs or homes, but they were always either hopeless or gone by the time he got there.

Margaret was desperate, for now, with William out of work and nothing saved, they could not afford the baby, besides having nowhere to live with it.

'William pretends he's terribly pleased about the child,' she told me, 'but I know he doesn't want it really. He just says that to make me feel better. It will be even more of a burden to him than I am already. His mother was right. We should never have got married.' Margaret had no parents. William had a mother, who had not come to his wedding and had not seen him since.

We tried to help. At last, Tick found him a job with a friend of his who had a dubious workshop for renovating second-hand motor cycles. He only lasted there three days, because the police came round looking for a stolen motor cycle, and Tick's friend said he did not trust William.

One day when he came back to give Margaret her lunch, she had gone out. He was after a job at the bus depot, so he could not wait until she came back. Coming out of the kitchen after the midday meal with the Goffs, I heard someone fumbling at the front door. Margaret came in, looking weary and plain. She took off her hat and tried to shake out her hair, but it clung together in hanks. It could have been pretty hair, but she did not wash it often enough, and did not know how to set it. She could have been quite a pretty girl, but although no doubt William sometimes told her she was, she had long ago decided that it was not worth trying.

'Any luck?' I asked her.

'What?' She looked half stupefied, like someone wandering about after an accident.

'With the rooms.'

'Oh, the rooms. No, no luck.' She started to climb the stairs. I followed her. 'You shouldn't have gone out.'

She turned, and looked at me with eyes that unaccountably seemed frightened. They were expressionless but widened, like a cat cornered by a dog. 'I had to,' she said, and went on into her room.

A few evenings later, before William came home, she went out again. I went down when I heard the front door, thinking that it was Margaret. It was William, but standing upright, not with that long thin stoop he had recently acquired.

His face was alight. He had found a room. A poky room, but cheap, and the landlady seemed kind. He could not wait to tell Margaret.

'How is she?' he asked, as he ran up the stairs.

'All right, I think. She's gone out, as a matter of fact.'

'Oh.' He stopped. 'Where is she?'

'I don't know.'

'Didn't she say where she was going? Oh dear, I do wish she'd come back.'

He kept coming up to my room and saying this at intervals while I was trying to write up an inquest on a lorry driver. He went to the garden gate and stared up and down the road, but she did not come back. My repertoire of reassurances was getting exhausted. He talked of going to the police.

I was worried about her too, because she had seemed so distracted these last few days. I kept imagining all the things that could have happened to her, and found with a shock that I was already concerned about not having a black hat for the funeral.

It seemed quite callous to go down to supper, but I was hungry. On the way upstairs again, I knocked on the Jacksons' door. William put his head out.

'She's back,' he said. 'She's laying down. She feels a bit queer.'

I could not get to sleep that night. When I did, I dreamed for the first time for weeks about the bathroom door. I was in the bath, with no water in it and my clothes on. The door was opening slowly, and as it opened, a feeling came in. Not a wind, or a change in temperature, or the suffocation that comes in dreams. It was not even an atmosphere, like tension, or malevolence emanating from someone else. It was a feeling of despairing sadness, and although it came in at the door, it was somehow part of me, and coming from me. I wanted to cry, but a river of tears would not relieve that feeling I had of utter hopelessness, that everything was lost.

The pounding on my door shocked me awake. It was Maimie in green pyjamas, her face white under cold cream.

I sat up in a fright. 'What's up? What's the matter?'

'It's Margaret. She's bleeding like a dustbin. Been there ages before that fool husband got me up. Tick's gone for a doctor.'

The doctor came in ten minutes, but it seemed like hours, while Maimie and I worked in a panic with towels and anything we could lay hands on, not knowing what to do and doing all the wrong things. William sat in a corner with his head in his hands, crying. We could not even get him to fetch water for us. Casubon, scenting trouble, had come upstairs in a flurry of distress and was hopping about on the landing, holding a blanket and a cushion, wanting to help. We sent him for water, and he panted up and down tripping over stair rods.

When the doctor came, he turned William out. He told us what to do, and we tried to help. 'Those damn Czechs,' the doctor said. 'I'll get them locked up for this.'

The ambulance arrived soon after the doctor. While they were carrying Margaret out of the front door, Mrs Goff came out of her room in a hair-net and a black quilted dressing-gown.

'What's going on?' she demanded.

'Margaret's having a miscarriage,' Maimie said.

'In my house?'

'Yes, in your house, and you know why, you horrible old woman. Because you wouldn't let her have the baby here.'

Mrs Goff made her face blank to the abuse. 'An abortion?' She gave the word its full ugliness. 'It's too much. No, it's too much. She needn't think she's going to stay on here by such tricks. There'll be things said when that young madam gets back.'

But Margaret never did come back from the hospital. She died from loss of blood within a few hours.

Naturally, we all hated Mrs Goff more than ever after that. We only spoke to her when absolutely necessary, but she did not mind. She had no remorse, but even a certain air of triumph about her.

Mr Goff did look a little uncomfortable. He kept opening his mouth to say something, and thinking better of it. He went out before supper and bought some bottles of stout to make William feel better, but William had already packed up and disappeared, and we all refused the stout because we had put Mr Goff into Coventry too.

Alice was affronted by the whole thing. She did not discuss it. Such subjects were not in the range of her vocabulary, which was limited to suspicion of the tradesmen and abuse of Barry. She went about looking thinner and flatter than ever, with her nose and mouth and chin drawn down to her arid chest, as if the tendons of her neck were too short. Maimie, whose vulgarity even tragedy could not dim, said it was a pity someone had not introduced Alice to the Czechs before little Barry was born. That was the day after he had crawled into their room and set fire to the eiderdown with a box of matches.

The run of *Mother Goose* ended at last. It was now nearly Easter, but pantomime at the Empire often went on as long after Christmas as that. It took a little time for the people of Downingham to decide whether it was worth going to see.

Maimie and Tick had the chance of an engagement in the north, and were going up to Sheffield to try and settle it. We did not want to lose each other, but I minded more than she did. It is always worse for the one who is left behind, especially when they are left at Five, Bury Road.

Maimie and I made the usual promises to meet again often and go on being friends, really believing that we should. I saw her once long afterwards, coming out of the Haymarket subway at Piccadilly. We had dinner together, and met two friends of hers from a band, who took us to dance. The friends became tedious, and we left them and went home in the all-night bus along Oxford Street. I got off at Notting Hill Gate and Maimie went on to Shepherd's Bush and I have never seen her since.

We had a farewell party before they left for Sheffield. We asked Casubon to come too, and he got drunk on gin and cider in the Feathers, and kept shouting slogans at people in the street on the way home. He finally collapsed in the market square, limp on the steps of the war memorial. We took him home in a taxi, and since Tick, who never drank too much, had elected to do so that night, Maimie and I put Neil to bed. When he was snoring on the divan, I looked round the room to see if there was a picture of Bunch, for he would not tell us how the affair was going.

There was no picture of Bunch, but the suitcase on the table was open, and lying on top of some papers in it was a snapshot of Margaret, taken in one of the water meadows by the river. She was wearing a short cotton dress and her hair was blowing about and she looked quite pretty.

Chapter Nine

MRS GOFF had lied about the Jacksons' room. It was not let at all. No one came there, but two girls took the front room, which had been Maimie and Tick's. One of the girls worked in a bookshop. The other was in the costing office of the bicycle factory. When you asked her what a costing office was, she never could explain it satisfactorily.

I don't believe she knew herself, or wanted to know. She had been engaged to type and file from nine till five, and type and file she did, and never talked about her work at home.

The other girl talked about her work at the bookshop all the time. There was a certain Mr Jaggers, for whom she was privileged to make cocoa, and we heard a lot about what Mr Jaggers had said and done and what he was going to do. There were also customers who had been ever so funny, but what they had been funny about was usually lost in a maze of side tracks before the end of the story.

The names of the girls were Connie and Win, and they never seemed to do anything but go to the cinema, and wash and iron their collars and cuffs. The bathroom was always hung with the drying accessories of their black working frocks, and there was much calling up and down the stairs for more soapflakes and: 'Shall I risk the green sailor, Win, or do you think it'll run?'

'Soak it in salt and water first, dear.' They were passionate readers of women's magazines and did all that they were told therein. They made little round crochet hats with gloves to match, and Connie had embarked on an embroidered beach bag, months before their holiday was due.

They set each other's hair in a new way every week, trying to discover what shape their faces were, to match them to the magazine charts. They steamed their faces over the bathroom basin and wore hand cream and gloves at night, and when Win was going to the works dance she lay down for half an hour with her feet higher than her head and slices of cucumber on her eyelids. It did not make any difference.

The front room on my floor was taken by a one-armed commissionaire from the Majestic cinema. He played his wireless too loudly, so I told him about the bread-knife murder. He told me he was psychic and would love to be haunted, and played his wireless louder than ever, for he said that ghosts liked music. Connie and Win did his darning for him and washed his socks and took him cups of malted milk, and altogether the atmosphere at Bury Road was cosy.

They tried to draw Casubon into the family circle, but he had gone back into his shell again. A woman writer, who paid the income tax on her novels by writing about Love in one of their magazines, had told them that the way to get a man was to encourage him to talk about himself, so at meals they were always asking poor Neil about his work. Mrs Goff would lay down her knife and fork and say, 'Yes, let's *hear* about that,' as if she were grilling a suspect. Neil would stammer and choke and bolt his pudding so that he could get away. I'm sure he had indigestion all the time Connie and Win were there. In the magazines, the stories were nearly always about misogynist men who had to be tamed to romance, so the girls pursued Neil by every means except the obvious one of natural sex attraction. When I went to the basement to return some pamphlets, I found that he had taken to locking his door, and he had given up his fortnightly bath for fear of meeting Connie or Win descending the stairs in a turbaned towel after trying out a new scientific miracle shampoo.

Connie and Win did not read the *Downingham Post*. When I asked them why not, they stared at me and giggled. They always answered questions like that: first a stare then a giggle, never the other way round. All you had to do was wait until they had finished and then put the question again, in simpler form if necessary.

Why didn't they read the *Post*? Why should they? There was nothing in it they liked, except some of the court cases, and they got enough of those, really, with the Sunday papers.

This encouraged me to tackle Mr Pellet once again on the subject of woman's angle. There must be thousands of girls like Win and Connie in Downingham, who would read our paper if only we would tell them how to get rid of blackheads and how to make a film star bolero for five shillings. I chose a bad moment, for an amateur contralto had just rung up to complain about a misprint in her name last week. Mr Pellet said that he was not so interested in getting new readers as in keeping the old ones, and that if I raised the subject any more he would fire me. I believe he would have, too. He had fired Vic last week, but Vic was still there, and talking about asking for a rise to make up for the insult.

Mr Pellet turned off the gas under the kettle and said that

if I was so keen on women's angles I could go straight off to the corset show at Harper's. I did not laugh at his joke. Murray did.

The corset show was upstairs in Downingham's largest store. Nancy was there, and I sat next to her on a high little chair. Most of the spectators looked as if they badly needed new corsets, but they tried to convey the impression of having just wandered in there to take the weight off their feet.

The show was compèred by a commanding woman, armoured from armpits to thighs in uplift and diaphragm support and hip control. She walked stiffly about, introducing the models in ringing tones, and Nancy took copious notes with Len's screw pencil. She was one of those women who love to use men's things. Len had given her his second-best cigarette case, and sometimes she wore his shirts or pullovers.

I suppose she was taking notes to show off the pencil, for I did not see how any paper, let alone the *Messenger*, could print the esoteric details about brassières which we were given. I did not think Mr Pellet would print anything about the show. He had only sent me there because he was cross about the contralto on the telephone. After we had suffered the embarrassment of seeing a fat woman, who must have needed the money badly, appearing without corsets and with, I left.

'Then don't go ringing me up this afternoon asking me for details you missed,' said Nancy as I got up, 'for I'm sure I'm sick of writing half your copy for you.'

I found Joe in the Lion. He was back at work now, trembly and grumbling, and needing to leave the office even earlier before lunch than he used to.

He told me that Mr Pellet wanted me back in the office right away to do the film notes for this week, since Mike – lucky Mike – had gone off on the first good story that had come our way for weeks. A patient from the Northgate Asylum had escaped from the activity method room and was now stuck in the top of a chimney, unable to move up or down.

I had my lunch and did not hurry back to the office, for I had a quicker way of doing the films than Mike. He would spend all afternoon poring over the handouts from the cinemas and old back numbers of film magazines, for the films that came to Downingham had seen the West End long, long ago. Many of the second features and Sunday films were westerns and custard-pie comedies that had never seen the West End at all, but we dealt with them gravely and gave them the same three lines allotted to the major epics.

I never wasted time looking up all the things that other people had written. The adjectives were not suitable for us, anyway. I used simply to take my list of films next door to the comps. Even if they had not seen the films, they had always heard or read about them. There was nothing they did not know. Maurice, the apprentice comp, who pulled the proofs, was like the memory man who knows the winner of every race since nineteen hundred. He could not be stumped.

'*Red Riders*,' he would say. 'Let's see. That was a remake of an old Tom Mix, wasn't it? Yes, that's right. Smashing picture. You saw a real scalping. The dame was Betty la Roche – only her second picture. She was still married to Leo Engel then. What you got next, dear? *Hearts in Paradise*. Ah, I seen that Monday. Lovely job. Coral Canning. What they call a star veekle for her. Listen, she's a knockout. She's got shape –'

'What's it about, Morrie? Downingham wants facts, not opinions,' I quoted Mr Pellet.

'Well she meets him in the park, see. Hugo Dilkes, he plays the millionaire, only he's pretending to be someone else, because he's sated with riches, see?'

'That's right,' Ernie stopped his machine and called across. 'It's all set in New York. There's a couple of super numbers. The floor goes round. All glass, it is.'

Ricky also stopped his Linotype and joined in. All work was shelved while we talked films. Harold came in from the reporters' room, glanced at my list, and sat down to light a pipe the better to tackle the subject. Between them, they wrote the column for me.

Mr Pellet came in while we were finishing off with Laurel and Hardy. 'Got a proof of the Snug-phit annual general meeting, Harold? I want to check something.'

Harold got up. Ernie and Ricky started their machines. Maurice stood upright and passed his roller busily across the ink table.

'There you are, girl,' said Mr Pellet. 'I wondered where you'd got to.'

'I just came in to see whether there were any proofs ready for us to read,' I said smugly.

'You're supposed to be doing the films,' said Mr Pellet, who knew that we were more likely to throw proofs back in Harold's face than go seeking them from him.

'I've done those long ago. Just waiting to copy them out when Vic's finished with my typewriter.'

'All right, you can go and do the B.D. and M.s then. Vic's got all the stuff.'

The Birth, Death and Marriage announcements were simple. You had to make a column of the details that people had sent, only altering the spelling and punctuation where necessary. Mr Pellet said that you should never alter anything in these personal announcements, but one could not let Downingham read on Thursday that Mable Emma Salter, aged 83, had passed piecefully away, sadly missed by husband, family and friends.

Above all, he said that you should never alter anything in the In Memoriam notices. This was difficult, for many of them contained home-made poems that only needed a little juggling to make them scan.

Many of them were old favourites, made up once by some-one and used again and again by other people.

> *Mother dear,*
> *We like to think you're near.*
> *We miss you every day,*
> *Since you went away.*

> *Pain and silence long you bore.*
> *Now you're at rest for evermore.*
> *A shining example you left behind,*
> *Loving and cheerful and wise and kind.*

This week there was a new one, 'from Jimmy to Mum':

> *She was beautiful and kind*
> *As a country day.*
> *I can't get her out of my mind.*

I did not like doing the In Memoriam column. It always made me cry.

To attend the Assizes, held three times a year in the county town twenty miles away, was one of the best jobs on the paper. The cases were those sent on from magistrates' courts, and there were always a few quite startling ones and often one important enough to bring reporters down from London. Everybody wanted to go to Assizes. Apart from the court, it meant a day out, with lunch at the paper's expense. Mr Pellet usually sent Murray. If something more important kept him in Downingham, Mike and Victor would argue with Mr Pellet about whose turn it was to go, and Mr Pellet would send Joe, who did not want to go, because the press bench in the county court gave him back-ache and the long bus journey made him sick.

I wanted to go, but short of everybody else in the office being asphyxiated by our leaking gas ring I would never have the chance. Mr Pellet, however, in one of his unpredictable bursts of goodwill, which fizzled out in a moment if you tried to take advantage of them, suddenly told me, in the middle of cursing me for coming in to the office too late and leaving it too early, that I could go with Murray to the next Assizes.

'Can I write up some of the cases?' I asked.

'You might try. Murray can decide which.'

Murray decided none of them. He was horrid to me all day, because he liked to go on his own and put on a big Fellow Journalist act with the reporters he knew and introduce himself as Assistant Editor, *Post*, to visiting newspaper men.

We met at the bus stop, in the rain. There seems to be a lot of rain in this story, but that was the way it was in Downingham that year. Murray said I was late, but as we had to wait five minutes for the bus, I could not see that it mattered.

There were two empty seats together on the bus. I sat there, thinking that it would look too rude if I deliberately went and sat with a stranger. Murray felt the same, and joined me unwillingly. Etiquette satisfied, we both opened newspapers and did not say a word to each other all the way to the county town.

Assizes day brought too much traffic to the jumbled old town with its narrow streets and its famous town hall, whose corner stuck right out into the main street, causing, like Scylla, its quota of accidents every year.

Murray took me into the building and then went off to the gents, leaving me stranded in the stone passage among the crowd of policemen and men with brief-cases and young barristers already robed. Everybody except me looked busy and important. I got out my notebook and tried to look like a special correspondent.

I was glad to be greeted by a detective-constable from Downingham who had come to give evidence.

'Never been to Assizes before?' he said. 'Never seen the trumpeters? Come on, you must see the judge arrive.' I abandoned Murray and went with him into the street. Police had cleared the roads round the town hall. A small crowd of idlers and some women with shopping baskets had stopped on the pavement to watch, but most people, blasé from many Assizes, were walking on, pushing past the sight-seers impatiently.

The judge arrived in a black saloon car, driven at walking pace, with two police cars escorting him behind. They skirted the town hall and drew up at the side entrance, where the two trumpeters waited, dressed in black jockey caps and rather dusty scarlet tunics with tarnished silver epaulettes and froggings, that looked as if they had come out of a child's dressing-up box.

The judge, in wig and robes, climbed out of the car in a rheumaticky way, and the trumpeters sounded a clarion call of three uninspired notes as he went up the steps and through the narrow door. I thought he should have entered with pomp through the main doors, but there were no steps there, and tradition decrees that an Assize judge must always go up steps. Prison slang for being committed to Assizes is 'going up the steps'.

The Assize court is full of tradition. One of them is that reporters must only enter the press benches from one end. I, of course, slipping in just in time before the judge made his entry, tried to go in at the wrong end. A policeman hauled me away and sent me round to the right end, and when I reached Murray and sat down next to him, he pretended not to know me.

'Rise, please !' shouted someone, just as I had sat down. We all stood up as the little procession filed on to the Bench. The judge looked like a monkey and kept blinking his eyes, as if he had been asleep in the car and was sorry to have been woken up. The High Sheriff was there in army uniform with medals, the chaplain in cassock and cravat, and two women who were somebody's wife and daughter came along in their best hats to see the fun. The judge's marshal unrolled a parchment scroll and in a flat voice which would make anything dull, read out the Commission of Assize, which was dull anyway. It was full of Know Ye, and All offences and injuries whatsoever within our said County, and was the most traditional thing we had had yet.

When we were all sitting down again, the two trumpeters, who were soldiers of the county regiment, came in without their jockey caps, climbed half-way up the public benches and sat down at ease on the steps. One of them put on a pair of tin spectacles.

Sex crimes of varying squalor took up most of the morning. They were startling at first. Until you go to Assizes, you don't believe that things like that really happen, but they do, and after two hours or so of them the only interesting thing is that the mild appearance of the defendants never tallies with the description of the passionate bestialities of which they stand accused.

Bigamists are the most baffling. They seldom look capable of getting one woman to marry them, let alone two, and the women for whom they break the law and usually go to prison are invariably dowdy, with fawn coats, untidy hair, and noses that speak of faulty digestions.

There was one important case at the Assizes that day, a kidnapping, which had already made headlines in the daily papers. A few London reporters had come down for it. One of them was sitting next to me and was making sure that everyone knew he was from Fleet Street and was more used to lounging among his peers at the Old Bailey than among people like me on the narrow yellow benches of the town hall court. All morning he had been yawning and fidgeting and giving little snorts of contempt, but when the kidnapper came into the box he ceased his slumming act and became the ace journalist, taking lightning notes with much jabbing of pencil and noisy flipping over of pages.

The defending counsel, a young and eager barrister who had been bravely but hopelessly trying all morning to defend the sex criminals with the time-honoured excuse that everything went black and an impulse came over them, now treated the judge to an impassioned harangue on the subject of the kidnapper's impulses. His Learned Friend, the prosecuting counsel, also young, with a wig made for someone with a smaller head, tied the accused in knots with an offensive cross-examination on the lines of: 'And do you really mean to tell his Lordship that, on the night of April 4th, you, etc. ... etc. ...'

When the accused stuck hoarsely to his guns, prosecuting counsel would say: 'Very good. Very well,' with the grim triumph of a Nanny defied by a small boy, but knowing that she will tell father when he comes home.

His triumph was justified, for the judge gave the kidnapper a very stiff prison sentence. Without a word, the kidnapper fell straight over backwards, out like a light into the arms of a policeman, who dragged him below to the dungeons with his heels going thump, thump on the stairs.

Sensation in court. Discreet sensation, but an outbreak of shocked murmurs and exclamations, sharply hushed by the clerk. The press bench was agog. There had not been a bit of excitement like this at Assizes since two years ago when a bigamist tried to jump out of the dock and make a dash for it. The London reporter shut his notebook, clapped on his hat, and began to push through the narrow space past our knees.

'Can't you wait a moment?' muttered Murray, who was writing. 'The judge will be rising in a minute.'

'Got to phone my story,' said the reporter with great superiority. He pushed on, dropped to the floor with a thud, and shouldered his way out through the policemen as if he were charged with a crucial dispatch from the Front.

Murray took me to lunch in the upstairs dining-room of the Blue Boar. He did not want to take me with him, but as I did not know anywhere else to eat in the town, I followed him, and when he sat down in a corner with two of his friends from other local papers, there I was.

The Blue Boar was doing a roaring trade, and trying to do it with the one defeated waitress who coped with the sprinkling of commercial lunchers on ordinary days. Murray and his friends talked of things I knew nothing about, and at last we were served – not with the dishes we had ordered, but time was getting on, so we ate them.

When I had picked all the currants out of my bread-and-butter pudding, I left the rest and went out to do some quick shopping. I was not quick enough, and I heard the last trump sounding while I was still in Boots. I ran back to the town hall, but the judge was already in court by the time I stumbled into the press bench, and he stopped speaking and gave me a fractious look which caused Murray not to know me again.

There had been some hundred and fifty people in that courtroom since ten-thirty in the morning, and tradition said that windows were never opened. The trumpeter with the tin spectacles, who with his mate had to stay until the end to pipe the judge over the side, dozed off. I slept nearly the whole afternoon, and the only thing I remember about it is the jury that tried one of the cases. After they had delivered their verdict, the foreman, a stout and serious householder, remained standing, clearing his throat and saying that the jury wished to make one more statement.

'Yes, yes?' said the judge, blinking at him.

'Well, your Lordship, we wish to lodge a complaint about the jury benches – that they are such that the heat of the body causes the clothing to stick to the paint of them.'

Everyone woke up. Everyone laughed, and the trumpeter with the tin spectacles sat up with a jerk and had the joke explained to him by his chum. Because the judge snickered, the public laughed with sycophantic immoderacy, like a B.B.C. studio audience. The foreman of the jury looked baffled, but then he laughed too, and the twelve good men and true filed out, popular figures of comic relief.

When the new jury was installed, a police sergeant came in and begged the judge's permission to disturb them, as one of the comedy team had left an overcoat behind.

'And the seat of his trousers,' said the young barrister with the perching wig, and got his laugh, to the bewilderment of a distressed mother who was in the witness box, telling the story of her daughter who was pregnant at the age of fourteen. Oh, it's hilarious fun, Assizes is.

The cases dragged on, and Murray began to worry about missing our bus. I thought we had plenty of time, and when the judge at last adjourned the court until tomorrow, and the trumpeters blew him down the steps and went away to put their uniforms back into the acting box, I dragged Murray into a café for a cup of tea. The waitress was slow, but I thought I would die before we got back to Downingham if I did not have a cup of tea, so we waited. There was not as much time as I thought, and when we reached the bus stop we saw the cream-coloured behind of the bus disappearing round a corner.

Murray was so cross that he would not come back for another cup of tea at leisure while we waited for the next bus. He stood on the pavement for an hour. I found him there when I came out of the café, propped against the bus-stop post with his collar turned up and his hands sagging his pockets. He was not knowing me again. I propped myself against the other side of the post and we waited in silence until the bus came. It was crowded. We had to stand most of the way home, swaying and bumping against one another without a word, while the bus rocked through the winding country roads back to Downingham.

We did not get back to Downingham until nearly eight o'clock. I should be too late for supper. I felt too tired to go and eat somewhere, so I went home to make tea and eat biscuits and chocolate in my room.

A small van stood outside Number Five. Mr Goff was watching a man unload from it an octagonal table with long, straight legs and a yellow top inlaid with black scroll-work. When it was on the pavement, the man dived back into the van and brought out a plaster statue the size of a six-months baby, which he put on the table. It appeared to be a nymph of some kind. It looked coy, like Nausicaa surprised bathing. Its hair fell over its shoulders in a decent way, and it clutched at lumpy draperies that for ever threatened to fall off. Mr Goff had been to a sale again.

On tiptoe with excitement, he hovered round the nymph, putting out a finger to her like a cat playing with a bit of fluff, and snatching back his hand as if she had stung him.

'Sorry I can't take 'em up for you, pal,' said the man with the van, 'but *she's* waiting.'

'Thanks, Charlie boy,' said Mr Goff. 'Thanks for obliging.' He made a pass with his cuffs, flexed his little arms, and braced his knees to lift Nausicaa. She was hollow and light as cardboard, and she came up so suddenly that he nearly fell over backwards. He grinned at me over the top of her coy head and staggered into the house with her, his legs wambling across each other like a stage-drunk. I pushed one of the dogs away from the legs of the octagonal table, picked it up, and followed him indoors.

When we were in the hall, Mrs Goff looked over the banisters and called down to us in the fluting, churchy voice which she used for strangers. She must have a prospective lodger up there. Sure enough, when she came downstairs, she was followed by a small dark girl with a melting smile and cheekbones so high that they pushed up her lower lids, giving her eyes a slightly oriental curve. Her black hair hung in a long, heavy bob like a tassel. She came down the stairs gracefully, just tapping the banister, her feet pointing down and outwards on every step.

I apologized for missing supper. To my surprise, Mrs Goff came quite close to me – she usually stood far off when she talked to you – and said: 'Never mind, dear. I'll get you a snack.'

Dear? A snack? I could only suppose that the girl had not yet made up her mind about the room. With a glance at her, Mrs Goff then asked me if I would like to have the octagonal table up in my room *for my writing*. She made it sound as if I were a best-seller come here to finish an important book.

Mr Goff was still carrying the nymph about, like a mother with her firstborn, unable to find anywhere to put it among the litter of his previous trophies in the hall and kitchen passage. I hoped Mrs Goff would not offer it to me as well.

I took the table upstairs before she could change her mind. It was not ideal for working on. It was too high, unless you sat on a pillow. The legs were in the wrong places, and the octagonal sides sloped away from you, so that papers fell off. The scrolls were irritating and distracted your eye, leading it along the whorls and curlicues trying to find an end. However, it was a table.

Either the 'Dear' or the snack or the gift of the table did the trick. Two days later there was a strange spongebag in the bathroom.

Chapter Ten

THE dark girl's name was Myra Nelson. She was eighteen
and a ballet dancer, working with a small but talented company, who were finishing their season with two weeks at the
Empire, and then staying on in Downingham, where they
had taken a studio, to train and rehearse new ballets until
they found quarters in London.

Few people outside the ballet world had heard of them, but
they were a promising young company, who were going to be
important one day. Their principal, a famous Italian dancer,
now middle-aged, but with a figure like a girl, set a standard
so high, both of dancing and behaviour, that the girls had to
work like niggers and live more or less like nuns. They accepted this, for to get into Signora's company was considered
a great chance. Two of her pupils had already gone on to
dance principal roles at Sadler's Wells.

'That's where I mean to go,' Myra told me, 'if only Signora
keeps me. She's always throwing people out who aren't good
enough, or who won't do as she says. She must keep me.
She's the best teacher there's ever been since Preobrajenska,
Signora is. She's incredible. She's never tired and she never
believes you are. Even at her age, she can still do everything
herself. She could dance Swan Lake if she had to. She was one
of the best Odettes there's ever been, you know, except Pav-
lova. Signora saw her. Signora says –'

Signora this, Signora that. We heard more about Signora
even than about Connie's Mr Jaggers. Signora was both the
goddess and the terror of Myra's life. If she had praised her,
the girl came home glowing and wanted to love everybody in
the house, even little Barry. If she had scolded her and told
her, as she told all the company at intervals, that she would

never be a dancer, Myra came home washed out, with her hair limp, and shut herself away in her room to mope.

With every smallest decision that cropped up, even a change of lipstick, it was: 'I'll have to ask Signora.' She had to be told everything, and if you did not tell her, she found out. She dominated Myra completely and worked her much too hard. Often I had to drag her out of bed in the morning, to get her off to class on time.

'Why do you let her treat you like this?' I asked her, when she came home one day in tears, because Signora did not like her new coat and said that she must change it. 'She's a monster, and she doesn't pay you all that much.'

'Oh, it isn't the money.' Myra's soft face looked shocked. 'We ought to be paying her, really, for what she teaches us. We can't expect to have a life of our own. If you're a dancer, Signora says, you must give up everything else.'

'Yes,' said Win, who was with us in my room, darning the commissionaire's socks, 'give it up to her. Jolly nice for her, but I think you're ever so silly to stand for it.'

'I must. Everyone does. She's like that with everyone, and if they don't like it, they have to go. Patty Grigg had a terrible time with her last year because she didn't like the boy Patty was going out with. She said she mustn't see him, and Patty only just met him once on the corner near our hotel to say good-bye, but Signora saw her, and that was the end of Patty. She's in musical comedy now, poor darling.'

'If she's like that,' I said, 'I can't understand why she lets you live here on your own. Why don't you want to be with the others, anyway?'

'Oh well, you see.' Myra dropped her eyes. She could never keep anything from you if she was looking at you. 'That's a secret, really. But I told Signora that Mrs Goff was a relation of mine.'

Win and I gasped.

'Oh, she's not, of course, thank goodness, but although

Signora doesn't like it very much, she let me come here in the end, because they're overcrowded where they are. I have to tell her though exactly what I'm eating, and what time I get in if I go out at night.'

'Well pooh,' said Win, getting off my bed and shaking threads off her skirt. 'You could tell her anything.'

'I couldn't. She'd soon find out if I was lying. Signora knows everything.'

'She doesn't know why you want to live here though,' I said, 'nor do we. God knows why anyone should. Come on, what's this secret?'

'I daren't tell you. It might get round to her. Oh, not that I don't trust you, of course,' she said hurriedly, afraid of being unkind, 'but you know how things get round, and that would be the end of me with Signora. Perhaps one day I'll tell you. I hate having secrets. It seems so mean. Shall I tell you? But you'd have to cross your heart and hope to die.' She licked her finger and drew it across her throat. Her gestures, though always graceful, were as childish as much of her conversation. Signora's Simon-Legree-cum-kindergarten treatment seemed to have arrested her development in everything except dancing.

Win and I licked our fingers and crossed our throats. 'Come on then,' I said. 'Shall I lock the door?'

Win giggled. Myra got up and went to the window, with that curious duck-like ballet dancer's walk.

'Shall I?' She looked out of the window, then suddenly turned round excitedly, and stood with her hands behind her on the sill and her eyes shining. She opened her mouth on a deep breath, and at that moment Connie blundered in from the bathroom with her head wrapped up in a towel and asked who was going to dry her. Myra shut her mouth on her secret and went downstairs to darn her tights.

Mr Pellet would not let me have the press tickets for the first night of the ballet. He sent Victor, and I had to buy my own. The theatre was barely full, for there had never been proper ballet in Downingham before, and the whole thing was viewed with great suspicion.

In the interval after *Sylphides*, a man said to his wife, 'Well, the tunes are pretty enough, I'll give you that, but it's that man with the bow round his neck I can't stomach. Can't we go now?'

'You'll like the next one, dear. It's all about skating –'

'Well, we'll see, we'll see,' he grumbled. 'I must say these seats are damned hard.'

Signora's little company gave a more beautiful performance than anything Downingham was likely to see for many years to come. I thought Myra was wonderful. It is always surprising to see someone you know doing something difficult. The rest of the *corps de ballet* were probably just as good, but then I had not seen them staggering to the bathroom in the early morning with their eyes half shut, or sprawling on the bedroom floor in a petticoat, stirring cocoa over the gas ring.

I went home exalted into a dream of a lovelier life, but when I started rhapsodizing to Myra, she said: 'Oh, it wasn't. It was terrible tonight. Didn't you see Mervyn come in half a bar late? And in *Sylphides*, Sally made a face at someone in the wings, when she was going upstage with her back to the audience, and Signora saw and gave her a terrible blowing up. So, of course, she was in a furious temper in *Patineurs*, and she and Prue, who do one of the variations, were having a row all the time. You should have heard the language.'

It could not have been worse than the language in the office next day, when Vic was trying to write his report on *Lez Sylpheedes* and *Patinewers*. He had hated it, and did not know why anyone should want to see ballet, much less read about it in the *Post*.

'Well, I don't know,' said Mike. 'I'm afraid I rather like ballet. I'm sorry. I can't help it,' he said, as if apologizing for an offensive infirmity.

At lunchtime, I took Victor home and smuggled him up-stairs, and when Myra came home from rehearsal, we got her to help him with the ballet notice.

We sat in her room, and Victor, who always said what was in his mind, asked her why she wanted a double room. 'I'll know where to come, shan't I?' he said, with a heavy and rather unsuccessful leer. That was one of his approaches to women – daring remarks of a hobnailed unsubtlety that were supposed to shock them into submission.

'Shut up, Victor,' I said. 'She's married.' I winked at Myra, but she did not wink back. She sat on that dreadful little tapestry stool that Mr Goff had bought from the sale at the old rectory, and stared at the wall, tapping her teeth with a pencil and wondering how many superlatives she could per-suade the *Post* to give Signora.

'This is bloody good,' Mr Pellet said, coming into our office with the ballet notice. 'I didn't know you knew all this about ballet, Victor.'

Vic studied his nails. 'Oh, I'm pretty versatile in my way, you know, sir.'

The editor looked at me. 'Did *she* write it?'

'If I had,' I said, 'you wouldn't say it was bloody good.'

'True. But did you?'

'Of course not. Why should I?'

'You did that filth about the pantomime, and I know these boys. They'll always get someone else to do their work if they can.'

Joe swore that he had not told him about *Mother Goose*. How did Mr Pellet know? He knew everything. He ought to meet Signora. They would make a lovely pair.

Signora, however, was married. Or had been. She had married a Milanese masher called Alessandro long, long ago when she was a foolish girl and thought that a ballet dancer could find room for love.

Alessandro soon tired of being a ballet husband. He took Signora round the neck one night and said, 'You must choose between me and *la danza.*' Signora chose *la danza*, and Alessandro went straight off to live with a woman of wealth and high social standing, who had nothing to do all day but lie on a couch and polish her nails until he came home.

This explained why Signora was so adamant in her rule that none of the girls in her company should marry. She did not have to bother about the men. The question never arose.

Most of the girls were very pretty, and quite often one or other of them came to Signora in fear and trembling to say that she had fallen in love, and could she *possibly* get married, please, Signora, or at least, as a great favour, announce her engagement?

Signora would then thump the girl in the small of the back to correct her posture, and say that she would not waste her time training someone whose mind was half on other things, and she would quote Alessandro's remark about choosing between the man and the ballet. The girl nearly always chose the ballet, and there were many wretched young men in England who might have been held on suspicion if Signora had ever been found with a bullet through the narrow blue-black head.

The girls did not seem to think of getting married without telling Signora. I suppose they knew that she would find out before long, and meanwhile the strain of wondering when would be too much.

It was getting to be too much for Myra. She had to tell someone. I had gone home for the week-end and Win was in hospital having her appendix out so she told Connie, who stayed awake on Sunday night to tell me as soon as I got back.

Myra's light was on when I came out of Connie's room, so I went in to her. She would know that Connie would be sure to tell me, for Connie told everything. News leaked out of her like a tap without a washer, and Mr Jaggers would have retired behind the Novels Reduced to Clear counter in some dismay if he knew that we had heard exactly what happened to him that time he had food poisoning.

Myra was sitting up in bed in a shawl with a blue ribbon round her hair, reading one of Connie's magazines.

'It's awful,' she said. 'I can't go to sleep, and we're rehearsing *Aurora's Wedding* tomorrow. I'm doing the *pas de trois*. Did I tell you?'

'Yes, you told me. You didn't tell me what this other bed was for though.' I sat down on it, remembering the night when Margaret had lain there and we could not stop her life ebbing away.

'Connie told you? I thought she would. Well, you'd have to know soon, anyway, because he's coming home. That's why I took this room. He's been out East, and he'll get leave when he comes back next month, and how I shall ever face Signora, I just don't know.'

'You mean you're going to tell her?'

'Heavens no. She'd kill me. To have got married at all is bad enough. I never would have done it, only it was Andrew's last week, and – well, you know – we had to be together. But a soldier ! She hates the Army, or anything like that which has nothing to do with any of the arts. And Andrew hates the ballet, and if Signora found out and was mean to me, he'd go and beat her up, you know. He really would. He's terribly violent.'

'But you can't keep it dark for ever.' It seemed a pretty poor lookout for Andrew if he was to be kept behind a baize door like a shameful secret. If he was so violent, he probably would not stand for it.

'While I'm with Signora we must. I must finish my training with her, and then when I'm good enough to go on to a bigger company, it won't matter everyone knowing. But Signora mustn't know now. She'd throw me out and that would finish me.'

We discussed the matter at great length. Myra told me all about the romance, from the moment when she had first met Andrew in a station waiting-room to the moment when, at another station, she had kissed him good-bye on the troop train, and gone behind a pile of empty ice-cream cans to weep while she took off his ring, which she had not been able to wear since. She could not even wear it tied to her shoulder-straps, because Signora was in and out of their dressing-rooms all the time.

She would not be able to wear it when Andrew came home, in case they met Signora in the street. She would hardly dare to go out with Andrew. They would have to stay in their room most of the time, and would he like the room? And Mrs Goff would have to know, and she might tell someone, and altogether married life was going to be very difficult.

'It's awful,' she kept on saying. 'Oh dear, I don't know what I shall do. It's awful.'

I did not think it was awful at all. I thought it was wonderful to have a romantic secret in those blatant days when everyone knew everything about everyone else's life. It was difficult, from the uninspired behaviour of most young married couples, to believe that they were in love, but with Myra and Andrew you could, because she had dared all for his sake.

It was like the princess secretly married to the shoemaker. One day, when I had learned how to write short stories, I would write a story about them, and I tried to memorize how she looked pattering across the floor in a torn nightgown to find his photograph for me, and sitting on the tapestry stool in tears, with her knees fallen apart in that jointless, almost ungainly way of a dancer at rest.

The season of fêtes was now upon us, and not a Saturday went by without some desperate village junketing to raise money for the memorial hall or the church roof. Usually, we got pick-ups on these from local correspondents, but if the village had managed to persuade any kind of a celebrity to open their fête, a reporter had to go along to get a first-hand story.

This was a job for the junior reporter, so it was always the job for me. There is nothing I don't know now about village fêtes. I have seen them in blazing sunshine when the ice cream had to be poured into the cornets, and the pig that was being bowled for collapsed from heat stroke. I have seen them in pouring rain, when the Rose Queen ran for shelter with a mackintosh over her head, and the tea tent came down like a wet sack on the vicar and most of his parish. I have seen them in a high wind, with boy scouts hanging on to the guy ropes, and I was privileged to be present on one occasion when the sausage rolls had gone off and people were laid out right and left with cramps. The St John Ambulance Brigade were beside themselves from excitement, for Steeple Bracken had not seen so many bodies lying about since a minor skirmish was fought there during the Wars of the Roses.

There were not many celebrities in our district, and the poor things, who started the season by thinking Noblesse Oblige, and one must do one's bit for the parish, soon became so overworked that they had not one free Saturday all summer.

In the old days, the lady of the manor used to open the local fête, but now the landed ladies had either sold up and gone away, or were living in small cottages in a far humbler way than most of the farmers. You could not expect people to get excited about seeing Mrs Heseltine-Raeburn on the platform in a floppy hat and long gloves saved from the good years, when they could see her any day at the village shop in corduroy trousers with her head tied up in a scarf, or lining up behind the fish van, which called once a week, for a bit of haddock, which might have been for her cat and might have been for her husband.

So a new class of fête openers had sprung up. They were the people of whom no one could say, 'She was one of the Shropshire Bletchleys, you know,' or 'Of course, he only inherited the Baronetcy through a cousin.' The new local celebrities were upstarts. People from town, who had made enough money to escape from it, invaders from a more sophisticated world, whose habits sometimes baffled the country people, but whose cottages and 'farms' (one pet cow, some pretty bantams, and a few self-conscious Muscovy ducks) were pointed out to visitors with as much pride as the ruins of the abbey where the nun had been walled up.

Authors, minor actresses, radio stars, and anyone who had ever had anything to do with films – these were the people who now opened fêtes. This was not Kent or Sussex, so we had not many of them, and those we had were bandied round from village to village, and must have got as sick of seeing me approach with my notebook as I was of having to interview them.

There was one wretched radio comedian, whose popularity depended on his pretence of personal friendship with his vast public. His voice over the air was intimate and confiding, and welcome as one of the family in millions of homes. When, therefore, he was asked locally to meet the people, he could not admit to being the lazy hermit he really was, but had to drag himself from his garden to register *bonhomie* among the children's fancy dress and comic dog shows.

I saw him at many fêtes, and he nearly always made the same jokes, but it did not matter. Nobody listens to an opening speech. They just want to stand round the platform and wonder if the rain will keep off, and think, well, he's quite old really. Not a bit like his pictures.

After his speech, the comedian, whose wife never came to back him up, would have to go round the stalls buying jam and bottled fruit, and jovially trying his hand at the skittle alley and the hoop-la stall, with face turned towards Hooky, the photographer we shared with the *Messenger*. Sometimes he would be given a consolation prize. I came up to him once when he had just been given some shaving soap, and then, his job done, his name having drawn the public, been abandoned in the middle of the field in the charming manner of amateur reception committees.

'You again?' he asked me morosely, looking at the shaving soap. 'What shall we write about this week? We can't very well put in about the vicar talking for so long they had to start the band to stop him.'

'It'll be the usual,' I said. 'I might as well have a block made of it to save the comps having to set it every time.'

He wrinkled his loose-skinned face. His professional humour was partly based on the idea that a man who is perpetually baffled by life is always funny. 'Do you have to go to all these shows?' he asked. 'Even more than I do?'

'Quite a lot,' I said. 'But then it's my job. It's not yours. I wonder you do it.'

'If you're an entertainer,' he said sadly, 'and get your money from the public, they expect you to be a public convenience.'

'Out of hours?'

'There is no out of hours. A factory worker knocks off when the whistle blows, but nobody blows a whistle for me.' He signed an autograph book for a child, who looked at his signature suspiciously before she walked away, as if afraid he might be somebody else.

'Isn't it worth it, though,' I asked, 'to be famous and successful?'

'They say so. But the point is, that if you let them, people would stop you doing the very thing for which you *were* famous. If I went to all the do's I'm asked to, I wouldn't have any time left for my own work. Look at authors who get caught up in lecture tours. They never have time to write another word and so after a bit the public forgets them, and then nobody wants them to lecture any more, and then what have they got? I tell you. People will destroy you. Like sucker fishes. Those things that feed on whales. Last week I had a letter from a sucker fish in Cumberland – hundreds of miles away – wanting me to open the vicarage garden party. "I'm sorry we can't offer to pay your fare, or any fee, my dear sir, as funds are low, but if you would honour us with your presence, you can be assured of a warm welcome." No thank you, madam, I've had a guess.' He bowed away a lady with a large fruit cake and a pencil and a notebook.

'I wrote back to say I was sorry but I couldn't support a wife and children on warm welcomes. Do you think that was too stiff?' He looked at me anxiously, fearful of having lost the ears even of one vicar in Cumberland.

'I say,' he said, 'none of this is for the *Puddlefoot Clarion*, of course. Officially, I just love to spend my Saturday afternoons this way.'

'Just one more, sir, if you'd oblige.' Hooky was suddenly with us in his curious tweed hat, throwing himself on one knee in the attitude in which he thought press photographs had to be taken.

The comedian tilted his hat and made his hangdog grin.

'Go away, Hooky,' I said. 'We don't want any pictures, except that one with the babies.'

'This isn't for the *Post*,' said Hooky, getting up. 'This is for the *Messenger*.'

'D'you have the same photographer for two papers?' asked the comedian. 'What happens if he gives you both the same pictures?'

'It doesn't matter,' I said. 'No one reads both papers.'

'I don't read either,' he said. 'Perhaps I should. Here, have some shaving cream.' He thrust it into my hands and loped off for the gate before two small boys and a jolly woman could reach him with grubby bits of paper for his autograph.

It was also now the season of horse shows. These were not popular among reporters because they went on for so long and there was such a list of names to get right. A lot of the children had tricky double-barrelled names, and their horses were worse.

I did not mind going to shows, except when it was cold and wet. When it was, I used to spend most of the time in the tea tent with the fat girl from the *Moreton Advertiser*, and horse shows for me are now for ever connected with the taste of Bakewell tarts and sweet tea made in a tin urn.

I took Connie and Win with me one Saturday. Win was back at work now after her operation, and I thought a bus ride and a day in the open air would do her good. Connie was very fond of horses. She stood by the ropes and called out, 'Isn't that sweet!' and went click-click as the children's ponies trotted by. She fell in love with a great Roman-nosed charger in the open jumping, because it had a noble face, and when it hit a jump she screamed, and Win and I were very ashamed of her.

We spent a lot of time in the tea tent. 'I'm silly about horses,' Connie said, as we waited in line by the urn. 'Well, all animals really. I wouldn't even tread on a beetle. There's a milk horse stops on the corner by our shop every morning, and I give him sugar, the dear. Mr Jaggers says he's sure I take his tea sugar for the horse, but I don't, of course. The tea things are kept locked up. Mrs Robb has the key.'

The open jumping went on and on. Horse after horse came into the ring and bounded agitatedly round. You were no longer pleased when you saw a clear round, because it just meant one more for the jump off. Connie was beginning to change her mind about horses, and Win was bored and irritable. She told me accusingly that the doctor had said she mustn't stand too much, so we sat her on the bumper of someone's car, and the car suddenly moved off backwards and jerked her on to the ground, and she said it hurt her scar. I had to stay until the end to get all the gymkhana results, but Win and Connie would not go home by an earlier bus. Outside Downingham they were helpless, and afraid of trying to find their way anywhere alone.

They perked up a bit when a child fell off in the bending race. Connie screamed again, and a man standing next to her, who was the father of the child, said, 'For God's sake! It's people like you who cause these accidents. Come back, dear! Angela's all right,' he called to his wife, who was running out into the ring among the galloping ponies in a felt hat and Newmarket boots, shouting, 'It's all right, Angie! Mummie's coming!'

'I hope she gets killed,' said Connie.

The gymkhana dragged on, until we were in danger of missing the last bus. I went to the secretary's tent to get some names that I had missed. If you are a reporter, you can usually barge your way in anywhere, and people at small country functions are delighted to see you; but the two tweeded men with badges and the woman in the square grey flannel coat and skirt did not want me in the tent. There appeared to have been some muddle about the money. Someone had been given too big a prize, and there was not enough for someone else, and the grey flannel woman was telling the treasurer that he must make it up out of his own pocket. The treasurer was telling the grey flannel woman that he would see her damned before he did, and furthermore, that she could do his job next year. He had done it for five years, and he'd just about had enough of it.

'Doesn't look as if there'll *be* another year,' the other man said. 'An objection has been raised about the judging of the light horses, and all the hack people are saying they'll boycott the show. You still here?' He turned on me savagely. 'I told you to clear off. And if you print anything about the objection –'

I assured him that our readers did not live or die by the

news of doings in the hack world. 'But if I might just have a look at the list of winners, for the *Post* –'

'For the Lord's sake, don't bother us now,' said the square woman. 'We're busy.'

'All right,' I said, 'if you don't want the publicity. It helps for another year though. If you're going to have the show another year.'

'Who said we weren't? Of course we are,' said the man who had said they wouldn't.

I left them to their wrangling in the little tent, which smelled sourly of trodden grass, and took Connie and Win home. As the bus drove past the field, we saw the riders still at it, playing musical chairs in the fading light.

Signora's company were not dancing at the theatre any more. When we got back, Myra, in a creased skirt and one of the shocking torn old jerseys that she would wear, was helping Mrs Goff wash up the supper things. Mrs Goff had quite taken to Myra, who she said reminded her of herself at that age. Win had giggled the first time she said this, and Mrs Goff, who had not liked Connie and Win from the start, now searched out reasons to find fault with them, although, apart from their activities in the bathroom, they must have been two of the most harmless lodgers she had ever had.

'I must say,' she said, as we came into the scullery to see if there was a hope of getting any food, 'it is nice to be given a hand for a change. That Alice – I can't get her near the sink. It's all knit, knit, knit now, but I'm glad *somebody* is willing to help me.' She smiled at Myra. Like Axel Munthe's housekeeper, it was worse when she smiled than when she did not.

We had often offered to help her wash-up, but she always said Too many cooks spoil the broth. Tonight, because she was power-drunk with Myra's tractability, it was Many hands make light work, and we all had to seize a cloth and

181

set to. Perhaps she hoped to distract us from wanting something to eat.

However, Mrs Goff had news to impart, and she could not resist telling it with full ceremony, so she made tea and cut bread and butter, and we sat at the table, laid for breakfast with the usual complement of sauces and pickles, while she told us.

It was about the commissionaire. There had been a smash and grab raid at the shop next door to his cinema, and his sole remaining arm had been broken trying to jump on to the running-board of the bandits' car. Mrs Goff was surprised to hear that I did not know about it. 'Though I suppose newspaper people are always the last to know of any news.'

I tried to explain that I had been out in the country all day, but she was pleased with her joke, and kept repeating it.

'Like jackals they've been, round here all day,' she said. 'A pert young lady from the *Messenger* and a young man with spectacles from your paper. Very interested, he was, in all I had to tell him about poor Mr Davies.'

Bother Mike. Not content with being lucky enough to get the smash and grab, he couldn't even leave the personal end of it to me, although I lived on the spot. Fancy missing such an excitement. I *would* have to be stuck out at the horse show when something really thrilling happened in Downingham. I always missed the best things.

We were terribly proud of our Mr Davies, as we now called him. He was a hero. We wished now that we had known him better. He had been a shadowy figure in our lives, coming and going quietly, shutting himself in with his ghosts and his wireless and never joining the bedroom tea parties. Connie said that she had known all along that he was the kind of man who would do a brave thing like that, and Mrs Goff said, 'More foolish than brave, I should say, interfering in what was not his business. That's how he

182

lost his other arm, I shouldn't wonder, for all he said it was the war.' She spoke like this because the commissionaire's heroism had cost her a lodger. He was expected to be in hospital a long time, and would probably give up his room.

'If he does,' said Myra, 'I know someone who'd like it. Someone in our company, actually, who's had a row with Signora about having to share a room, and would love to come here, if Signora allowed it.'

'A dancer?' said Mrs Goff, dropping a cigarette stub into the dregs of her tea. 'Another girl for ever holding on to the backs of chairs and swinging her legs about?'

'Well, it's a man actually,' said Myra blushing.

Mrs Goff caught on to the blush and immediately assumed that the man was Myra's boy friend. I went down to tell Casubon about the smash and grab, and when I was coming up the back stairs, I heard her in the kitchen talking to Mr Goff about No nonsense, and We'll have to keep our eye on that young lady.

When Mervyn came, however, with some odd-looking luggage and a black Spanish shawl to drape over his bed, it was plain that there was no cause for anxiety. I went in for supper before the others, and heard Alice telling her mother scornfully that she could have told her that all male dancers were like that.

'Like what?' asked Mrs Goff who, although she was libidinous about straightforward sex, was fairly innocent about its finer points.

'Well – like he is.' Alice made her disgusted face and knitted faster. 'You know. I wouldn't put my lips to the word, but you know.'

'And what does your mother know?' inquired Mr Goff, coming over from the sink with wet arms, eager to share the conversation of the family circle.

'Oh, you wouldn't understand,' said Alice, in the kicking-around voice she always used on her father. 'I wasn't talking to you anyway.'

'What do I know?' asked Mrs Goff, bringing in the potatoes without a lid, long before anyone was ready for them.

'Well. That he doesn't like women. One could put it that way.'

'Oh, but he does. He has been ever so charming to me, and most polite. I wish all would follow his example.' The deliberate way in which she did not look at me made the remark as pointed as if she had. I sat down and began to eat bread.

'Don't be so simple, Ma,' said Alice, rolling up her knitting and jabbing the needle through it. 'I don't mean like that, you know I don't. I mean, he doesn't like women *in that way*.'

Mrs Goff's eyebrows went up. 'Oh, I see,' she said. 'You mean he's One of Those. Well, I don't know. They say it takes all sorts.' Her reactions were always unexpected. She was outraged about ridiculous little things, and then suddenly tolerant of something that should have shocked her.

'One of what?' asked Mr Goff, sitting down and tucking a napkin under his chin.

'Oh, be quiet,' snapped Alice. 'I told you, you wouldn't understand.' And he never did. He had one joke for each of us, and to the end of Mervyn's stay, he pegged away at the one he had thought up for him, calling him a Lady killer, and asking him : 'And how many hearts did you break last night, young man?'

Win and Connie did not understand about Mervyn either. Their magazines had never told them about anything like that. They were skittishly excited when Mervyn took the front top room. Although he was much too small for strapping girls like them, he was very good-looking, with soft brown eyes and a delicate pink mouth. He wore Indian sandals with curly points on the toes and coloured shirts and bow ties, and he talked with a slight faked American accent, which gave them the illusion of living in the same house with a film star.

When he behaved in a way they did not understand, like the time he found a spider in the bath and went screaming about the top two floors clad only in a towel, they simply giggled, 'Oh, isn't he funny? Oh, he's a scream, that Mervyn, honestly, isn't he?' They pursued him unsuccessfully all the time he was there, and Mervyn, who liked to be snug, enjoyed their attentions and the cosy chats in bedrooms, which were such a feature of our life at Bury Road. Sometimes the place seemed more like a nurses' home than a boarding house, with coffee brewing in an enamel jug on the gas ring and people in dressing-gowns curled up on each other's beds, talking endlessly about themselves, until Mrs Goff, like Night Sister, knocked on the door to inquire if we thought she was made of electricity.

Mervyn made friends with everybody, even little Barry, with whom he would romp rather sweetly on the kitchen floor. He took Alice to the pictures, he came to socials and amateur concerts with me, he helped Mrs Goff in the kitchen, and he went for walks with Mr Goff and the airedales, although he was nervous of the dogs, and squeaked if they came smelling round his legs. Mr Goff took to him so much that he gave him the plaster nymph for his room. Mervyn had to accept it. We put it on his table, and he walked round and round it wringing his hands in distress and crying that his life would never be the same again. Finally he put it on the chest of drawers, turned its face to the wall and draped it in the top half of his yellow silk pyjamas.

He was often down in the basement, playing racing demon or having soulful talks, for while Connie and Win were chasing Mervyn, Mervyn was chasing Casubon.

He and Myra were very thick. He was like a girl friend to her, only safer. She could confide in him without the complications that arise when women confide in other women. They

185

talked ballet shop together all the time, and when Signora had upset her, she would weep on Mervyn's bosom, and he would hold her hand and pat her thin shoulder. If Connie or Win saw this, they would be jealous, and give him the routine tossing the head with indifference treatment, until he oozed into their room begging for cocoa, or for someone to cut the nails of his right hand.

He was in my room one morning having a splinter taken out of his finger, when Myra, who always watched for the postman, came in like a small tornado and flung herself on the bed, with the skin over her high cheekbones fairly bursting with the smile that was springing from her face.

'He's back, he's back!' She waved a letter and kicked her legs about. 'Oh, isn't it wonderful! He's back. He's in Yorkshire, and he's getting leave in a week's time!'

Mervyn was bowed over his tiny splinter. I made a face at Myra over his back.

'Oh, that's all right,' she said. 'He knows, but he'd die rather than tell Signora, wouldn't you, darling? Mervyn knows everything. He was one of the witnesses when we were married.'

'Yes,' said Mervyn sadly, 'and now I shall play cupid for your second honeymoon. Herbs under the pillow, and all that glorious pagan stuff. I shall sleep on the mat outside the door, like Charmian did for Cleopatra. When's he coming, the great lover?'

'Next week.' Myra rolled on to her stomach and began to read the letter again, pushing up her hair with her fingers.

'Oh dear. There'll be no more crosswords then. Never mind, I shall do them with Neil. He's really much better at them than you are.'

I asked Myra if she had told Mrs Goff yet. 'Oh, don't be sordid,' she said, with that smile still shining out of her face like the sun. 'I'll face that when I have to. She won't mind,' she convinced herself boldly. 'I say, imagine, you know, that

Andrew's actually in England. It doesn't seem possible, does it?'

We agreed that it hardly seemed possible.

'How much does it cost to ring up Yorkshire, I wonder? But then I don't know. They might not let him come to the telephone. He's only a corporal, you know. He was a sergeant, but they put him down for saying what he thought. They're horrid to him in the Army. I'll send him a telegram and tell him where to come to, and look,' she said to me, 'if he comes while I'm at class or anything, you will ring up at once, won't you, and tell Signora you're dying, or the house is on fire and my clothes burning, or something?'

'Wouldn't matter if they were,' I said. 'You'll have to give up those old jerseys when Andrew comes.'

'Oh, he won't mind. He doesn't care about things like that.'

'He will, dear,' said Mervyn, who had been reading Win and Connie's magazines, 'when you're going off a bit and can no longer rely on the fresh charm of youth.'

'He won't. He's not like that. D'you know, once he said – No, I shan't tell you, because Mervyn will only say something cynical. Mervyn's awfully cynical, did you know?'

'Mervyn will now say something very cynical indeed,' Mervyn said, snatching his finger away and slapping my hand as I probed too deep. 'Have you forgotten that next week you and I and the entire company are supposed to be going to Buxton for two nights to adorn the Hydro centenary of arts and music with our rendition of *Coppelia*?'

Myra had forgotten. She buried her face in the pillow, and then came up not smiling any more, but suddenly grown up and determined. 'I shan't go. I shall have my chest again. I can always say I've been to a doctor –'

'As if Signora didn't always insist on going to the doctor with us,' said Mervyn.

'I'll manage it somehow if it kills me. I'd die rather than go to Buxton. It'll be all right.' She sat up with her legs crossed.

'If you only want a thing badly enough, you know, you do get it. Oh, you do.'

'If you've quite finished messing about with my finger,' Mervyn told me, 'I would remind you that I have a class in exactly half an hour, and that it takes twenty minutes to get to the studio from this neck of the woods, and furthermore that I have had no breakfast. I would remind you of all that too, Mysie.'

'Oh class,' she said. 'Breakfast. What dull things you talk about.' She lay down to read the letter again, and then suddenly rolled over and jumped off the bed in one movement.

'Class! Why didn't you tell me what the time was? Gosh, I'll have to simply dash. I was late last week and Signora nearly murdered me!'

Chapter Eleven

WHEN the fruit was ripe and onions growing to monster size, the Women's Institute held a produce show in Downingham. They said in the office that the Women's Institute was the only thing that made them glad to have a girl on the paper. Before I came, it was always Mike's job. The other papers all had girls to send, and when he went to the annual meeting of all the branches, he was the only man among hundreds of women with hats and cavernous handbags. When a delegate got up to speak, she would say: 'Ladies and – er – gentle*man*,' and all heads would turn to Mike and he would have to take off his glasses and start polishing them on his handkerchief.

The produce show was in the upstairs room of the town

hall. The Women's Institute craved publicity, and I was well received and shown round by Mrs Phelps, the organizer, who was all in a dither over some contretemps about the judges' lunch. She was a tall, waistless woman with treading shoes and a brown velvet hat and a lot of pepper and salt hair, coarse, like a horse's tail, that seemed to be bothering her as much as the judge's lunch.

The exhibits had been judged in the morning. Bottled fruit was tested for sealing, cakes cut open, and pickles and jams tasted with a long-handled spoon and much delicate smacking of lips. It was a wonder the judges wanted any lunch, because there were hundreds of pickle entries, and some of them were made of things like quinces and turnips and elderberries.

Each exhibit was labelled with its marks, and some had gold stars. Mrs Phelps offered to let me taste, but I was still tasting Mrs Goff's luncheon roll and thought that it would not mix. I took copious notes of prize-winners, and she told me many more things that I must put in the report: 'Because, you see, this is the *greatest* day of the year for us. The members all work so hard to keep up the *standard*.' She had a way of stretching her lips in a grin when she emphasized words, which made them come out as *greetest* and *steendard*. She was keyed up with enthusiasm, and clasped her hands ecstatically over the strawberry jam, which was the highest *steendard* so far of any other *yeear*. I had not the heart to tell her that she could only have one column, or less if the cricket news was big this week, so that none of what she was telling me about the triumph of the eggless sponges would ever reach the public eye.

When the doors were opened at two-thirty, a mob of women surged in and spread out like water tracking through sand, searching for their own exhibits. Mrs Phelps and I were at the bottling counter. I was taking down names, and she was fighting yet another round of the losing battle to get all her horse hair secured under the brown velvet hat.

'Where's my blackcurrants?' A small woman in black lunged up and down the table, searching among the bottles. 'Florrie, I don't see my blackcurrants anywhere. Come and look. Come all this way on the bus to see my currants, and then – Well!' She held up a jar. 'Look at that if you please! Only fifty out of a hundred, and there's Mrs Pryby got the gold star and her fruit not graded half as well as mine. Look at this, Florrie. Where's Gran? Gran, have you found your popovers? Look how they've marked my blackcurrants. It's not good enough, that's what it isn't. Let's go and see the cakes. If they've put me down on my simnel, there's going to be trouble for someone. It's not good enough.'

'I think you will find, Mrs Warren,' said Mrs Phelps, taking an extra large hairpin out of her bag and thrusting it under her hat, 'that where you lost marks was on the sealing.' She wiggled the bottle lid and it came off quite easily. 'There, you see. It's no good if it isn't sealed.'

'But it *was* sealed,' said Mrs Warren, 'when it left home. I know these judges. They'll fiddle and fiddle with the cap and take a knife to it as like as not to get their way. I've never had a batch of bottling yet that didn't all take. And look at this. Unsealed, and now the currants won't keep. I shall have to use them tonight for His tea, or lose them.' She put the bottle into her basket with baleful tenderness and walked off, like a mother leading away the child who didn't win the hundred yards race.

'Some of our *meembers*', said Mrs Phelps to me, 'are a little touchy, you know, about their exhibits. They work so hard at them, good souls, that one can *understeend* . . .'

We drifted away via the root vegetables and fancy biscuits to where a lady in a green smock was giving a talk on flower arrangement to a group of sceptical country women. She had some roses and leaves and a piece of wire-netting, which she bent to hold the flowers at different angles in a shallow glass bowl. She took about ten minutes to make each new arrangement. One could hardly imagine these women fiddling about at home with wire-netting and rhubarb leaves, with the washing still to do and the chickens to feed and Dad and Johnny coming back for their dinner at midday. Anyway, they could get much better results with a handful of marigolds or a row of geraniums on the window-sill.

Back in the office, Victor was on the telephone, making his bets for Saturday's racing. Joe had his shoes off and his feet up on a chair, and was rolling cigarettes and cramming them into the pocket of his buttonless waistcoat.

Mike was playing the gramophone, which was the latest addition to our office furniture. Mr Pellet did not mind it so much as he minded the tea kettle, and would even sometimes come down and ask us to play him 'that waltz thing, you know, that goes tum, tum, *tum*, te tum'. He would lean on the window-sill with his muscular behind stretching his tight trousers, and gaze dreamily out down into the street while we played him 'I'll see you again'. He was getting quite dulcet these days, and Victor said that the red-haired widow was always at her best in summer, in spite of the sun not agreeing with her skin.

Sylvia had given Mike a new record of 'Tiger Rag' for his birthday. She was a hot number and she liked hot tunes. He was playing it for the hundredth time, and young Maurice, who had been lured by its strains from the comp room, was tapping his feet and clicking his fingers and making breathy hotcha noises.

Murray had cottonwool in both ears and was pasting press cuttings into the morgue. He waited until I had sat down, put the paper into my typewriter, and started to grind out the epic of the Women's Institute in a rival rhythm to Tiger Rag before he asked me to go downstairs and look up something for him in the files.

I went down the ladder staircase to the basement, climbed over some bales and boxes and hunted about among the dusty

191

copies of old newspapers. I was going home for the week-end, so I did not mind about Murray, or Mike's gramophone, or Joe's socks, or Vic's eternal 'Right . . . Right . . .' on the telephone.

Heavy feet came slowly down the steep stairs, dropping from step to step as if carrying a weight. It was Mr Pellet, bringing down some large old volumes. I stood up, and he started when he saw my head appear above the bales and packing cases.

'Oh – hullo, girl. I didn't know you were down here. Thought I'd turn out my office a bit,' he said quite apologetically. 'You can't move in there for junk. Give the place a bit of a tidy up.'

'Shall I help you?' Anything was better than writing up the produce show.

He seemed pleased. 'Well, thanks,' he said. 'It's always more pleasant to do those sort of jobs with someone else.'

Mike was right. He ought to get married. It must be a dreary life, trying to run the *Post* without anyone at home to grumble to about it. I wondered whether we could possibly mate him with Win or Connie. They were young for him, but Win would do anything to get out of the costing office. She had lately joined a pen friends club and was writing letters to lonely soldiers and frustrated men in Wales who were fond of music and cycling. She would jump at Mr Pellet. She would whisk round his flat with feather dusters and darn his socks and iron his shirts and cook macaroni dishes for him and grill up left-overs with bits of cheese. In the evening, she would work on a *gros point* fire-screen and say: 'Fancy' when he told her about the rising cost of newsprint. I saw it all.

Mr Pellet put down his books and waited while I found the paper that Murray wanted. 'Er – look girl,' he said, as we came to the foot of the ladder. 'You know the civic banquet tomorrow night? I've got to go. Big do, you know. General Berkeley's guest of honour, and they've got some cabinet minister speaking.'

'What fun,' I said politely.

'Not much. But better if you go with someone. Like to come? I can fix another invitation.'

I was staggered, but dismayed. As far as I was concerned, he was a bear, and I was still a bit nervous of him. To get this favour was cheering – but I did so want to go home for the week-end.

I hesitated. He started up the stairs and said without looking at me, 'Of course, if you don't want to come . . . I know these shows are not always. . . .'

'But of course I do.' I hurried after him, which was difficult on the steep stairs. 'It's terribly kind of you to ask me. It was just that I –' He had gone on ahead, going fast along the corridors. He had reached his office and shut the door before I panted in and said: 'Please, I would like to go. Very much. It would be lovely.'

'All right,' he said ungraciously. I stayed and helped him to tidy his office, and he did not mention the banquet again. When we had finished, and I was going out with two wastepaper baskets full of rubbish, he called me back.

'And by the way,' he said, as if we had not left the topic, 'I – er – well, you'd better not mention the banquet to that lot downstairs. Cause ill feeling. They'd like to have the chance to go.'

Strange. He knew as well as I did that none of the others would want to go to the civic dinner. They were only too thankful that he had to be there, so that none of them had to go and report it. He knew that. He was having an intrigue with me. Not much of a one, but still an intrigue. I was glad I had given up my week-end. I would go with him, and work on this promising start, to get him humanized for Win.

He called me back again. I stuck my head round the door, because I had a wastepaper basket under each arm. 'Evening dress, of course, girl,' he said. 'Your best. Meet me downstairs in the town hall at seven.'

My best evening dress! I had not got any evening dress. It was five o'clock and I had jobs that would keep me busy all day tomorrow. I would have to do the Women's Institute at home. I dumped the rubbish and dashed back into the reporters' room to get my typewriter. Victor was using it. He had thrown away the beginning of the produce show, and was pounding out the unsavoury story of a man committed to trial at the Assizes for bigamy with three women. I knocked Vic's hands aside, pulled his copy off the roller, told him: 'That ought to be polygamy', shut the typewriter, and ran with it out of the building to buy an evening dress for Mr Pellet's delight before the shops closed.

I spent more than I could afford on a dress for Mr Pellet, and only hoped that it would come in for something else. It was as pretty a one as you could get in Downingham, but he did not seem to notice it. I was groomed for stardom by Win and Connie, who were as excited about my night out as if they were going themselves. They made me take a foam bath and lie down with my feet on a pillow while Connie did my nails and Win tortured my eyebrows. They slapped my face with astringent and combed the back of my hair round their fingers, and finished me off with a touch of perfume at pulse points and daringly down the neck of my dress.

Mr Pellet did not notice any of this either. He greeted me without a smile at the town hall and told me I was late. In his dinner jacket, with his curly hair already springing out of its brushing, he looked more like a farmer than ever, dressed up for a gala Harvest Home.

He seemed abstracted. He did not enjoy himself at the banquet, and was probably sorry that he had brought me. I think I made him nervous, although I used the right knives and forks and did not try to smoke before The King. We had quite a lot of drink, because it was free, but it was difficult to find things to talk about. Obviously we could not talk about the office, since the fact that he and I were sitting side by side in evening dress eating vinegary hors d'œuvres and *sauté* of chicken and ice-cream with unripe fruit salad was such a very unoffice situation. As he had never before talked to me about myself, and never talked to me about himself, he could not start now.

The speeches were interminable and full of laboured wit. Mr Pellet dozed off with his eyes open, but glazing. I stiffened my back, stiffened my jaw against yawns, and tried to look bright, hoping that people were impressed by the sight of the junior reporter out with the editor.

When it was over at last, and the sad waiters were left to clear up, Mr Pellet said with a bad grace that he would see me home. I did not want him to. He had had too much port and was morose, and although he did not seem to like me tonight, I had half a feeling that he might suddenly savage me in a bear hug under the glass arcade. When he was disgruntled, you never knew how he would vent it.

We walked together for a while, and when we reached the market square, we saw that the fair was still on. Lights, racketing dodg'ems, shouts, shots and blaring music, and dominating all, the roundabout, the flags round its crown spinning, the horses rising and falling, the riders floating by with a fixed smile of ecstasy to see their world go whirling by below them.

As we turned the corner into the square, the noise and lights hit us like the clash of a cymbal. We stood for a moment to watch, outsiders in evening dress, carriage folk watching the peasantry at play.

The stall nearest to us had a circling aeroplane and a glass case like the train indicator at King's Cross Underground, which flickered with changing names. Several people were standing round holding tickets and waiting for something to happen, while a man in a white scarf and a decayed golf jacket was shouting: 'Only two more; who'll try their luck?

Ev-ryone a chance to win! Just two more ladies or gents and then the game begins. No waiting! Who'll try their luck?'

The people round the stall looked restive. They had been lured to buy 'the last two tickets' and then found that there were two more to sell and two more after that before the game could start.

'Just two more! Come along, that lady and gentleman, be a couple of sports. Two more only – chance of a lifetime, the very last two!' he shouted at Mr Pellet and me. The crowd looked at us. The aeroplane whizzed round, the china and glass and trumpery glamour piled up in the middle of the stall sparkled with the allure of a gamble.

'Oh, come on,' I said to Mr Pellet. 'Let's have a go.'

He let himself be dragged up to the stall, where he stood glumly clutching his ticket, while the aeroplane spun faster and the light flashed madly up and down the indicator and at last slowly came to rest, hesitating, jumping on to one more name, and just reaching the next.

Mr Pellet had not the faintest idea what the game was about, and his surprise when he received a three-foot high pink rabbit was tremendous. He turned and walked away, holding the rabbit with the helpless dismay of a man given charge of a baby. Then, suddenly, the drink that was in him bubbled up out of its sluggishness and flooded him with the joyous passion of capture. He grinned at me for the first time that evening, his bright blue eyes electric.

A klaxon on the Rocket Ride ('Thrills! Speed! Laughter!') yelled just by our ears, and: 'Come on!' he shouted above it. 'This is bloody good fun!' He ran up the wooden steps and climbed into a car. I followed him, and had to pay our fares because he was too encumbered by the rabbit and by excitement to find the money when a man jumped on to the outside of our car and balanced there with a dirty palm thrust out while the rocket gathered speed.

Round and round and up and down it went, faster and

faster, until you knew that you would die if it did not stop. Hanging on to the rail with one hand, and trying to stop my precious dress billowing out of the side of the car with the other, I glanced at my editor. With the pink rabbit in his lap, he was leaning forward clutching the rail with stiff arms, his eyes fixed, his mouth half open, his head jerking back every time we took the steepest corner.

One would have given a month's pay if only it would stop. Just when you knew that it never would, the car jerked and slowed, your body slackened, your breath came back, the top of your brain returned to you from the stars, and you were suddenly at rest and wondering what all the fuss had been about.

'Let's have another go!' we both cried.

'And shut your mouth this time,' shouted Mr Pellet, as the rocket started again. 'Screaming like a bloody hyena!'

'Was I?' I did not know that I had screamed. The car whipped into the speed of the delirious torture, and I felt myself screaming again, although I could not hear it. Again I prayed for the rocket to stop, again I knew that it never would, again I was sorry when it did. We had another turn, and at last climbed out and staggered down the steps, more dizzy and drunk than all the port in the town hall could have made us.

Mr Pellet was beside himself. It is banal to say that he was like a little boy, for stocky, blue-eyed men are always likened to their childhood when they get excited, but I can think of no other way to describe him. In prodigal abandon, he changed two pound notes into silver, and we went on every single sideshow that moved, and tried our luck on all the ones that didn't. We bought treacle rock and toffee apples and Mr Pellet spilled half an ice-cream down the lack-lustre lapel of his dinner jacket. We saw the tattooed lady and the man with india-rubber skin and the smallest horse in the world, which was only a Shetland pony standing in a pit to make it look shorter. We played the slot machines until our pennies ran out, and at last we tottered out of our third ride on the ghost train to find the lights being dimmed all over the fairground, stubble-chinned men putting up shutters, and ourselves among the last of the crowd to wander away exhausted over the littered cobbles, clutching three glass butter dishes, the rabbit and a quantity of tiepins and beaded brooches.

Sober now, we walked back to Bury Road, surprised to remember who we really were. A junior reporter in a creased and dirtied evening dress and an editor in an old-fashioned dinner jacket, who never floated on the roundabouts of life.

We did not talk much. Our elation had gone, and there was nothing to say. When we were under the glass arcade, Mr Pellet did not give me a bear hug. He gave me the pink rabbit instead.

It sat on my window-sill with a ribbon round its neck, and made me feel like a girl of the nineteen-twenties with limp Spanish dolls and harlequins strewn on the zigzag divan cover of her emancipated bed-sitter.

Mervyn was wildly jealous of the rabbit. He offered to swop it for Nausicaa, but I would not part with it. It was all I had to remind me that Mr Pellet had ever cut loose. In the office, we neither of us ever mentioned our night out, and he treated me exactly as before, even a little more churlishly, as if he feared that I would take advantage of his midsummer madness.

The week after the civic dinner, Myra was so excited that we thought that she would have to tell Mrs Goff about Andrew soon to explain her high spirits. She went singing about the house in a sweet, flat voice, crouched on the floor and barked at the dogs until they nearly went demented, and could hardly sit still through a meal. She spring-cleaned her room and bought a picture for the wall, which Mrs Goff removed, tutting at the nail-hole, and hung from the picture rail, too high to give any pleasure.

She danced to the wireless with Mervyn on the first floor landing, and Connie and Win danced together, like two girls in a palais de danse. Mr Goff, who had been on the beer, came up and hopped some polka steps and asked whose birthday it was.

'Nobody's,' said Myra, 'but something much more wonderful.'

'Aha!' chuckled Mr Goff, producing his special joke for her. 'You've found that millionaire at last.'

'Even better than that,' hinted Myra, but she refused to tell Mrs Goff until the very last minute. Nor had she yet told Signora that she was not going to Buxton. She was a coward, that Myra. Even the thought of Andrew did not embolden her.

Two days before he was due, she knocked on the bathroom door while I was in the bath. I dripped across to unlock it, and she came in crying. She gave me a letter which turned to pulp while I held it in my wet hands to read it, and what with her tears and my dripping bathwater, the place was nearly awash.

The letter was from Andrew. It was short and furious. It began with just 'Myra', and did not end with love. It said that he was not coming to see her. His leave had been cancelled and he was confined to barracks because he had hit an officer. I wrapped myself in a towel. The bathroom door was open and Mervyn came in to see what the keening was about. He sat on the edge of the bath and read the letter.

'Well, you always said he was violent, Mysie, didn't you?' She was crouching on the linen basket still sobbing, and he took her hand and kissed it.

'He is,' she gasped, 'but why must he do it just now?'

'Man's a fool,' said Mervyn. 'Got no sense of timing.'

'Oh, he's not!' Myra stopped crying and looked up. Her narrow eyes had almost disappeared above the puffy cheeks. 'If he hit the beastly officer, it must have been the officer's fault. I hope Andrew hurt him. But oh . . .'

She slumped on the linen basket, staring at the blank door, seeing all her plans of joy vanishing down the pitiless corridor of disappointment.

'Oh, pardon me,' said Connie, opening the door. 'I didn't know it was engaged. I only wanted to rinse my stockings through.'

'Come right in,' said Mervyn. 'Bring all your friends.'

'Well, Win's gone out, as a matter of fact,' said Connie. 'Why? Are you having a party?'

'A wake,' I said. 'Andrew's leave has been cancelled.'

'Oh dear,' said Connie, noticing Myra's face and looking embarrassed. Then she quickly jollied up. 'Oh well,' she said brightly, 'they do say it's an ill wind that blows nobody any good. Now you won't have to worry about making excuses not to go to Buxton.'

Myra looked at her and began to cry again.

'Go away, Connie,' said Mervyn. 'Can't you see this bathroom's occupied?'

'If you'll allow me to get to the basin *please*.' Connie pushed past him and turned on the taps. We took Myra away to my room, and Alice, prowling up the stairs, asked me if I had a dressing-gown, and if so, whether I did not know what it was for.

Chapter Twelve

MYRA went off to Buxton with Mervyn. Win had to do her packing for her, because she had gone limp with disappointment and could not give her mind to anything. She cheered up a little just before she left when she remembered that for two nights on the big stage at the Hydro, she was going to dance the *pas de trois* in *Aurora's Wedding*. In the morning, when they went off to meet Signora and the rest of the company at the station, she was talking ballet quite animatedly on the stairs with Mervyn.

'Maybe,' he said, 'but if you forget to put that silly little ruff round your neck again, Signora will never let you dance it in London.'

'Oh, she will. I'm going to dance so well tonight, she'll never give Felicity the part again. You never know, I might even get a chance to do the *Bluebird*, if Norma's really leaving. You'd dance it much better with me. She's too heavy for you.'

'I dance it very nicely already, thank you,' said Mervyn. 'I got a better press here than anyone.'

'Only because I wrote the notice for the *Post*. You wait. When you dance the *Bluebird* with me, you'll get a good press everywhere. I'll make you famous. I'm going to be famous. Oh darling Merv, I know I'm going to be good one day, I *must*.'

'You will dear,' he said in the hall. 'Hang on a minute. I must just pop down and say good-bye to Neil.'

If it came to a showdown, I wondered which would come first with Myra – the ballet or Andrew.

On the second night that they were away, Marjorie Salmon was at supper. She looked plump and pleased with herself and talked a lot about My flat and My kitchen and My new curtaining material.

'But it is nice to be back home,' she said, as Mrs Goff brought on the cracked soup tureen, which I suppose reminded her of her childhood. It had probably been cracked even then.

'You should come home more often, baby,' said her father, putting butter on her plate.

'Of course you should,' said her mother. 'It would save your reason. You look thoroughly washed out and overworked. I don't like it at all.'

'Oh, she doesn't Ma,' said Alice. 'She looks as fat as a pig.'

'I do *not*,' said Marjorie. 'Anyway, it's better than being skinny like you.'

'Well!' Alice put down her soup spoon and wiped little Barry's chin savagely. 'Of all the cheek. You rude little brat.'

'Just because you're older than me,' said Marjorie. 'I'm married now, don't forget. If Cecil heard you, he wouldn't stand for it.'

'Oh, he wouldn't?' Mrs Goff's bosom rose. 'And who is he, pray, to presume so on his family connexion? I'll give him not stand for it. Goes jaunting off like this into the blue and leaves his wife to run home to her family for comfort. And who knows when he'll come back, that's all I say. Who knows? I've had experience of sons-in-law, thank you.' She nodded at Alice.

'Oh, don't be silly, Ma,' said Marjorie. 'He's coming back tomorrow, I told you. It isn't his fault if he had to go up to the engineering exhibition.'

'That's what they all say.' Mrs Goff shook her head sorrowfully. 'Never mind, my chick. You've always got a good home here, when things go wrong.'

'Oh Ma,' said Marjorie. 'Don't carry on. What will everyone think?' She looked at Connie and Win and Neil and me, and we smiled brightly, to show her that we did not think. 'You know I've only come here for the night because I don't like being alone in the flat.'

I wondered where she was going to sleep. In the double bed with her mother and father? In the narrow bed with Alice? In Barry's camp bed and he on the old mattress in the scullery with the airedales?

I soon found out where. I sat up late, finishing some work on my inlaid octagonal table. Since it had come to Bury Road, it had somehow developed a crippled shortening of one of the legs, and had to be propped with a folded newspaper. The top had come right off one day when Mervyn and Myra were practising a lift in my room, and we had stuck it on again with nail varnish.

When I had finished, I hung out of the window to clear the twitter of petty sessions out of my head. It was a beautiful night, with a great yellow harvest moon standing over the corner of the hill by the breweries, so I put on a coat and took a walk up to the park before I went to bed.

When I got back to Bury Road, a soldier was standing under our lamp-post. He was biting his nails. While I was having my struggle with the gate, he took a step forward, hesitated, and then came up to me, clearing his throat. He was a solid, sunburnt soldier with a short nose, a boxer's jaw and a deep frown pleated between his sandy eyebrows.

'Oh, er –' he said. 'Excuse me.' He cleared his throat again, and I waited.

'Do you, by any chance – I mean, do you happen to live here?'

'Yes.'

'Who – oh, dash it, no. You'll think this very odd. I mean to say – are you one of the family?'

'I hope not,' I said. 'No, I'm only the lodger.'

'Thank goodness.' His frown grew shallower. 'I say, you're not by any chance the girl who works on a newspaper?'

'I am,' I said. 'But what's all this about?'

'Oh, that's all right then. She's told me about you. I say, what a colossal bit of luck you coming along. I've been hanging about here wondering how to get in to her.'

'Who?'

'Myra. My wife.'

'You're Andrew! But that's wonderful. Why didn't you ring the bell?'

'Well, you see – oh, never mind. Where is she? can you sneak me up to her room?' He leaned forward, quivering like a terrier.

'She's not here.'

203

He fell back on his heels, his jaw sullen. 'You mean she's moved. Why the hell didn't she tell me?'

'She's only gone away for two nights. She wouldn't have, but she thought you weren't coming when she got your letter about – you know. You said your leave had been stopped.'

'Oh, that worked itself out,' he said hastily. 'The point is, I'm here. And she isn't, blast her.'

We discussed what to do with him. He said he could not go to a hotel because he had no money. I offered to lend him some, but he refused. He seemed unnaturally anxious, even a little furtive, and I supposed that Myra had communicated to him her own worry about the Signora finding them out. I decided that the only thing to do was to take him up to Myra's room and let him sleep there, and get him away in the morning before Mrs Goff was up. I was not going to have the task of telling Mrs Goff who he was. Myra could do that when she came back tomorrow evening.

As we tiptoed up under the arcade, I saw that he had no luggage.

'I left in a hurry,' he said. 'Only just had time to catch the train. I'll buy a razor and things here.'

'I thought you said you had no money,' I said. A cat tore the night with a squall and we both jumped, and I forgot to notice that he did not answer.

I got him safely up the stairs and showed him the door of Myra's room. 'I'll come and fetch you at six,' I said, and started up the stairs.

Before I got to the top, there was a scream like a pig-killing from Myra's room, and Andrew shot out, hurtled down the stairs, and was out of the front door with a bang like a bomb blast.

Marjorie appeared at the door of Myra's room, pot-bellied in a satin nightdress, white and shaking and about to have hysteria all over the first person she met.

I left her to it. I locked myself in my room and refused to

come out even when Alice came banging at my door crying: 'Burglars! Burglars! We shall all be murdered in our beds!'

If the Goffs had the nerve to put Marjorie in Myra's room, they could cope with the consequences by themselves.

My chief worry was how to get hold of Andrew again. He would not dare come back, and I hoped that he would have the sense to find me at the newspaper office.

When I went off to work next morning, I was startled, as I passed under the arcade, to hear a low whistle from behind me on my right. It came from the direction of Casubon's window, but he was not given to whistling at girls in that clandestine way. The whistle came again. I turned and stepped between the pillars into the garden. Casubon's window was shut, but from behind the dustbins in the area, a head rose and then ducked quickly down again. It was Andrew.

I went down into the area and pretended to be putting something into one of the dustbins. Andrew crouched there looking up at me, his frown like chisel cuts.

I told him when Myra would be back. 'I'll tell her to meet you – let's see – in a pub somewhere?'

He shook his head.

'What about the war memorial? You'll find that easily. Or the Downingham Arms?'

'Too public.'

'Well, think of somewhere quickly. I can't stay here any longer, or someone will wonder what I'm doing.' Why was he being so hole-and-corner? No one had seen him last night except Marjorie, and she only in the dark. He must be as frightened of Signora as Myra was.

'The park,' he whispered. 'That's where I slept last night. I climbed over. Tore my blasted pants. What time do they shut it? Nine o'clock? It'll be nearly dark by then. There's a little summer-house. Tell her to meet me there at a quarter to.'

I shut the dustbin in which I had been poking about

pretending to look for something I had thrown away by mistake. 'Have you got any money for food?' I asked.

'That's all right.'

'Well look.' I gave him a shilling. 'Get yourself a shave for heaven's sake before Myra sees you.'

'Go and hold the gate open,' he said, 'and I'll skip.'

I opened the gate. He swung himself out of the area without using the steps, streaked past me, swerved like a polo pony and was gone round the corner of the street.

I went on to work, pleasantly elated by the adventure and the thought of telling Myra tonight. It is not always easy to see what other women see in the men they choose, but you could with Andrew. She would be silly if she did to him what Signora had done to Alessandro.

Myra was due back about eight o'clock. At five, when Joe and I, who had been reading proofs all afternoon, were thinking about going home, Mr Pellet came into the office with his hat on and his thick stick swinging.

'Sorry girl,' he said to me. 'I forgot to tell you. The Labour candidate is speaking tonight at Frierley. You'll have to go.'

'Can't someone else? I've got a date.'

'Got yourself a man at last?' asked Mike who, now that he was engaged to Sylvia, was always trying to settle me down.

'He'll keep,' said Mr Pellet. 'Reporters can't make dates. You'll have to go and hear this Red. Everyone else has got something already.'

'I can't get to Frierley. There aren't any buses.'

'You've got a bike.'

'It's raining.'

'It's stopped. What's the matter with you? You're getting as lazy as the others. So long, Joe.' He pushed the swing door open with his stick and went out.

I cursed him, and Mike said: 'Well, I wouldn't go, if you've really got a fancy date. You can get the notes of the speech from the committee rooms probably.'

'Don't worry,' I said. 'I wouldn't dream of going.' If Mr Pellet found out, I would say that my bicycle had had a puncture. I would say that I had been stranded for hours in a country lane, and that would make him feel bad. Or would it?

At home, I waited about with my door open so that I could hear the minute Myra came back. When I heard the front door, I ran down, pulled her up to my room and told her about Andrew. Although it was much too early, she insisted on running off at once to the park, in case he was there before time.

'What's eating her?' asked Mervyn, coming into my room as the front door slammed. 'Passed me on the stairs like a dose of salts. Where's she gone? She and I are going to go a bust and have supper at the Dover.'

I told him. 'Well, damn her,' he said. 'What about my supper?' He was very put out. I hoped he was not going to be like that all the time, if Andrew was going to stay here.

Later in the evening, Mrs Goff came up to my room and stood portentous in the doorway, nodding her head. I wondered what I had done, but for once it was not me.

'It's too much,' she said. 'This house is becoming a den of indecorum. First that horrible man last night – I don't suppose the police will ever catch him. They never catch anyone. Frightening my poor little Marjorie half out of her senses. I doubt if she'll ever get over it. And now tonight. Just now. That Myra Nelson. That innocent little minx. Oh yes, indeed, I'll give her innocent, never fear.'

'Why?' I asked. 'What's happened?'

'You pretend, no doubt, though so friendly with her, to know nothing about her goings on. You pretend, no doubt, not to know that she's just gone into her bedroom with a Man.'

'A man?' I echoed stupidly, trying to gain time to think what to tell her.

'A man. I was in the kitchen and I saw his legs through

the banisters. Don't tell me I don't know a man's legs when I see them.'

'It was Mervyn, of course.'

'Oh, it was Mervyn, of course,' she mocked me. 'You know as well as I do that Mervyn is in the basement playing whist with Connie and Mr Casubon.'

She would have to know some time, so I told her that Myra was married to Andrew. I had to, to stop her bursting in on them.

I braced myself for her wrath, but to my surprise her flat pulpy face lifted into one of her rare and hideous smiles.

'The dear little thing,' she said. 'Fancy her not telling me. I suppose it was because she was so happy here, and was afraid I might turn her out. And why shouldn't she have a husband, pray? Though, of course, she'll have to pay more if there's going to be the two of them, bless her heart.'

Myra came up to my room early the next morning.

'It's awful,' she said, sitting down on my feet.

'Don't keep saying it's awful about Andrew,' I said, waking myself up. 'He's lovely. There was nearly a bit of trouble last night, but it's sorted itself out.'

'It hasn't,' she said. 'It's awful. He's deserted. Run away from the camp because they stopped his leave. The police will be after him all over England. Now say that isn't awful.'

'It is, but it isn't the end of the world. He must go back and give himself up. Perhaps there'll be a sentimental colonel, who'll understand why he ran away.'

'He says he's never going back. He hates the Army.'

'They're bound to find him sooner or later. Then it will be much worse. You must make him go back.'

'You don't know what Andrew is. You can't make him do anything. He says he's going to stay here with me. I want him to, of course, but if he stays too long, Signora is bound to find out. It's awful.'

It was worse than awful. To be hiding from Signora and

the police at the same time seemed more than anyone could stand.

However, we worked something out. We called in Mervyn, and the idea of an intrigue tempted him out of his last night's sulks. We arranged that for the time being, Andrew would have to stay in Myra's room. We would tell Mrs Goff that he was not well, and if he wanted to go out, he would have to sneak out at night when everyone was in bed. If Mrs Goff would not send up any meals, we would all help to feed Andrew off gas rings. Mervyn insisted on telling Neil all about it. It did not matter, since he seldom spoke in public, but he did not tell Connie and Win the truth. One might as well have advertised it on the front page of the *Downingham Post*.

Apart from the fact that we all lived under a great nervous strain and jumped every time the door bell rang, and went out of our way to avoid policemen in the street, everything went fairly well. Mrs Goff did not object too violently to Andrew, although she said his manner was abrupt. She agreed to provide his meals, and as her idea of invalid food was plenty of starches to build up the strength, he did all right. We could not stop her going in there when we were all out. She made the excuse of doing his room, although she had never dusted any of our rooms, and it was no wonder his manner was abrupt, because he said that she fiddled about in there for ages telling him all the stored-up grievances of her life.

Connie and Win were in their element with an invalid in the house. They made jellies and blancmanges for him. He and Myra hated blancmanges, and once Myra threw a vanilla shape out of the window, because she did not know how to get rid of it without them seeing. In the morning, there it was, sitting on the path like a jellyfish, and Mervyn had to engage Mrs Goff in conversation in the front room, while Neil went out and buried it in the back garden with a spoon.

Andrew was restive, but behaved himself well. We all liked him, and he fitted in well to our family circle. We used to play vingt-et-un in his room at night, with Andrew in bed and Myra solemnly giving him his medicine of water tinted with gravy for Win and Connie's benefit.

How long we could have gone on like this, I don't know. Myra was getting thinner than ever with the worry of it. She hardly slept, because she was always listening for trouble. Her dancing suffered and she regularly came home in tears because of what Signora had said to her. It was all we could do to stop Andrew jumping out of bed and going out to knock her in the teeth in the pyjamas which we had clubbed together to buy for him.

One Sunday evening, the Goffs went out to the cinema. We were all in our own rooms for a change, except Mervyn, who was in the basement writing poetry with Neil. When I heard the front door bell, I thought that the Goffs had forgotten their key, and went downstairs to let them in, as I was stuck with what I was writing.

It was a man in a trilby hat and a mackintosh. When he stepped into the hall, I recognized him, for I had seen him many times giving evidence in court. Beyond him, I saw dark uniforms moving about in the garden.

A letter from Myra to Andrew had been found at the barracks. I prepared for a last stand.

Why the detective sergeant did not search the house at once, I did not know, but it seemed the correct order of things to question us all first. When he had finished with me, I took him down to the basement. While he was talking to Neil, Mervyn said that he would run up and fetch Connie and Win, and I knew that he had gone to warn Andrew. I could not think why the detective let him. Perhaps the films were right, and the police really were dumber than the crooks.

Mervyn had managed to explain briefly to Connie and

Win, and although pop-eyed with mystification, they repeated their piece staunchly.

'Right,' said the detective. 'Well, I'll just look through the house if I may.' He was very polite. When we went up the stairs, I saw why he was not hurrying. A policeman was posted at both the front and back doors. A constable that I knew quite well was in the hall. He would not return my smile.

'Come on, Martins,' the detective said to him. 'We'll just have a look round.'

We trailed after him as he went into all the rooms and looked methodically in cupboards and under beds. The airedales slept peacefully on their mattress, and he patted them, and laughed: 'Good house dogs, eh?' We did not laugh with him.

We followed him in a silent, hostile bunch. At last he came to Myra's room. She was in there alone, sitting on the tapestry stool pretending to sew, but she had not got any thread in her needle. Idiotically, she at first denied that she was married to Andrew. When the detective said kindly: 'Oh, come on, my dear,' and showed her the marriage certificate and her letter to Andrew, she went limp, but continued to protest that she had not seen him. She said it too often and too fast.

'He might have gone to Ireland,' she said wildly. 'His mother's there. Yes, that's where he must be. In fact, he wrote and told me he'd be going to see her. No, I don't know where she lives. Dublin. Yes, that's where. I don't know where he is.' She was the worst liar I ever saw.

The detective gave her a disappointed look, as if he were used to a better performance. 'Come on, Martins,' he said. 'We'd better take a look on the top floor for this soldier.'

Andrew was not in Mervyn's room. He was not in my room. They found him in the bathroom in his pyjamas, kneeling in the bath, trying to open the door that led to nowhere.

Chapter Thirteen

MR PELLET went away for his annual holiday to his sister at Angmering. He always left it until the autumn, because he did not want to go, but finally Mrs Murchison, the owner of the paper, appeared in the office, and when I took tea upstairs for her, I found her ordering Mr Pellet away.

Murray was the editor for a fortnight. 'Two weeks' hell,' said Joe. 'Dictator complex, that's what he gets. You wait. He'll probably take the opportunity to fire you.'

'I shan't accept it,' I said.

'You might have to,' said Joe, surprisingly ethical. 'He's the editor. He's *in loco Pelletis* and we've got to swallow it, or else.'

Murray sat up in Mr Pellet's office smoking cigarettes in a holder which he brought out every year for his editorial season. He affected a spotted bow tie and would not come with us to the Lion at lunchtime. We lost all our darts matches against the *Messenger* that fortnight, because whatever his limitations, Murray could play darts. He kept summoning us upstairs to impugn us for some slip that Mr Pellet would have put right himself without a word. He kept lists of things that had to be done, and ticked them off in red pencil, and if all current proofs were not read and rechecked by the end of the day, we had to stay on and finish them, instead of knowing happily that tomorrow was another day, as we did with Mr Pellet.

Murray would not come down for his tea. I had to take it up to him. He had to have the only saucer in the office, so I slopped it into that, instead of on to the stairs.

'Careless you are,' he said, tipping the saucer into the cup. 'Just a moment,' he called me back from the door. 'Magistrates' court tomorrow.'

'Yes, I'm down for it, I think.'

'I'll cover it. You can come with me and learn how.'

'But look here,' I said. 'I've been dozens of times on my own. I can do it.'

'You never get your cases set out as I would like to see them,' said Murray, taking a biscuit out of Mr Pellet's tin and biting it with his front teeth. 'You'll come with me to-morrow and learn how to do it properly. Mr Pellet may be soft with you because you are a girl –'

'I hadn't noticed it.'

'There are more things that I notice in this place than you think,' said Murray. Had he somehow, in his nasty way, found out about the fun fair?

We had another skirmish the next morning, when I announced that I was not going to Sessions with him. There was no children's court, and it was a waste of time for two of us to go when it was press day and there were so many other things to do.

'You'll do what I say!' Murray flared up, red in the forehead and white round the corners of his nose. 'I will not stand for all this laxness and answering back. If you can't behave yourself, you'll have to go.'

'There you are, Poppy. What did I say?' said Joe without looking up from his writing.

Murray ignored him. 'You can do what you like for the rest of the year,' he said, drawing down his upper lip, 'but while I'm editor, we'll have this place run like a proper newspaper office.'

'Then you should wear your hat,' said Vic, 'and have six telephones on your desk all ringing at once, instead of wasting time arguing with your juniors. Don't you know what time it is? You'll be late for Sessions.'

Murray looked at his watch and hurried out. I followed him more slowly. Murray had never been late for Sessions. I always was.

The magistrates were already on the Bench. Colonel Burrows wore his summer suit of creased gabardine with a regimental tie and the last rose of summer in his buttonhole. The large lady, who looked hot even in winter, wore much the same clothes and looked hotter. The old gentleman in the wing collar had had his holiday and was sun-burned on the top of his head. Mrs Chase wore a white straw hat with a kind of walkie-talkie aerial sticking up on one side of it. She wore a linen suit and white crochet gloves, and if she had had her holiday, she must have had a parasol up all the time over her alabaster face.

I pushed into the press bench over the knees of Nancy and Ronnie, and sat down next to Murray, who was making neat headings of the cases on the list on his half sheets of paper. The first case was not on the list. There was some dispute about hearing it. The clerk, standing in the well of the court with his chin on a level with the Bench, talked to the magistrates. Colonel Burrows leaned forward and cupped his ear. The little old man had no hope of hearing. Mrs Chase inclined her neck and looked sceptical and the large lady supported her bosom on the Bench and looked at the clerk as if she were Mussolini. I borrowed Ronnie's penknife and got on with the elaborate engraving of my name which I had started the week before. If Murray ever did succeed in firing me, I would at least leave my epitaph in the magistrates' court.

'Oh, I see – mph,' grunted the Colonel. 'Got to get the train with him. I see. Mph.' He nodded to the clerk, the clerk nodded to a police sergeant, and Nobby took a deep breath and called out, 'Andrew William Phillips!'

I sat up with a jerk. Andrew came in with his uniform creased and stepped smartly into the box. He looked once into the body of the court, saw me, and looked away.

He did not look at the magistrates, or at the detective who gave evidence. He stood at attention and kept his eyes in front of him all the time, as if he was afraid that if he looked at anyone, he might jump out of the box and take a swing at them.

The case only took a few minutes. It was simply a formality before sending him back to Yorkshire under military escort for his court martial.

The M.P. who had come in with Andrew touched his arm and he stepped down and walked out with his head up, looking as though he could fight the whole War Office. He looked worth ten of anyone else in that court, and I saw why Myra loved him.

I began to get up. If I dashed out, I might just have a chance to wish him good luck, even if I was not allowed to talk to him.

'Sit down,' said Murray, taking my arm and pinching it as he pushed me down. 'What do you think you're doing?'

Nancy leaned across and said to me, 'Sorry dear. I was talking to Ron and missed something. What was the name and address again of the wife?'

It was only then that I realized the consequences of Andrew's appearance in court. It would be in the local papers, and Signora would either see Myra's name herself, or be told about it by some sycophant who wanted to dance the *pas de trois* in *Aurora's Wedding*.

I pretended to look at my notebook, then I gave Nancy a false name and address. That would settle the *Messenger*, but there was still the danger of my own paper betraying Myra. Murray was already writing out his brief report from the notes he had made about Andrew.

'Please,' I said, 'Murray. Don't report that case.'

He stared at me as if I were a tropical fish, then looked back at his paper and went on writing.

'I'll explain afterwards,' I said. 'Please. It matters terribly and it's not as if –'

'Ssh!' He dug me in the ribs with his pointed elbow. 'Behave yourself.' The next case had arrived, and was standing

215

in the box being asked if its name was Ann Maria Sedgwick. Murray drew a fancy line under his story about Andrew and began to take fresh notes in his pin-neat shorthand.

He shut me up every time I tried to speak to him during the morning. When we went out I tried again, but he hurried away through the crowd, jumped on a bus, and left me in distress on the pavement.

I went back to see Myra. We did not have any lunch. We sat in my room and she cried and cried. She cried for Andrew, but she cried about Murray too, and it was no use thinking that she would ever snap her fingers at Signora, and tell her that she was married and so what?

'She'll see it, she'll see it,' she moaned. 'And she'll know I'm married and she'll turn me out.'

'Suppose she does? There are other companies, plenty of other teachers.'

'Not like Signora. Anyway, I wouldn't have the heart. If she throws me out, I'll never dance again.'

'Well then,' I said, trying to jolly her up, 'you could settle down with Andrew and have lots of children.'

'If I can't dance, I'll die,' she said melodramatically. 'You must help me. You mustn't print that story.' Like Maimie, she could not understand that I had not supreme powers to do what I liked on the *Downingham Post*.

'If you don't help me,' she cried, 'I'll kill myself.' I knew she would not, but I had to help her.

Murray was out when I got back to the office. Half-way through the afternoon, Harold came in with a roll of proofs. Since this was press day, Murray had written up his court cases during the lunch hour, and among them was the little story of Andrew, giving Myra's name and address and even her stage name and the fact that she was a dancer. Murray, who was usually against too much human interest, had chosen to make quite a sob story out of this, playing up the romance of a husband risking punishment to see his wife, and heading it: 'THE SOLDIER AND THE DANCER,' so that everyone would be sure to read it. Just a small paragraph, it was; a mere two inches of print, but it was enough to ruin Myra's career.

Mike read out the story, and despondently I corrected the proof. 'Husband leaves wife, four children,' he went on. 'I say, that last case. You've got a girl who's a dancer up at your digs, haven't you? Wasn't her, was it? She must be quite a piece for him to do a silly thing like that.'

'Of course it wasn't her,' I snapped. 'Get on about the wife and four children. Get on for heaven's sake, or we'll never be done.'

All afternoon, I thought and thought about what I could do, and rehearsed different things to say to Murray. If only Mr Pellet were here, he might have understood. If I had known where he was, I might have rung him up. Only Murray knew his address in Angmering, and he would never give it to me.

I thought of cutting the story right out of the column, but Murray would notice it when he corrected the page proofs. I could not even alter Myra's name and address, because after what I had said in court, he was cunning enough to check that paragraph carefully, probably from his own copy.

Later in the afternoon, when all but the last two pages were made up and screwed tight in the formes, and Maurice was pulling page proofs for Murray to read when he came in, I went into the comp room to torture myself with the sight of Myra's fate in type. There it was, half-way down the middle column. Even with the letters the wrong way round, it seemed to leap direfully to the eye, like a notice on palace gates telling of the passing of a king. The very shape of it looked ominous. There it was, a little lump of type not much bigger than a matchbox, but by tomorrow it would have spread its back-to-front secret all over the town.

'What's the matter, ducks?' Harold tiptoed up behind me.

'Got nothing to do in there? because if not –' He held a roll of proofs.

'Plenty thanks. I was just checking something.' I heard Murray's feet going up the corkscrew stairs to the editor's office, and ran up to appeal to him once more before he got busy with something and would not listen.

He was not busy. He was rolling up his umbrella as carefully as if he were to walk with it in a bowler hat down Bond Street, but he still would not listen.

He was very cross. He had been to a buffet social. Having missed his lunch, he had taken a big tea there, and something on the buffet had not agreed with him. He asked me who I thought I was, and when I told him, and followed it up with what I thought *he* was, he threw me out of the office.

'You'll regret this!' I shouted from the bottom of the stairs. 'I'll tell Mr Pellet. He wouldn't have let that story go in. I'll pay you out for this. I'll get you fired. I'll –' Murray slammed his door.

'Calm yourself, Pop,' said Joe, leading me back into the reporters' room. 'We've all been saying that to him for years. Forget it, whatever it was. It'll all be the same a hundred years from now. Make the tea and forget it.'

I did not forget it. It was my turn to stay on with Murray and see the paper to bed, and after the others had gone, I sat on in the twilit office, not bothering to turn on the lights, trying to think of something to do.

I kept getting up and looking into the comp room. If only they would all go out for a drink, I might go in there, unscrew the forme of page five, and pick out the fatal paragraph. But even if whoever carried it to the lift did not notice the gap, Murray would never miss it when he checked through the specimen copy from the machine before they started printing the edition.

Should I risk it? I heard a lot of walking about in the comp room, and when I looked in again, they were all going out.

'Coming out for a beer?' asked Ernie. 'There's a bit of a hold-up downstairs.'

'No thanks.' When they had gone, I went like a thief to the metal table where the forme of page five had lain. It was not there. It was not waiting by the lift. It must have gone down to the press already. I went down to the basement. All the formes were leaning against the wall by the machine. I wondered why they had not been clamped into place. The pages were all complete and there seemed no reason why they should not start printing.

Murray was standing with his hands in his pockets, looking pinched and annoyed. He looked more annoyed when he saw me. The machine minder had his head and shoulders inside the works of the giant machine. His mate, in dungarees, was lying on his back in the well underneath, making noises like a garage. If I pressed the starter button now, they would both be killed and there would be no paper printed.

'Anything wrong?' I asked.

'Anything wrong. Anything wrong. Of course there's something wrong,' said Murray testily. 'Don't be a fool, girl.' His impersonation of Mr Pellet embraced even my soubriquet.

The machine minder withdrew his head and shoulders and faced us with oil in his eyebrows.

'Take a good two hours yet, Murray,' he said. 'Damn nuisance. We'd better send the boys off and get 'em back to start printing about ten. It'll mean overtime.'

Murray swore. 'I'm ill, dammit,' he said. He looked it. 'I want to go to bed. I'm damned if I'll sit up half the night with this damned paper.' He did not often swear, so when he did, he had no variety of words.

My brain jumped. 'I'll do it, Murray,' I said brightly. 'I'll check the copy. I've done it often with Mr Pellet. I'll be terribly careful. You go off to bed. You do look pretty bad. I'll take care of everything.' My whole plan was as neat as a geometry theorem worked out down to Q.E.D.

Murray turned on me. 'Of course you'll stay on,' he said ungraciously. 'I don't know about being *able* to do it, but you'll just *have* to do it. I'm off home. You be back here at ten sharp, and don't go home until you're sure everything's all right. And don't expect overtime either. You're not a printer.'

He thought he was punishing me, but he was playing right into my hands.

He went. 'Aren't you going out, then?' asked the machine minder's mate from his supine position.

'I think I'll hang on here,' I said. 'Might as well.'

'I thought you might go and fetch us in some sandwiches,' he said. 'There's some money in my jacket over there.'

'All right,' I said. He too was playing right into my hands. I went down the High Street to the Feathers and got them to make me some ham sandwiches. I bought cheese rolls and two pieces of treacle tart. It was quite a meal. I laid it all out in the reporters' room and I made tea and went downstairs and told the machine minder and his mate to go and feed themselves.

'Bring it down here,' they said.

'No, it's cleaner up there. And there's tea made and everything. You go on up.' I held my breath. Presently, they stopped working and went upstairs. I had got some of Harold's tools in my pocket. Feverishly, I searched along the row of formes by the wall for number five. With Harold's pliers, I loosened the screws. It was more difficult than I imagined, but it was easier than I expected to pick out the lines of type that made up the paragraph about Andrew. I put them in my pocket and screwed up the forme just in time before the two men came down the stairs wiping their mouths and picking bits of pastry out of their teeth.

When at last they had finished tinkering with the press, I watched them fit on the formes and clamp them down. They did not look at number five. Harold and Ernie had come back with two bottles of beer and were waiting upstairs in case there was any resetting to do. There wouldn't be. Not on page five, anyway. The machine minder pressed the button, with a groan and a clank the rollers started turning, and in a moment, the first copies were jerking out at the end.

The mate threw the first few dozen away without looking at them. I picked one out of the next lot that were coming through. 'I'll check it down here,' I said. 'Can't be bothered to walk upstairs.' I did not want to risk Harold and Ernie seeing the paper. The machine minder lit a cigarette and went into a coma with his back against the wall. He was tired and was not going to bother to look at the paper. His mate started to go round the machine with an oil can.

I spread the paper on a table and looked through it with my back to them. I did not read page five. I turned it under quickly in case one of them came over.

The rest of the paper was all right. 'O.K.,' I said. 'Let her go.'

The button was pressed, the rollers turned, the papers jerked out in dozens, and the machine minder's mate began to lift them off and stack them in labelled bundles ready for the vans to collect them.

The *Downingham Post* was out on time next morning. It was in the shops. It was tucked through letter boxes. It was lying on front steps with the milk. It was being sold on street corners.

Every single copy had a two-inch space right in the middle of page five. It looked most odd.

'Well, there you are,' said Mrs Goff. 'Life has its changes, and we can't stand still and watch it. There's things have happened in this house that I could write a book about if I had the time. And now you tell me this, and there's Myra and Mervyn going away next week too, to London, so it's said. 'She made it sound very wicked. 'And well, I don't know, but I fancy that when all's said and done, you've been less trouble in your way than all the others.'

It was the first really nice thing she ever said to me. And the last, for I left her house at the end of the week.

When Mr Pellet came back, Murray told him who had tampered with the print and mutilated the *Downingham Post* for all the world to see. There was nothing for it. I went upstairs to hand in my notice and met him half-way coming down to give it me. It made quite a friendly transaction, and we agreed that women were a nuisance in an office, anyway.

We all had a tremendous party in the White Lion to celebrate my disgrace. Mr Pellet got a little drunk and said he did not know how they were ever going to get the paper out without me.

'We'll miss you,' he said, and they got a promising young lad of sixteen, fresh from school, to take my place on the *Downingham Post*.

MORE ABOUT PENGUINS
AND PELICANS

Penguinews, which appears every month, contains details of all the new books issued by Penguins as they are published. From time to time it is supplemented by *Penguins in Print*, which is our complete list of almost 5,000 titles.

A specimen copy of *Penguinews* will be sent to you free on request. Please write to Dept EP, Penguin Books Ltd, Harmondsworth, Middlesex, for your copy.

In the U.S.A.: For a complete list of books available from Penguins in the United States write to Dept CS, Penguin Books, 625 Madison Avenue, New York, New York 10022.

In Canada: For a complete list of books available from Penguins in Canada write to Penguin Books Canada Ltd, 2801 John Street, Markham, Ontario L3R 1B4.

MONICA DICKENS

'Miss Monica Dickens gets better and better. It is a pleasure to record such steady and admirable progress in a world in which so much gets worse and worse ...' – J. B. Priestley

THE FANCY

THE HAPPY PRISONER

THE HEART OF LONDON

MAN OVERBOARD

NO MORE MEADOWS

ONE PAIR OF FEET

ONE PAIR OF HANDS

THURSDAY AFTERNOONS

THE WINDS OF HEAVEN

and

AN OPEN BOOK,

her autobiography

'Entertaining, often touching, always humorous and, best of all, extremely readable.' – Margaret Forster in the *Evening Standard*